T0199099

Praise for Patrick C. Greene and His Haunted Hollow Chronicles

Red Harvest

"Greene has brought a brilliant level of complexity and humanity to a horror novel."

—Book Nerd's Brain Candy

"I found myself getting completely lost in this sleepy little farm community and wishing I could live in a town like this…until the killings started, of course [. . .] Patrick C. Greene doesn't hold a single thing back."

—Cameron Chaney, YouTube

Books by Patrick C. Greene

The Haunted Hallow Chronicles

Red Harvest

Grim Harvest

Demon Harvest

Published by Kensington Publishing Corporation

Demon Harvest

The Haunted Hollow Chronicles

Patrick C. Greene

LYRICAL PRESS
Kensington Publishing Corp.
www.kensingtonbooks.com

LYRICAL UNDERGROUND BOOKS are published by
Kensington Publishing Corp.
119 West 40th Street
New York, NY 10018

All Kensington titles, imprints, and distributed lines are available at special quantity discounts for bulk purchases for sales promotion, premiums, fund-raising, educational, or institutional use.

Special book excerpts or customized printings can also be created to fit specific needs. For details, write or phone the office of the Kensington Sales Manager: Kensington Publishing Corp., 119 West 40th Street, New York, NY 10018. Attn. Sales Department. Phone: 1-800-221-2647.

First Electronic Edition: September 2020
ISBN-13: 978-1-5161-0832-9 (ebook)
ISBN-10: 1-5161-0832-9 (ebook)

First Print Edition: September 2020
ISBN-13: 978-1-5161-0835-0
ISBN-10: 1-5161-0835-3

Printed in the United States of America

Author's Note

We live in a world of wonderful and amazing technology that gives us instant access to each other and the rest of society. Ember Hollow is not in that world. No cell phones, no internet. Its residents need wit and courage to survive. Quite often, that won't be enough.

Prologue

Cronus County, Eastern North Carolina
Modern day

"Such beautiful country," Maisie commented, smiling over the edge of her half-open window at another of countless farm fields. Most were desolate and weed-pocked. A few, like this one, were dotted with orange spheres. "Forgive me, Ysabella, but I wish you were wrong."

Ysabella Escher nodded, staring across a similar field from the passenger side of her Mercedes. She had removed her sunglasses and let her window all the way down a few miles back, happy to accept the scents and sounds carried on this October day's warm wind.

The elder witch clutched her left hand in her right, knowing it was a giveaway. No sense in hiding it. Maisie had surely read her growing unease by now.

Maisie slowed the Mercedes. "Is it…?"

"Getting stronger," answered her elder. "Worse."

"I'm turning around."

"No, Maisie!" Ysabella raised her trembling hand to her neck. "Just stop. Here."

Maisie pulled off the road, pained to see Ysabella fumbling with the door handle before the car was even fully stopped. Yet, even in physical distress, the sixty-two-year old's grace was admirable.

Ysabella stepped to the edge of the pumpkin field and dropped to her knees, just as a thick stream of crimson fluid burst from her mouth like a firehose opened full-throttle.

Maisie clamped her mouth to silence a pained gasp as she watched her elder witch jet-vomit across a quintet of pumpkins and surrounding soil. The red fountain flowed in an impossible volume of fluid.

Maisie ran to Ysabella, kneeling beside her teacher, despite her revulsion at the spill. She rubbed the old woman's shaking shoulders and spoke words of comfort and healing under her breath. At twenty-four, Maisie had already seen a lifetime of strange, wonderful, heartbreaking and terrifying things. But it was never easy to watch her mentor suffer.

A minute later, as Ysabella began to gulp shuddery breaths, Maisie held the petite enchantress tightly to keep her from collapsing. Ysabella allowed her weight to rest in Maisie's arms. The younger woman stroked the elder's gray-streaked brown curls out of her pained face.

Hearing a rising hiss, Maisie dared a glance at the jagged line of smoking and charred ground—like a spent gunpowder fuse—rising from Ysabella's violent regurgitation. The splashed pumpkins lay collapsed, rotted, disintegrating.

It was small comfort for Maisie that it wasn't actual blood her teacher had spewed, but an etheric by-product of her visions.

The crone took Maisie's hand. "It's much worse than I could have foreseen here," she weakly croaked. "This town. This...*evil.*"

Maisie traced a sigil of vitality on Ysabella's back with her finger. "And you won't let me take you away from here. No matter how I beg."

"Call...the others," Ysabella said. "Get them here now."

"Ysabella, respectfully...we...we're not complete. We need to make our coven whole before we—"

"No time. It's too close to Halloween," said Ysabella, eyes blazing blue with late-day sun and earnest wisdom. "Samhain. If we don't start now... no number of us will be enough to save this place."

Chapter 1

American Witch

Ember Hollow settlement
Circa 1670

Hezekiah Hardison smiled at the memory of childish fear that had descended upon him like a vulture the first time he made this nocturnal sojourn back in midsummer.

On this night, the half-moon provided more than enough light for him to traverse the footpath between fields and forest from Conal O'Herlihy's place on the hill. He could usually count on the company of neighbor Friedrich Schroeder up to this point, but the Dutchman had not attended the meeting.

These late, clandestine gatherings with Conal O'Herlihy and his other followers, coupled with his wariness of these strange lands, had once left Hezekiah a nervous wreck, requiring a jar of dandelion wine and a long smoke of his pipe to calm him enough for sleep. He was glad to say he barely noticed the odd noises and shadows of the forest night any longer.

Until he reached the cornfield, where a mute army of scrawny troops formed across several acres of Schroeder's land.

It would be shorter to cut through the middle of this field. But Hezekiah was not about to traverse the narrow aisle in the dark between tall, ever-rustling rows whose inhabitants seemed to lean forward and inspect him as he passed.

Worse, neighbor Schroeder had built what he called a *bootzaman*—a figure made from old clothes dressed on a frame and stuffed with straw and leaves to appear human. Raised on a cross with arms spread like a mocking idol of Christ, it was meant to scare away the ornery crows that brazenly helped themselves to the crop.

Smiling with satisfaction befitting an acclaimed painter, Schroeder had shown the false man to Hezekiah under blazing daylight. It had left him in such a state of unease that he came to dread opening his door after dark, for fear the crow-scarer would be there, issuing its perpetual, silent threat.

Hezekiah knew that Schroeder often moved the man-thing around the field to keep black-feathered thieves on their toes. It was somewhere among the stalks.

Hezekiah did not wish to ever encounter it again, in *any* light. He hadn't grown that brave.

However, he had overcome his fear of the odd orange fruit that grew here in the new world this time of year, the one the settlers discovered growing alongside corn and apples when summer began to wane.

Hezekiah had once imagined the huge fruits as monstrous bald demon heads waiting for him to come close so they could rise to the full heights of their misshapen bodies. They would drag him to hell as they mockingly cried out a litany of his frequent impure thoughts for Margaret Worthington, Mary Hodgins, Glory Brightwell, and a good many other of the settlement's womenfolk.

Now, Hezekiah saw only another harmless crop, no different from the hay and potatoes that filled their barns and barrels as winter threatened. A shortcut over the quiet, musky soil of the pumpkin patch only made good sense.

Peering through the steam of his own breath for the candle lantern he'd left hanging outside his door, still a good two dozen yards away, Hezekiah caught a whoop of surprise in his throat as he tripped on the vine of one of the ubiquitous squashes.

"Damn you!" He kicked the mute obstacle, thinking of Conal O'Herlihy's fiery rail he had listened to less than an hour ago, against the evil the Irishman was sure had infected the settlement, wickedness that the Lord had shown to the fiery zealot via the fungus, despair that would run rampant and claim them all if not soon addressed.

Looking toward the clearing where his homestead stood, Hezekiah again strained to spot the candle lamp. Since that afternoon, a steady autumn wind had come and gone. But it shouldn't have been enough to unsettle the lantern hung on a peg outside his door. The beacon was as sturdy as they came, and the candle set within had many hours yet.

No matter. Just past Friedrich Schroeder's cornfield, his clearing would be unmistakable, even under this weak moon.

The cornstalks rattled against each other in the steady wind, like the dying leaves of poplar trees all around his homestead, or the tail tips of the deadly snakes that had them all wary of where they trod during the hot season.

Hezekiah knew that he and others from the settlement would soon be called upon to help with harvesting the well-bred ears of the field he was passing, though Schroeder himself often mysteriously seemed to fall ill when his time came to reciprocate.

Still, the Dutchman's special wine was as good as his corn, and often given freely.

Hezekiah wondered why Schroeder had not attended the evening's meeting. It was the first he had missed, though Schroeder seemed well devoted to O'Herlihy's cause. Hezekiah already bore a measure of distrust for Schroeder, owing to the Dutchman's growing love of his own product—the one other than corn, of course.

Surely, with all he stood to lose, Friedrich Schroeder would not betray his friends to—

Hezekiah froze in his tracks.

A strange amber glow appeared, cresting the hill a few yards to his left.

The Devil.

Sinister eyes and mouth burned orange, floating and dancing in the sharp air.

To mock Hezekiah's secret fears, the Author of Evil had taken the form of a pumpkin.

A low snicker, at once childishly innocent and wickedly ancient, issued from the fire-filled gourd.

Hezekiah felt the urge to run, like the pull of a strong mule, and did not resist it. But no sooner had he pivoted than his feet again tangled in the vines of the new-world fruit—servants, after all, of the encroaching, orange-faced Satan. He pitched forward and fell upon the cold, earthen rooftop of The Devil's hot home.

With sharp grunts, Hezekiah kicked and scrambled, reaching for the matchlock at his side. But it too was trapped, twisted at an unwieldy angle by his fall. He tried rolling to his side to free the weapon, but the vines twisted tighter. He needed to twist his body the other way.

He did—just as the childish mirth sounded closer.

The burning-eyed demon floated above him, held aloft by something its inner flame—Hezekiah's own lamp candle—revealed to be far worse.

Schroeder's scarecrow.

Behind ragged strands of rough fabric, very real eyes and teeth reflected the candlelight. Real, yet only vaguely human.

This was not Lucifer, but Hezekiah prayed it was Schroeder, having a cruel ruse at his expense. He prayed but *knew*, by the madness those eyes held, that it was not.

"*Trrrick!*" said the scarecrow in a gleeful voice, as it held high in its right hand the pumpkin it had carved.

"Trrrreat!" it continued, as it raised a shiny hand sickle in its left, the blade stringy with pumpkin innards.

Hezekiah renewed the struggle for his weapon, exposing the side of his neck, the part the scarecrow knew would splash and spray blood so wonderfully.

In his nifty new scarecrow costume, Everett Geelens, many centuries later to be known as the Trick-or-Treat Terror, played with his pretty new toy, sharing it, in his way, with Hezekiah Hardison.

* * * *

Modern day

"When I'm sheriff, I'm gonna get a helicopter for stuff like this," Yoshida had quipped to Hudson as they set up the hunter's blind. That was three days ago. It seemed like three years.

The culmination of months of planning, this "stakeout," for lack of a better word, had the Cronus County Sheriff's Department's two ranking officers camped out in what was essentially a treehouse for potentially as long as four days.

It was no pleasure outing. Despite consisting of precious vacation and sick time, this outing was pure duty.

The elevated shelter, which Hudson and Yoshida had started planning and building the previous winter, sat nearly two dozen feet off the forest floor, wedged in the strong fork of a towering elm and hidden from below by strategically placed poplar branches and camouflage netting.

Eight feet square, the wooden box barely accommodated the duo. Food supplies were limited to bland necessities meant to provide energy and limiting waste scent production. Water was consumed sparingly. Latrine buckets were emptied into heavy-duty garbage bags that were hoisted through the roof above the hide and left to hover over them like a disgusting sword of Damocles. A flashlight, wax paper taped over its red lens and pointing straight up, gave a modest hint of illumination in the cramped shack.

Rugged as these conditions were for the deputies, they were mild compared to those suffered by their bait down on the ground, a juvenile fawn. They had placed her in a painless snare just for this purpose, to keep her relatively comfortable while they watched her through the scopes of their tranquilizer rifles, which lay poised in the narrow slot that was the blind's third opening.

They passed notes using legal pads—they were on their fifth—and traded off watching the bait while the other did push-ups and sit-ups, read or napped. Long before day three, the cramped solitude had begun to wear on them. If the two longtime friends had allowed themselves to speak at this point, they would surely have screamed at each other.

Hudson peered through the night-vision scope of a tranquilizer rifle loaded with high-dosage darts, which he had ordered from a gunsmith in Eagle Ridge. Beside him, Yoshida peered through an identical scope attached to a more traditional hunting gun.

Unlike Hudson's, his rifle was loaded with silver-tipped bullets, for a worst-case-scenario shot.

They had good reason to remain vigilant. This spot was less than a mile from where the first of many cattle killings had occurred, starting less than a year ago. It had been abandoned by bears and other known predators. This was a sure sign that a more dominant carnivore had taken over the area.

After the events of the previous year's Devil's Night, they knew that only one animal could be more dominant than bears and wolves.

Nearing the end of twilight, their inertia was violently shattered when their sights fell on a hulking, dark shape stealthily approaching the fawn.

The shape was familiar. It raised a terrifying memory Hudson and Yoshida had shared with a pair of punk rockers, a memory less than a year old.

Hudson drew the breath that braced his body to take the shot.

The skulking black hulk got set—and made a leap. It covered over twenty feet, landing upon the fawn. Following deftly with the luminous sights, Hudson pulled the trigger; no more than a mute clink.

"You got her!" Yoshida said, breaking the three-day silence. "She's moving!"

"Keep eyes on her!" Hudson rose and hurried to the trapdoor, clicking on the radio clipped to his belt. "Maybe I won't have to chase her too—"

"Get away from that hatch!" Yoshida sprang up and aimed his rifle at the square door. The way the weapon shook in his hands, he might have stepped on a live wire. "She's coming to *us!*"

Hudson leaped back from the hatch and reached for the knapsack slung across his back. The sound of scattering leaves in the wake of something massive—coming lightning-fast, and snarling with carnivorous rage—sent their adrenaline soaring.

Hudson's hand went to the silver chain in the sack, found the lock that coupled the links. He pulled the loop taut, as he had practiced hundreds of times.

The hunter's blind quaked when the bulk of the beast hit the elm. The growing volume of its growl told them the creature was climbing the trunk as deftly as a spider.

The enormous wolf's head burst through the plywood hatch like a torpedo, sending convulsions of terror through the seasoned deputies. Then the beast was upon Yoshida before he could pull his trigger.

Hudson lunged toward the monster with the chain loop held out—and missed, landing awkwardly across the monster's sinewy back.

The werewolf sprang to her hinds, sending Hudson face-first to the floor. Seeing stars, he thought for an instant that he was ascending into the night sky.

"The chain!" Yoshida's cry and the beast's ear-shattering roar brought him back. "Now!"

Hudson posted his foot to stand—and stepped right through the shattered hatch.

He caught himself on his hands, as he made out, in the dark mass of movement, Yoshida on the creature's back, pulling the rifle across its throat. He was sure to be tossed off at any second.

Hudson got his footing and launched himself again, aiming the chain loop for the pointed ears that nearly touched the ceiling. This time the hoop found home—only to get stuck halfway down the werewolf's thick head. Hudson cursed that he had made the loop too small. He had to push hard against the monster's head to get it over her ears.

Smoke rose where the silver made contact, giving off the sharp stench of burning hair. With a yelp, the wolf sank to all fours, shaking her head violently in an attempt to toss off the burning lariat. Hudson and Yoshida both backed against the walls to get a safe distance from the flailing marauder.

Hudson picked up the flashlight and tore off the wax-paper diffuser, focusing on the monster's clawed hand. She dropped the trank dart on the floor, looking up at Hudson with glowing eyes that promised annihilation.

Then the eyes softened, and the creature formerly named Aura gave off a keening whine.

"Easy girl," Hudson said, extending a comforting hand, well clear of her fangs.

* * * *

"Aaaagh!" DeShaun Lott's cry echoed in the rafters of the Community Center's basketball court. "I can't see! I'm…blind!" He fumbled around until his hand fell on his best friend's face. "Stuart!? Is that you, ol' buddy?"

"Ha," answered Stuart Barcroft. "And also…*ha.*"

DeShaun roughly ran his fingers across Stuart's mouth. "Yeah, it's you, all right. Big goofy grin and all. That must be what blinded me."

Stuart didn't push his friend's hand away, just walked away from it to the Community Center's loading doors, where his brother Dennis's tricked-out hearse sat with the rear door open. Truth was, Stuart was soaking up every minute he had with his lifelong friend, uncertain how many were left.

He couldn't resist a barb. "Maybe you can grope your way over to the freeway and stand around over there a bit, if you're not going to help me with the gear."

"Nah. You'd miss me, bro."

Stuart looked back at DeShaun, who smiled as always, but with a hint of sadness. Stuart leaned into the hearse, grabbed the handle of his brother's coffin-shaped guitar case and pulled it toward him. It was a much easier task now than the last time, some months back, thanks to a growth spurt during the band's extended hiatus. "Maybe not."

"Maybe you wouldn't, what, miss me?"

"Maybe I won't have to."

"Don't talk about it right now, dude." DeShaun reached in for bassist Pedro's case. As the teens lugged the instruments toward the center's stage, the clean purr of an antique Indian motorcycle rose in the parking lot, bringing the goofy grin back to Stuart's face

DeShaun burst out laughing.

"I can't help it, man," Stuart confessed. "Right now, everything is just so…"

"Perfect," DeShaun finished. "That's just your meds talking, sonny."

"Change of plan, losers," Pedro Fuentes called out as he leaped off the stage, where Dennis—aka Kenny Killmore, vocalist and lead guitarist of Ember Hollow's resident horror punk band, The Chalk Outlines—and engineer/chemist Bernard Riesling, an odd pairing if ever there was one, intently discussed something undoubtedly so technical in nature that Stuart and DeShaun often commented they should get college credit just for showing up.

"Dennis says we're setting up dead center of the joint," Pedro said.

"Dead center, huh?" Stuart repeated. "Bet he really hit the emphasis on 'dead,' didn't he?"

"Says he wants a 'cavernous' sound."

Stuart set his big brother's guitar case down against the wall, next to a spanking-new portable Yamaha keyboard, and glanced expectantly toward the open door. He should have known better.

"Ooooooh, Caaaaaandaaaace!" squealed DeShaun. "I neeeeed youuuu!"

Stuart punched him in the shoulder. "Shut it, ass brain."

"Well, it's not a big secret there, Stewie," remarked Outlines drummer "Thrill Kill" Jill Hawkins as she sashayed in, her hair dyed for the first time in months, jet-black this time. She carried a helmet airbrushed with the band's "voluptuous victim" Chalk Outline logo in one hand and a backpack covered in punk band patches in the other. Red drumsticks jutted through the zipper.

Carrying Jill's spare helmet, fourteen-year-old Candace followed. "You *neeeed* me, Stewie?" She set down the helmet and clasped her hands, casting a dreamy smile at him. She fluttered her eyes, swooned and "fainted" dead away on the glossy hardwood floor.

Her big mastiff, Bravo, leaped down from the stage to greet her, tail slashing the air behind him as he made his way to lick and sniff his girl back to giggly life.

Stuart loved this, as he did Candace, as he did this moment, this event. His brother's band back together—at least for rehearsals—after a painful breakup, his best friend, the girl he loved and her big ol' dog, all in one place and not terrified for their very lives, for a change.

Dennis came to the microphone at stage front, took one look at Jill and made an expression of lust so intense it resembled pain. "Tell me something, lady. How'm I supposed to get any work done with a smokin' hot number like you slinkin' around?"

Jill turned her blackened lips into a sultry smile and gave herself a spank.

Dennis shook his head. "I might have to sit down a lot."

Pedro and the teens rolled their eyes and groaned.

The troubled, yet loving couple, on advice from Dennis's rehab counselors, had vowed to remain platonic, purely bandmates, for at least six months or until their new demo album was finished. The sexual tension between them was a tightly wound spring; pent-up energy they did their best to channel into their music.

But the flirtation and innuendo flowed nonstop, to the extreme annoyance of anyone in earshot.

"Thanks for helping, everybody," Dennis said. "It's been a rough road."

Applause, a whistle from DeShaun. Bernard intently straightened cords behind the singer.

"I have to say how proud I am of you guys. All of you. We've all been through hell."

Bravo trotted up to the foot of the stage and sat watching Dennis with ears perked, curious about the microphone and what his friend was doing with it.

"I wrote a lot of stuff while I was in rehab." Dennis drew a folded sheaf of papers from his back pocket. "We're going for a new sound. You'll find out in a minute."

Stuart smiled for his brother.

"This studio in Asheville will invest in us and produce this album—if this demo is any good. Pedro, Jill, we gotta work our asses off like never before."

Stuart's excited smile spread to everyone else.

"DeShaun, Candace, little bro—thanks for pitching in. Now, let's kill it."

* * * *

"You'll just have to make do without me, Maisie," Violina said into the phone, as she traipsed to the bay windows to check the roundabout drive. "I have bookings into the middle of next year."

It was an exaggeration. Violina had become wealthy and successful through the craft. Indeed, she was truly set for life. But when it came to the others in her business, and especially what was left of her coven, inflation of even her formidable success was mandatory.

Violina Malandra *had* to be the most famous, the most in-demand, the wealthiest, the best, and in due time—The Only Witch.

"What can I say to change your mind?" asked the younger witch.

Violina was both contemptuous and resentful of Maisie's humility. The girl was young, well aware of her own lack of knowledge and experience. At thirty-five, well-established in both business and social circles, Violina could never allow herself to be so humble.

"Ysabella wants you here," Maisie continued. "She says we can't do this without you."

The sitting room of her three-story Victorian, with its occult trappings, was meticulously designed to ride the fence between theatrical and inviting.

Violina waved a hand over the table she'd prepared for her expected guest, with an ornate, gilded tarot deck and velvet-lined tray of crystals. "Me specifically?"

"All of us," the girl answered. "Those of us left."

This was not what Violina wanted to hear. "Like I said dear, I'm very busy."

"Violina, I have a feeling this might be too much for her," explained Maisie. "I'd feel better having you here."

Violina strolled to the window. In the driveway, the expected gleaming-white Bentley crept over fresh-fallen New England maple leaves.

"I have a client, Maisie," Violina said. "Sorry I can't help."

"Would you at least call me back when you're free? We're at the Blue Moon Inn in Ember Hollow, North Carolina."

Violina raised a manicured eyebrow, her interest suddenly sparked. "Did you say Ember Hollow? Where they had that parade disaster? And all those awful murders?"

"Yes. Matilda Saxon was here, up in the hills. We think there's a connection."

"Give me the number there," Violina allowed. "I'll consider it."

"Oh, bless you, Violina!"

Violina wasn't interested in the naïve apprentice's gratitude or "blessings." But she had wanted to get out to Matilda Saxon's isolated farm since meeting the solitary witch some years ago. She wished she had learned of her fellow baneful practitioner's death earlier, in time to scour her substantial inventory before the police or anyone else got to it.

Nonetheless, Violina's elegant nostrils flared at her favorite scent: opportunity.

With Ysabella weakened and supernatural forces clearly at work in the troubled town, Violina realized she could easily come away from the job with greater power than any witch. *Ever.*

Chapter 2

She Wolf

Covered in a blanket that was bound with Hudson's silver chain, the monstrous gray wolf lay motionless on her side. Though her head remained uncovered, a leather strap was tied around her snout, and this strap was wrapped with a Saint Christopher medallion on a chain. The necklace had served a similar purpose on Bravo's collar a year ago.

The wolf's eye lolled from Hudson to Yoshi and back. She displayed her long, gleaming teeth in an eerie, silent snarl.

"That's starting to freak me out," Yoshida admitted. "You sure she can't move?"

"Well, I skipped the day they covered skinwalker biology at the academy," Hudson deadpanned, "but the boys have been reading everything they can get their hands on about werewolves."

"The boys" was how Hudson Lott referred to both his own son DeShaun and DeShaun's best friend, Stuart Barcroft, whom he considered just as much a son. "But I doubt she's playing dead just to see if we'll give her a doggie treat. So stay alert."

As they squatted to grasp the edges of the thick mover's blanket on which the chained beast lay, Yoshi gave a faux-bitter laugh. "Now I know where DeShaun gets his smart-assery."

"Honestly, I think I caught it from him," Hudson said. "And it's probably contagious, so…"

"Now you tell me."

Hudson couldn't know that the word "contagious" made Yoshida bristle with dread.

They hoisted the monster and slid it into the chain-link cage—essentially an oversized kennel—they had fashioned two weeks earlier.

"I'm still not sold on this dinky pen," Yoshida said.

"If those silver chains don't hold her, the cage is meaningless anyway."

They closed and locked the cage door, dropped the heavy canvas tarp flap over the front and raised the tailgate.

"The fawn's okay?" Hudson asked.

"Scared shitless, but not a scratch. She ran off without so much as an *'Eff you.'*"

"Good work, my friend." Hudson offered his gloved hand.

Yoshida clasped it. "That's what I'm gonna say to my shower, because it sure has its work cut out for it."

They climbed into the front, and Hudson started the engine. "We'll stop and look in on her in ten or twelve miles."

Yoshida checked the chamber of the trank rifle and propped it against his leg. "You really think the witch's farm is the best place to take her?"

"We damn sure can't put her in the drunk tank."

Yoshida chuckled at the image. Not so much of a gigantic wolf in a cell full of sots, but of Hudson explaining it to the chief. The wisecracks were a welcome diversion. But his thoughts would not stray far from the tiny tingling nick on his arm, where the werewolf's fang had pierced his skin half an inch deep.

* * * *

Flipping black locks out of his eyes, Pedro cocked his head sideways and grimaced. "What do these words mean…'too loud'?"

"Just your backup vocals," explained Dennis, as he muted the preprogrammed rhythm track on the new keyboard. "Understated. Not screamed."

"Am I even audible?"

"You will be," reassured Dennis. "That's why we're so wide open." He arced his arm to indicate the Community Center's vastness. "To get a good echo effect."

"What about me, babe?" asked Jill. "I mean…*Dennis.*" Though her tone was playful, it carried an edge of frustration. "You sure you even need me? You could set the keyboard to…"

Jill didn't finish, and she didn't need to. Dennis hadn't mentioned the addition of a keyboard to any of them before this very session. She might even have harbored an ounce of jealousy toward it.

Dennis just looked at her the way he always did these days—like she had just walked in naked. "Even if I didn't need you on the skins, I'd be a sad little sicko without you around to gawk at…"

Holding eye contact, Jill parted her black lips and narrowed her eyes, playful and sultry.

"…and the hypnotic purr of that sexy-ass voice."

Sitting together nearby on folding chairs, Candace, Stuart and DeShaun gave dramatic reactions—Candace giggling, Stuart covering his eyes and shaking his head, DeShaun launching himself to a stand to simulate a violent vomiting attack.

"I swear you're making me celibate over here," griped Pedro. "Your shrink is gonna have to start giving me hazard pay for my chaperone services."

"Look, I know it's a learning curve, guys." Dennis reached for the sleeve of his Mephisto Walz T-shirt and the pack of cigarettes that used to live there. "Damn this oral fixation…" He smoldered at Jill again, and she smoldered back.

"Get 'em, Bravo!" ordered Stuart. "Go for the throat! Kill!"

Bravo hopped up and wagged his tail, but that was all.

"Dude, it's just not who we are," Pedro said. "The kids love our songs. And our shtick. No apologies. We're horror punkers! Not…Goth…death rock…bat cave…cold wave…"

"It's like I told you, Petey. The studio guy wants it dark and stark. These songs are our *biographies,* bro. Shit that we went through was not fun, or fun-*ny.*" He raised the new song sheets, clutched like a stick of dynamite. "This is genuine. And we have it in us. Let's just roll with it and see what happens."

Pedro swiped his hand through his unruly, neck-length mop and shrugged. "You're the boss."

"Hey, that's right." Dennis narrowed his eyes at Jill yet again. "Are you ready to submit to my will, drum slave?"

Candace bumped Stuart and scooted into his chair a little, laughing like Dennis's allusion was the funniest thing she had ever heard. DeShaun got up in a huff, dramatically stomped to the exit, and slammed the door behind him.

Candace leaned into Stuart, looking at him just a little bit like Jill and Dennis always looked at each other, and they laughed, easy and natural.

"Let's hit it." Dennis counted down, and they started again, with a number called "Cinders of Summer."

The song was a testament to his versatility. Dennis eschewed his usual punkabilly voice projection for a gloomy, dreamy sound somewhere between Rozz Williams and Johan Edlund. He strummed rather than pounded his guitar and kept his eyes closed a lot.

Pedro raised his confused look from the paper on his music stand to Dennis, then to Jill, then back, noticeably straining to stand still and carefully finger his strings without slashing.

Jill choked up on her drumsticks to keep from hitting too hard, but soon found herself staring at her drum set like it was an alien artifact.

She stopped, then Pedro stopped, and finally Dennis. "Okay, guys," he began. "This transition might take longer than I thought."

"We wanna play ball, babe," Jill said. "I mean, Mister Platonic Bandleader, sir."

"I could get it. No doubt about it." Pedro looked around the basketball court. "Just not feeling it here."

Dennis leaned forward over his guitar and peered at him like an interrogating detective. He sat like this for a long time, until Candace cleared her throat, purely to break the stiff silence.

"You're right, Petey." Dennis murmured into his microphone.

"Of course I am." Pedro's puzzled expression belied his agreement.

The door opened with an echoing clack, DeShaun returning, peering in between fingers. "You guys aren't doing it, are you?"

"Get in here, deserter." Dennis had called DeShaun that, plus "traitor" and a variety of other, less palatable names, since the day back in March when the Lotts announced they would be moving away. "We got band business to discuss."

"Swell." DeShaun made his way back to his seat. "Then can you guys keep your disgusting mush talk on a strictly telepathic wavelength?"

"I wanna try a different location for rehearsal. Maybe even for recording." Dennis stood and unshouldered his guitar. "This place'll be off limits for the Devil's Night shindig anyway, and we can't spare the time."

"Where then?" asked Stuart.

"I want everybody to think about it before you murder me. This could be good."

"Okay..."

"I mean really good."

"Dammit, just spill already!" demanded Jill.

Dennis walked out to stand roughly in the center of the group. "The church catacombs."

* * * *

"Unlike your Jamestowns and your sponsored settlements and whatnot, Ember Hollow was totally independent," DeShaun would explain to witches Violina and Maisie, just a few hours later, across a table at the Kronus Café.

"Wilcott Bennington knew a trapper guy who had already been over here. That dude dropped some crucial info that nobody else in Europe knew," Stuart would then say. "The trapper dude found a nice big spread, ya know, a piedmont, with lots of flat fields kind of closed in by the mountains and hills."

"Benzo knew that, sooner or later, Ol' Lady England was gonna claim all this dirt," continued DeShaun. "The Cherokee stayed near water, which our little burg isn't, so it was basically there for the taking,"

"And these local natives were 'docile.'" Stuart frowned before his next sentence. "Lots of Europeans thought of Indians as less than human."

"Our boy hired this guy to get a crew and come back to survey it." DeShaun drew an imaginary map on the table with his fingers. "Meanwhile, he got up some investors to foot the bill for making the settlement, with him in place as governor, so they could beat the king to laying claim on this bucolic death trap you see all around us."

"Ol' Wilcott started recruiting 'partners' on the D.L. two years before ever setting sail. Difference between his deal and, say, the French settlements of the time was that Wilcott knew what to expect."

"And he wasn't such a hard-ass on religious beliefs, since his own were pretty radical for the time."

"Rather pagan-esque, I take it," said Violina, "given the Saint Saturn appellation."

"W.B. did some studying. He believed Christianity was actually Saturn worship. A few folks shared this belief, once he explained the backstory."

Chapter 3

Valley of The Scarecrow

Settlement era

Friedrich Schroeder rubbed the back of his neck, his hand coming away damp. But there was no sting of sunburn, and for that he prayed his gratitude, if absently, as he did for every little thing, including the mild euphoria he got from his dandelion wine and, of course, the paying patronage of his fellow settlers.

Soon after arriving, the settlers encountered the natives and found them kind and welcoming, a contrast to the terrifying rumors they had all heard in the port taverns back in England. That is, until Conal O'Herlihy introduced the tribe to his vaunted mushroom, and promptly scared them away.

All except a few young males who were captured and imprisoned.

Schroeder was ashamed to have played a role in their oppression and enslavement. But Conal, in his uncompromising wisdom, had declared that it was God's will that man hold dominion over beasts, which these natives were to him, no different from horses or cattle.

Still, keeping the small troop of young Tsalagi men and boys secretly encamped in the woods a few miles from the settlement was a logistical challenge. Schroeder's special wine was a persuader for the settlement men in Conal's confidence, for the young Indians themselves and for his own pesky conscience.

His wine had secured his position among O'Herlihy's most trusted lieutenants. But his absence the previous night might strain their friendship. Expressing his growing qualms would not salve it.

At the moment, plans for the harvest of his corn and pumpkin crops were at the fore, and that labor would fall to his friends, neighbors and fellow disciples of Conal.

There was a good bit of preparation to be done before he would call on them. First, he would need to make more wine, of course, and have Olga bake her special bread.

For now, his task was to move the *bootzaman* to the eastern edge of his cornfield, beside the pumpkin patch. The crows, though mostly uninterested in the strange orange squash, often gathered there and perched atop the spheres, as if awaiting marching orders. They had heeded well his towering strawman here in mid-field. The move would keep them confused.

At Schroeder's invitation, a handful of settlers had come to behold the unveiling of his uncanny false man. They had all been left uneasy by it.

Schroeder understood the fear of a thing that could not be real. His grandmother had ruined a good many of his dreams with her stories of the *Sensenmann*, or Death Angel, forever lurking out of sight, waiting to separate souls from bodies with his curved blade.

By comparison, Schroeder's straw-stuffed guardian was laughable. These Anglos could count themselves fortunate to have evaded his grandmother's stories.

Schroeder counted the rows and lanes he walked, his only way of knowing one identical section of field from another, and reminded himself to make a few more of the effigies. Stopping to part two familiar stalks, he found the scarecrow just where he had last placed it.

But this was *not* his scarecrow.

Just as Hezekiah Hardison, before dying, had believed for a split second that Schroeder was giving him a fright, Schroeder thought the opposite.

It was Hezekiah *himself* who hung from the sturdy cross frame Schroeder had made. Hardison's head lay at a hideous angle. His clothes were soaked through with something meant to recall blood.

"Oh, stop this…game…" Schroeder chided, his voice trailing as early decay met his nostrils. This man, his neighbor, was dead—his neck torn open like a grain sack.

Schroeder spun to look behind him, then up and down both lanes, then back to the ersatz scarecrow. He leaned as far forward as he could without taking a step, to touch Hezekiah's hand—and recoiled, despairing that the hand felt so cold, here under the warm sun.

He pivoted and ran to get his horse, blasting past cornstalk leaves so fast they cut his face. He needed to be near as many living folks as he could find, to hide from Death until it was wiped away in the Second Coming—oh, holy God, please let that be a true thing!

* * * *

Modern day

Yoshida watched until Hudson's taillights disappeared into the trees beyond the drive, then went back into the strange scents and sights of the barn.

He switched on the portable stereo he had brought and tuned to local station WICH. Their two-month-long Halloween celebration for the region's dwindling population, which had deejays assuming cornball Cryptkeeper-type personae, was always good for a few laughs, even if it seemed half-hearted at best these days. The deputy kept the volume low for the sleeping guest.

The barn's towering steel shelving units, filled with what the deputies had taken to calling "hoodoo potions," had been pushed back to make room for the cage weeks earlier. As Yoshida and Hudson wrestled with one of the cabinets, a squat asymmetrical ceramic jar fell onto the plywood floor, and the lid fell off.

The jar appeared empty, but when Yoshida went to pick it up, he was stunned to find it far heavier than it looked—it weighed at least sixty pounds.

Hudson thought Yoshida was pulling his leg, until he too went to lift the jar. "Maybe we better not touch any more of this stuff."

"You don't have to tell me twice."

Now, after three miserable days, and with Hudson heading back to Ember Hollow to greet incoming guests—consultants in this very case—Yoshida felt more alone than he ever had. The massive, chain-wrapped wolf in the cage had remained subdued from the tranquilizer dart throughout the drive. But when they slid her cage down from the rear of the truck, it slipped from the hands of the exhausted deputies and dropped the last few inches to the floor.

Aura's eye popped open—and instantly focused on Yoshida. She followed him around the room with her amber stare, straining to the very limits of her periphery to keep him in sight. Her wet nose twitched fastidiously, perhaps assessing her environment or the strap wrapped around her snout.

Yoshida rechecked the chamber of his tranquilizer gun and the cylinder of his sidearm before settling into a lawn chair sitting just within the open barn doors. He couldn't see Aura's rolling eye from here, but he had no doubt it was directed toward him. He watched the steady rise and fall of the blanket that protected her against the burn of the silver chains.

After all the vicious biker had done both as woman and wolf—a body count on par with Everett Geelens himself—she hardly deserved to be pampered.

Then again, she had helped save the lives of his friends Candace and Jill, and that was worth something.

Weighing whether to switch off the overhead lights, Yoshida caught himself rubbing the nagging tingle on his arm again, where her tooth had nicked him. He pushed up the sleeve of his flannel shirt, dreading to see angry redness and watery discharge.

Instead, he found that the wound was nearly healed.

Other than a red mark, which could well have been from his constant rubbing, there was no sign of the bite, no indication his skin had ever been broken.

Chapter 4

Settlement era

The new scarecrow costume was not Everett's favorite.

Life had been very strange for him lately. He had awakened from a strange dream in which he had burst from a pumpkin, like a baby raven leaving its egg.

Then he played Halloween games with a witch, some motorcycle men, and a pretty girl with shiny black boots. His sister Candace was there! And he was so happy and ready to play with her too, to give her a mask he would make from the nice face of the girl in the boots.

Then a big werewolf came and attacked him! And then Bravo did too! Why? The girl in the boots smashed something over him that made him burn up.

The next thing Everett Geelens knew, he was lying in a field full of corn, naked and cold. He was sad that he hadn't really gotten to spend time with Candace.

There were colored leaves in this new place, and a cold breeze all around. The scarecrow could only be…a Halloween decoration! He had awakened just in time for his favorite day!

The scarecrow was just standing out in the middle of the cornfield. Not many people would see it way out here, so Everett decided it would be okay to put on its clothes.

The costume fit him just okay. It was itchy and too tight, but it looked like a really real scarecrow, and it was better than being naked.

Everett walked around for a while to try to figure out where he was, though he didn't know the names of places. He just knew it was time to start celebrating Halloween and to help others celebrate too.

Lo and behold, he found a pumpkin patch! So many big beautiful Halloween squashes wanting him to carve them into jack-o'-lanterns. Everett could almost hear their voices, scratchy and low like his, but not from what evil church men did. Just because they were full of seeds and stuff.

Everett picked up one of the pumpkins and carried it with him, reassuring it he would get it ready for Halloween, as he would do for each and every person he found.

Just as soon as he found a good knife.

He had followed a trail to a little old barn and found a nice sharp hand sickle. He sat down on a stump to carve the first pumpkin jacko ever.

Last night, he finally found somebody—a man in a funny, old-timey pilgrim costume. But it wasn't spooky enough, so Everett helped him get spookier with the sickle. A scarecrow like him! Everett didn't know the man's name was Hezekiah.

Everett ate the pumpkin's seeds and some of the corn. They tasted weird and sweet. Very different from the meat and potatoes and pumpkin pies his Mamalee used to make for him back when he lived in his little haunted shed, behind the big house where Mamalee and his grumpy old father and his sweet little sister, Candace, and fuzzy dog, Bravo, lived.

Father would never let him out of the shed, except for on Halloween. Then one Halloween not very long ago, Everett realized he was grown up and could decide for himself when he could go out.

Now he walked around the fields and found footpaths but no houses. He saw a column of smoke, so he ventured out of the cornfield to find where it was coming from.

A house! A cute little one, made of skinned trees, like a fairy-tale house. There was no car outside and, even worse, no Halloween decorations. Someone inside was singing, and her voice was nice. But she was singing about the mean old man in the sky that those priests always talked to, the priests who hurt him and made him feel so wrong.

Maybe this lady was nice, though. The best way to find out if someone is nice is to trick-or-treat them.

Everett got his scary sickle ready, trying to hold back his giggle as he crept to the door. There was no ding-dong button. The lady didn't even have any paper skeletons or toy black cats put out front. Maybe she didn't know it was Halloween time.

He would have to help her get ready, like he had so many others.

* * * *

The harder Glory worked, the louder she sang praise to the Lord, and Glory Brightwell was surely the loudest-singing woman in the settlement, perhaps in all of the new world. Certainly, her husband, Allard, was the hardest-working man, and he deserved no less. Chopping these carrots for his rabbit stew was the Lord's work.

Allard was always eager to avail himself for the unexpected needs of their fellow settlers. When he wasn't leading hunting parties to keep the settlement well-stocked, he was helping to raise barns and houses.

Then there were frequent, secret meetings with Conal O'Herlihy and a growing group of men. That was a matter that was none of Glory's business, and just as well.

Glory's ordained purpose was to keep Allard's one-room domicile as tidy as she had their rented flat back in England.

Tending this home and the land around it was more than enough work for a woman, especially one belonging to such a busy and important man like Allard.

Allard's frequent vague promises of a bigger and better home, like Bennington's, were as certain to bear fruit as God's promise to Moses of a land filled with milk and honey. For now, there was only a bed, a dining table, and the fireplace, which took up nearly a quarter of the house.

Still, Glory was grateful for a new life in a new world. This poor street girl, who had bitterly considered prostitution before the miracle of meeting Allard, then becoming his bride and helpmate in Wilcott Bennington's wilderness settlement across the sea, would forever offer thanks in work and in song.

An oddly cadenced knock at the door severed her psalm.

Whenever Allard returned from a hunting excursion or a barn raising, he always knocked and gaily called out so he wouldn't frighten her.

But this was not his knock, and he did not call or enter afterward.

Glory stared at the door, finding small comfort behind the barrier of the big oaken table. She sought to sense something familiar in the shadow that broke the light between cracks in the wood of the door.

Burly Hezekiah Hardison came to mind. Whenever he tipped his hat at her in the town commons or at gatherings, it accompanied a penetrating, lustful stare upon her bosom.

And Hezekiah would surely know Allard was out hunting. Thinking of Glory all alone, he might have got himself a head full of carnal mischief and corn-liquor courage.

"Who's there!?" she called.

The answer was the kind of stifled snickering that came from a shy child. But its timbre, and the size of the shape filling the cracks—these were far from childlike.

Glory found herself wishing, then praying, that it was Hezekiah. She had rebuffed him before, and she could again.

In the early days, the Indians had visited on occasion, but they had since been driven away, somehow, by Conal O'Herlihy. All that aside, something about the knock and laugh told Glory this was no Indian.

Other than the giggle, there was nothing to suggest it was even human.

"Answer me!" she called. "I'll have no foolishness!"

The response came as a curved blade, sliding between the cracks and slowly scraping down till it met the cross plank.

Then, the blade softly, teasingly, pecked against the plank. As with the initial knock, there was no rhythm to it.

"Go away!" Glory dashed to the matchlock resting in the corner, grateful Allard had insisted on leaving his secondary weapon loaded and in easy reach for her. "I will shoot you!"

The blade halted, resting atop the cross plank of the door like a giant talon pointing straight to hell.

"I'll shoot you right through the door!" she yelled. "I do mean it!"

The blade withdrew.

From this viewpoint, Glory could not see whether the blackness between the cracks had gone as well. With her back pressed against the dry mud wall, she began to sidestep to her left until she could see through the cracks again.

They were still filled with black.

Yet there was no sign of movement. Glory relived the last few minutes, wondering if she had imagined…

"Triiick…" came a raspy call. Glory reflexively pulled the trigger before she could even aim, punching a hole through the thatch roof. A dusty ray shone onto her chopped carrots.

She screamed, even before the door was splintered to kindling by the boot of a bloody scarecrow.

Glory convulsed as she fell back against the wall, aiming the matchlock across the dining table, repeatedly squeezing an unmoving trigger on a weapon that wasn't even cocked, much less loaded.

The scarecrow raised the hand sickle and pointed it at her. "…or treeeat!"

Both stood frozen for so long that Glory's knees began to shake. She hurled the gun at the invader and lunged for the paring knife that lay amid the carrot slices, snatching it as Everett swatted the rifle aside. He flipped the table toward the fireplace as if it was a branch of dried poplar. She lunged at him with the blade. Everett yelped like a suckling pig as the point entered between his ribs.

Glory took a split second to decide whether to run away or stab him again. Choosing the latter, she despaired to find the blade held firm in his flesh.

Her hopes for survival plunged as she recalled that inner suction often took hold of Allard's skinning knives when he dressed out a deer.

She yanked and yanked. But the ragged demon just stared at her with a mix of disappointment, dejection and what could only be madness.

Everett raised his sickle in a swift upward arc. It entered just below Glory's belly, sliced cleanly through her breastbone and exited just under her chin.

The only treat she had to offer was the sharp pain in his ribs and this splashing scarlet mess at his feet.

* * * *

Modern Day

"They're heeere." Only after she had spoken did Leticia Lott realize she had just echoed a line, complete with childish inflection, from *Poltergeist*, her son DeShaun's third-favorite movie on the annotated list he maintained and frequently updated with utmost gravitas.

"You mean…here?" asked Stella Riesling as she sidled through the door carrying four-year-old Emera in one arm, a bursting bag of groceries in the other. She brought a puff of crisp fall air in her wake that gave Leticia a quick thrill of dread.

"At the Blue Moon Inn," clarified Leticia. "Maisie called when they arrived. They'll be here within the hour."

Leticia closed the door and took one of Stella's burdens—Emera, of course. "Hi, Emmie!" she cooed.

The little girl, adorable in a Scooby-Doo top and leggings, gave a shy smile and buried her face in Leticia's shoulder.

Then came a squeal from the living room, and thumps of happy little feet. "Meh-meh!" It was three-year-old Wanda, overjoyed that her friend had come to play. Emera returned the sentiment. "Wandaaaah!"

"Show her your spooky drawing, baby." Leticia put Emera down, and the girls raced to the living room. "God help us all, Wanda is copying DeShaun's scary comics—and she's very good at it."

"Do you still feel weird about this meeting?" Stella asked.

"Don't you?"

"Mmm…touché."

"Weird or not, I'm glad you had this idea." Leticia gave Stella's arm a reassuring pat. "I couldn't leave you guys if I didn't know you were going to be all right."

"You can thank Abe," Stella whispered. "He doesn't want it getting out, but he came up with the whole thing."

They went to the counter of Leticia's ever-immaculate kitchen, which these days doubled as an art gallery for Wanda's crayoned masterworks, and started setting out groceries.

When the doorbell rang again a minute later, both baby girls squealed with faux fright from the living room, then giggled at one another.

"Speak of the devil." Leticia stopped to dim the lights minutely, then went to the door while Stella looked over the groceries—all organic, as requested by the guests—that would comprise dinner for two housewives, two little girls, two pagan witches and a Christian minister.

"Thanks for letting me borrow your assistant, Reverend." Leticia said, as she led Reverend Abe McGlazer to the kitchen.

"Yes!" exclaimed McGlazer. "Assistant, not boss! Thanks for playing along, Leticia." McGlazer dug into a bowl of cashews left on the counter just for him. "Any idea how Hudson and Yoshi are doing?"

"Due back tomorrow. I'm trying not to worry."

"DeShaun?"

"Helping The Outlines at the Community Center."

McGlazer gobbled cashews as he cast a glance at the front door.

"Don't tell me you're nervous," said Stella.

"Anxious is the word," McGlazer answered. "But not about tonight."

Leticia and Stella did not ask what, then—and did not need to. With Halloween approaching, they all bore the same abiding apprehension. Two consecutive autumns of harrowing, county-wide peril had conditioned them to expect something terrible and terrifying to happen, some horrific disaster surely brewing even now as they futilely rushed to prepare for it.

Chapter 5

Seasons of the Witch

In a raucous race, the little girls answered the door before the adults could. "Twick o' tweat!" Wanda yelled to the two guests.

Emera giggled and repeated the phrase.

"Trick-or-treat to you, little cuties!" responded Maisie, her smile as wide as a crescent moon.

"Here you go!" said Ysabella, handing the children confections she had made herself. "For dessert. All right?"

"Dee-zert!" said Emera, though she mimed eating it then and there, to the delight of her friend as they darted back to the living room.

"I didn't know what to expect—but you're both so pretty!" Leticia told Ysabella and Maisie after hellos, as she took their jackets.

"Hey, look!" Emera and Wanda were back, both holding up rumpled crayon illustrations.

Ysabella and Maisie each took one and examined it. There was not the slightest irony in their smiles of admiration.

Emera's was a forest. The trees were black at the bottom but became green at the tops, under a fat, smiling sun.

Wanda had rendered a powerful mother figure, black like her, with rainbows sprouting from her hands.

Ysabella knelt, though her knees popped and cracked. "This is far beyond their age level. Have you had them in classes?"

"Neither one," answered Stella.

"They seem to feed off each other's talent," said Leticia.

"A little coven of two," said Ysabella, touching each girl's head "That is as magical as it gets."

Stella got the little girls in their high chairs, McGlazer got the guests seated in gentlemanly fashion and Leticia gave orderly and concise introductions.

The name Maisie came easily to the girls' little tongues, but "Ysabella" proved to be a challenge. The elder witch suggested "Miss Iss." They repeated it to each other dozens of times.

"I feel underdressed," added Stella. Looking down at the guests' feet, she gave a quick laugh. "I'm sorry," she said, pointing to their slip-on loafers. "I must have expected pointy black boots."

Ysabella and Maisie were far from offended. Hyper-aware of the general public's perception of witches, they always did their best to present a comforting appearance. For the dinner meeting, they had worn casual-elegant dresses and understated makeup.

Rings and necklaces bearing pentacles and other so-called pagan symbols were either concealed or left back at the inn, save for a braided leather bracelet Ysabella wore, woven through a carved jade Green Man head, the tiny polished face sculpted with a gleeful smile.

Emera's eyes fell to the jolly little man, and she mirrored its smile.

Once everyone was settled at the table, the dinner guests joined hands and looked to McGlazer.

"Right," he said. "Time to say grace. You…don't mind?"

"We always give thanks," said Ysabella.

McGlazer offered a broad, nondenominational thanks, which little Wanda punctuated with chubby hands held high and a hearty "Maaaay-mim!"

The witches tucked in and gave their compliments on the décor and furnishings. Then it was time for business.

"I felt it," Ysabella said. "Not long after we crossed the county line."

Maisie rubbed her elder's shoulder and looked at McGlazer. "You were right to call us, Reverend. It's only getting stronger."

"We've contacted our sisters, but I must tell you, you've caught us at a bad time." Ysabella's voice was still scratchy from the earlier vomiting spell. "We're far from full strength."

"Suffice to say, we'll need anyone in town to participate who will," Maisie added.

"It's our town," Stella said. "Of course, we'll help."

"There's a good deal of risk involved."

Leticia and Stella exchanged an uncertain gaze.

Maisie broke the heavy pause. "We understand you're moving away, Leticia."

"Hudson is taking a job in Henderson County."

This assertion was mostly positive thinking. The deal was far from sealed on her husband's new position.

"It's good of you to host us. But I can tell you have reservations."

"I was raised Lutheran." Leticia cast a self-conscious smile at Maisie. "Or did you already know?"

"I'm not reading your mind," Maisie said. "The tells are all there. It's more important to you to help your friends."

"Sure sounds like mind reading," Leticia responded.

"Tell me," began Ysabella, "do you folks know of any practitioners here in Ember Hollow?"

"Witches?" Stella wondered if she should mention her own psychic moments or her success with dowsing as a teenager.

"We can't afford to be fussy. Wicca, Vodun, Taoist." Ysabella looked at McGlazer. "And you, good Reverend."

McGlazer's eyebrows rose. "Me?"

"Of course."

"You surely must believe in ghosts," Maisie dabbed at her mouth with a napkin, "after having been possessed by one."

"Well…yes."

"Then you know what we're dealing with. You're invaluable to this process."

"I'm sorry, but I don't see how all these conflicting beliefs can work together," Leticia remarked.

"The conflict is imaginary. Everything has the same source."

Maisie's answer struck Leticia as ridiculously obvious.

"Maaay-mim!" Wanda said again, to everyone's delight, twin points of candlelight alive in her brown eyes.

"How long do we have you, Leticia?" asked Maisie without credulity.

"We should hear from Henderson County any day now."

"So you might leave before we can finish?"

Leticia frowned, reluctant to answer.

"What about your church?" asked Maisie.

"Closed and locked up since last Halloween," Stella answered. "Only a handful of us know what was down there."

"I couldn't see any good coming of telling everyone what happened and having the old place condemned…" explained McGlazer. He was pained to say the next word. "…destroyed."

"We told everyone there was a massive mold problem, which is not entirely untrue," Stella added. "Moved services to the Community Center."

"Saint Saturn's is a crucial part of this town. We've prayed and brainstormed ever since, to come up with some solution other than condemning it." McGlazer's fork shook in his hands. "Thinking of the witch in the hills. Matilda. I thought it couldn't hurt to contact you ladies, if only to learn more."

Maisie smiled. "You love your church. We'll do our best to save it."

"Miss Iss," whispered Emera with a giggle, drawing everyone's gaze.

The elder witch was holding an intense stare with the little one. In less than a second, both the woman and the girl cycled through expressions of sympathy and understanding.

Ysabella laughed, and so did Emera.

"We've found one of our new recruits," explained Ysabella. "Maybe two. Tell me about her and her sister."

"Emera and Candace? They've already been through so much…" Stella said.

"So often, that's exactly what makes a powerful witch," explained Ysabella, as she continued to hold the loving gaze with Emera. The child smiled and smiled, like she did when big sister/best friend Candace was near. "Tell us more."

Stella gave the short version: Candace's parents were murdered by her brother, Everett Geelens, the Trick-or-Treat Terror, during his Halloween night rampage two years earlier. She was placed in a group home as Emera's roommate. The house parents had sought to provoke Candace into violent behavior, to exploit the rights to her story.

"The Fireheads gang had a different plan for Candace," added McGlazer. "To sacrifice her. They were in wolf form when they kidnapped her."

"Thanks to Matilda Saxon's magic," said Leticia.

Maisie raised her hand to her mouth. "The poor child must be traumatized beyond our understanding."

"Then Everett returned, quite literally, from the dead."

Maisie reached across the table and grasped Stella's hand. "You're a saint, to adopt these troubled babies."

While everyone else took on grim faces, Ysabella and Emera continued to hold a smile filled on both sides with wisdom. "Don't worry. We would never endanger any of these precious children. It's only their imaginations we need."

Ysabella untied the leather and jade Green Man bracelet from her wrist and handed it to Emera. The little girl raised it in both hands with awe. "Thank you, Miss Iss!"

As Stella tied it on Emera's wrist, she realized she felt…jealousy? She would tell the witches about her own experiences. But now was not the time. "How do we get started?"

"To heal the town, we'll have to start with Matilda's farm," Ysabella said.

"We need to go as soon as possible," added Maisie.

After a pause, Ysabella pronounced "Tonight."

"Why tonight?" asked Leticia.

Just as Ysabella stood, Hudson opened the front door, looking weary and smelling of woods and sweat.

"Daddeee!" called Wanda.

"You're home a day early, babe!" said Leticia.

Ysabella stood. "Deputy Lott, I'm sorry. There's no time for rest or pleasantries. Please take us to the farm. Before something terrible happens."

* * * *

Settlement era

Not long ago, this daily ritual had been a form of relaxation for settlement founder Wilcott Bennington, nothing more than pleasant time spent with his quarter horse Jupiter, appreciating the new-world acreage he had claimed and conquered.

With the enmity growing between him and the forceful Irishman O'Herlihy, it felt less like a leisurely ride these days, and more like patrol duty. There had been threats, implied by both words and mere looks, from O'Herlihy and his growing group of followers. Given the size of the house and estate Bennington had made for himself and his loyal maidservant, Chloris, he knew it was best to keep a lookout for trespassers, and to make sure everyone knew he was doing so.

Bennington inhaled the unique scent of southeastern autumn air and absently patted Jupiter. Though wary, he did not expect an ambush. Matters had not decayed to that level just yet.

He had a sense that they would, soon enough. There were rumblings that O'Herlihy was holding organized gatherings, to discuss—and perhaps breed—dissatisfaction with settlement affairs and with Bennington's odd beliefs. That was their right, of course, but it made Bennington sad and regretful that he had been too eager and forthcoming in discussing his evolving spiritual philosophy when winnowing potential partners for his new-world settlement.

Still, it was hard not to lose himself in the unique beauty of the land, especially at harvest season. Its beauty whispered a song of dread and a promise of difficult times ahead that made these short days feel all the more precious.

Jupiter whinnied and snapped his head sharply, alerting Bennington that he was pulling the reins too hard. It was a bad habit that accompanied his dark ponderings. The pioneer eased his grip and scratched the horse's neck. "Very sorry, old friend."

Yet Jupiter remained stiff and alert, keeping his busy snout to the left. He issued a soft snuffle, as if sensing a predator.

The only movement was that of the poplar and locust trees somberly and steadily giving up their colorful dead—bat wings of red and gold. Softly as they landed, this was all that Bennington heard. Jupiter knew of something else, though.

Bennington drew his matchlock pistol and peered down its barrel—as if it offered the magnification of a sailor's glass scope—toward the direction Jupiter was staring and cocking his ears.

"Is someone there?" he called, in the most powerful and booming voice of all the settlement. "I'll let you be on your way, if you show yourself to me! If you hide, I'll presume you mean me harm!" Bennington allowed a moment for this before resuming with a warning. "I will see you—and shoot you!"

Only falling leaves and Jupiter's breath answered.

Bennington called a greeting in what he knew of the Cherokee tongue.

Did he hear a moan?

If so, Jupiter heard it too. The horse took agitated steps backward, until Bennington halted him and leaped off. If there was to be trouble, he wouldn't endanger his loyal friend.

Bennington took four steps. Though he trod lightly, his boots crunched like burning maple branches on the newly carpeted forest floor. He listened and took another step, repeating the process until he found himself at the top of a shallow slope.

Halfway down, a long-fallen oak lay crosswise amid its own broken branches. From the far side of it, a man's leg protruded at an odd angle. Bennington grimly hoped that he would find the rest of the body there as well.

A glance back at Jupiter did not offer reassurance. The fidgeting beast had backed itself to the full length of its tether.

Bennington eased his way down the slope, his cumbersome weapon at arm's length. He walked wide of the fallen tree until he was just within a comfortable range of accuracy. Leaning over the oak, he saw the full figure—and laughed.

It was the false man from Friedrich Schroeder's cornfield, discarded here for some reason. The strawman had been a subject of much curious chatter when the cheerful Dutchman made and displayed it.

Then Bennington recalled the soft moan he'd heard a moment earlier and braced himself again. "Ho there!"

There was no answer, but the leg shifted minutely, in a way that Bennington recognized as a sign of injury. He stepped over the oak and sidestepped until he could see the man clearly. There was blood on the old clothes, and a fullness to the frame that was too meaty for a mere effigy.

The handle of a reaping tool poked out from under nearby leaves. Bennington examined it—and found bloody fingerprints.

Bennington lowered his pistol and went to the man. "What's happened to you, sir?"

The burlap-masked face of Everett Geelens rose. His eyes were nearly closed, hiding from Bennington the madness that dwelled within.

"Tricked..." mumbled Everett as he showed Bennington the wound in his side.

"Hold here." Bennington ran back to Jupiter, cursing the beast for resisting with all his might as Bennington dragged him down the slope.

* * * *

Modern day

"Jesus!" grumbled Dennis. "You'd think I pissed in the water cooler."

"My question is...are you sure you're not drunk right now?"

"Not even funny, Stuart."

"Yeah, well, neither was casually tossing out the idea that we should record down in the bowels of hell, where a bunch of us nearly got our tickets punched."

"That's why I'm so sure we *should,* little bro. Authenticity." Dennis lowered the volume of the hearse's stereo, playing Alien Sex Fiend again, which Stuart now realized should have been a dead giveaway of his brother's growing infatuation with death rock.

"Look, we'll take all the precautions. Have Hudson check it out, keep somebody on guard..."

"First, you gotta get past Reverend McGlazer."

"He's always been on board." Dennis returned a wave from excited kids in the back of a pickup. "He's our biggest supporter."

"Yeah, well, something tells me you already hit the end of that rope," Stuart said. "Not just with him, but with everybody."

"*Jeez,* you're a buzzkill tonight, man. Sleep on it, at least."

"Oh, sure! Can't wait to see what nightmares you've conjured up in my poor young melon with your cockamamie—"

"Dude! Ice it, already."

Dennis turned the stereo back up until it was too loud to hear Stuart if he did say something.

As for Stuart, long accustomed to stepping on eggshells for fear of sending delicate Dennis back to the bosom of the bottle, he didn't press it. But he couldn't ignore his disappointment in his brother, after what he, Stuart, had experienced, along with his friends, down in that goddamned moldy chamber of horrors.

Out on Main Street, thin evening fog had already settled on the streets, sidewalks and the many piles of gathered leaves. Two years ago, the shops would already have had their windows and signs decorated for Halloween. So far this year, only occasional pumpkins, left uncarved, or yellow-and-red wreaths gave any hint of the holiday.

Stuart was saddened, though not surprised. It was taking all he had to muster any Halloween spirit himself.

He recalled again the horror of being lost in the soul-crushing darkness of Saint Saturn Unitarian's secret basement with DeShaun, Reverend McGlazer and the Rieslings as the ubiquitous fungus triggered horrifying hallucinations.

And that was before the super-aggro ghost of Conal O'Herlihy took possession of McGlazer. Then, of course, the effing mushroom demons made the scene.

Dennis's suggestion wouldn't really be causing Stuart bad dreams, because they were virtually guaranteed anyway. Luckily, just like Candace and a good double fistful of his fellow survivors, he had his meds to keep the terrors beaten back. And he didn't even need as high a dose as Candace. His brother was only an alcoholic music genius, not a psychotic killing machine, like hers.

Still, Stuart could almost understand where Dennis was coming from. His older brother's devotion to the integrity of his music was not just intense, it was damn near insane.

And there could be no doubt: any music recorded in those dank, ancient subterranean chambers was sure to be authentic all right. Authentically terrifying.

* * * *

Yoshida was beginning to doze when the monstrous wolf stirred awake. She began with a series of heavy puffs—fit to blow a house down, Yoshida grimly thought. Then came low growls and a rattling of the silver chains.

The biker-turned-beast should not be able to break the chains, of course—yet there was no known precedent for a lycanthrope that had been in wolf state for nearly a year.

She had grown even larger than the near-seven-foot height she and her fellow gang members—make that pack mates—had stood, back when he and Hudson's posse of punkers did battle with them.

This reminded him of something else. Except when running, the wolves had all stood and walked upright. But Aura had moved about mostly on all fours.

Even her once very human breasts had gotten smaller, regressing into her torso to make her body more streamlined. Her teeth, eyes, hands—all were much more wolflike than human.

Had her extended time "in skin" erased all vestiges of humanity?

What if the "magic" effect of the silver chains also no longer applied?

Yoshida switched on the barn's overhead light and raised the trank rifle, approaching the cage from Aura's blind side.

She had rolled onto her stomach to raise her head. Yoshida found her glowering at him with eyes that shone like hot coals under the barn's low-watt bulbs.

She stopped growling and just stared at Yoshida, cocking her head sideways.

She wriggled and shook, rattling her chains like Dickens's Marley, glaring intently at Yoshida. As if she fully expected him to set her free.

"H...how about you just go back to sleep now, okay?" Yoshida said.

When the wolf shook again, Yoshida deduced she was attempting to loosen the chains. Was she going to try to break them? She jerked her head from side to side as if to test how tight the leather muzzle was, to see if she could shake it off.

"No, come on, dammit!" Yoshida said. "Just sit still."

The chains rattled again, louder. Yoshida raised the tranquilizer rifle and took a step closer. "I said, *sit still.*"

She narrowed her eyes, regarding him without fear. Yoshida lowered the rifle, surprising himself.

"Maybe it'd be best to let you go," he muttered.

He shook his head and put his back to her, finding resolve only once he broke eye contact.

But still—it made sense. To let her go.

She growled again, shaking the chains. Yoshida knew he should go ahead and dart her—but felt like he couldn't. It would be...disloyal.

The tiny spot where her tooth had punctured him tingled, but it wasn't an unpleasant feeling. He pivoted to meet her glowing gaze again.

"Yo!" came a deep-voiced call from the doorway. "'Shida!"

Yoshida spun quick with the rifle.

"Hey, hey, hey!" said the big deputy, hands out. "Easy, Yosh!"

"Oh, God. Sorry." Yoshida lowered the rifle. It took some effort. "Little on edge, I guess."

"Sure, sure." Hudson held out his hand to take the rifle.

Yoshida found some part of himself fighting not to relinquish it—and to pull the trigger. "She's, uh...starting to come around."

Hudson took a few steps though the doorway, leading his companions—Ysabella, Maisie and McGlazer. "Ladies, meet Deputy Yoshida."

Aura issued a low growl, causing the newcomers to stop in their tracks. Their eyes widened as they beheld the monster. McGlazer stepped in front of the witches, instinctively protective of them. "She's enormous!"

"Yeah," said Yoshida. "And she's not in a good mood." He went to draw his sidearm for safety and decided against it. Increasingly, he did not trust his own hands.

Looking at Ysabella and Maisie, he found himself surprised. He hadn't known what to expect, but it was not this pair of sweet-faced ladies. Maisie, the younger one, was attractive and unassuming, while Ysabella, the older witch, bore wisdom untainted by cynicism.

"You're certain she's secure?" asked Reverend McGlazer.

"Stay here a minute, Abe." Hudson patted Yoshida's shoulder, leading him toward the cage. He checked the dart rifle. "You okay, Yoshi?"

"I'm ready to do something else for a while," he answered, stopping within a few feet of the cage.

Narrowing her amber eyes, Aura growled and snapped, startling them. Hudson brought up the rifle. "Maybe you should draw your weapon now. Just in case."

Meeting Aura's ferocious gaze, Yoshida reached for his sidearm. The alarming feeling that, once in his hand, the gun would point to Hudson, or to his own temple, was stronger than before. Avoiding the wolf's stare banished the sinister urge—partly. "Go ahead and give her another dose."

"They need her awake." After warily circling the cage, Hudson relaxed and motioned for the guests. "She's locked up pretty tight anyway."

Hudson saw how Yoshida avoided eye contact with the hulking captive, how his gun hand shook. "I think you should go home now, Yoshi. Get some rest."

"I'm all right."

"Since this is volunteer time, I can't order you," Hudson said firmly. "But I can have Leticia withhold your annual pumpkin loaf." He motioned for the newcomers.

Aura shifted suddenly, rattling the chains. Hudson pointed the trank rifle at her haunches. "What do you need us to do, Ysabella?"

Ysabella stepped around McGlazer to stare into the wolf's eyes, much as she had little Emera's just a short while ago. She knelt, indifferent to the dirty plywood floor soiling her dress. "She's…suffering in there."

"Suffering?" scoffed Hudson. "She's wanted for murder. The *human* her, that is."

"In any case," Ysabella began, reaching for Maisie's supporting hand, "we can't leave her like this. Not any longer."

"What would happen?" asked McGlazer.

"The balance of nature is at stake," explained Ysabella, reaching out for McGlazer to help her stand. "We won't be able to hold her for long."

Maisie helped on the other side. "Wait. We're going to try to do it now? With just two of us?"

"The deputies will have to assist. And the reverend, of course. Maisie, look around and see if Matilda has…*had*…anything we can use." She touched Hudson's arm. "We'll need our bags from your truck."

"Yes, ma'am." Hudson was more than happy to relinquish oversight of this strange situation to this strange woman. He nodded to McGlazer and Yoshida. "If you would, fellas? I'll stay here with the trank rifle."

* * * *

"I guess I could've grabbed both of them," Yoshida said, hefting Maisie's enormous antique canvas suitcase. "I was thinking they'd be heavy as hell."

He told McGlazer about the vase in the barn that, despite appearing empty, was startlingly heavy. The minister stopped and looked at him.

"What?"

"You would think we'd start getting used to this kind of thing." He cast a nervous glance around the scene where so much strange carnage had occurred.

"Look, Rev. I have to ask. Aren't you a little conflicted about this? Working with witches?"

McGlazer thought about it. "Mysterious ways, and all that."

"So you still…believe?"

"I believe that I believe," answered McGlazer. "I *hope* I believe."

They trudged, in silence, along the worn pathway where Jill had fought for her life against "deceased" slasher Everett Geelens almost a year earlier. Within a few yards of the barn, Yoshida stopped again. McGlazer met his worried gaze.

"What's wrong?" the reverend asked.

"If you had to, could you change her back?"

"With faith in God, we can do anything," McGlazer answered.

"How is your faith in God holding up, Reverend?"

As McGlazer struggled with the lie forming in his mind, a low growl rose from the barn and grew to an eerie whine, a howl suppressed by the muzzle. It filled the farm and the men with a dark vibration.

Yoshida bolted into the barn to help his…pack mate?

Chapter 6

Wolf's Blood

"Cannisssss!?" Emera called at the very instant Stella opened the front door.

"In the kitchen, Emenemenema!"

Bravo appeared, panting a greeting.

Stella set down the little one and followed her to the kitchen, where husband Bernard and Candace filled puffy cooler bags—Snow White–themed for Emera, *Nightmare Before Christmas* for Candace—with the next day's lunch. Though Emmie didn't go to school yet, she insisted on having a packed lunch every day like her big sister.

"Don't forget her noon pills," Stella told Bernard as she gave him a kiss and rubbed Bravo's head.

"Way ahead of you."

"Almost time for tonight's." Stella said, as the older girl accepted Emmie's hug and kiss.

"I know, Mom."

Throughout the bedtime routine, the family exchanged accounts of Leticia's dinner party with the witches and the setup for The Chalk Outlines' rehearsal at the Community Center. Stella and Bernard smoothly traded off, seeing to the needs of one little girl or the other as needed. It was a near-mastery of the chaotic dance called parenthood.

Helping Emmie brush her teeth, Stella felt Bravo's meaty haunches brush past her. Looking up to talk to the dog's reflection, she caught sight of herself smiling in the toothpaste-spattered mirror. Yes, it was satisfying to be providing the orphan girls and the big dog with a normal home and a future of relative certainty, especially after the many horrors they had suffered. She was proud of Bernard, how he had evolved and taken to fatherhood like a natural, leaving behind a pattern of self-absorption and emotional inaccessibility.

But she wasn't ready to tell him what the witches had said, about "recruiting" Emera. Not until she knew more herself.

Bernard checked the hallway overhead light, a blazing hundred-watt bulb that both girls needed to sleep. Their bedroom door remained open so they could listen for any slight sound from the girls. Stella and Bernard had gotten used to wearing sleep masks and taking turns getting up at least twice a night to look in on them. After all they had gone through both before and after the girls came into their lives, Stella and Bernard were all the more fiercely loving these days. Their parental instincts were alive and kicking, their marriage better than ever.

Though they helped keep their bad dreams in check, the girls' meds didn't eliminate them. Only recently, through counseling, had the Riesling family learned to accept that the nightmares might never go away.

"Don't forget, we're going to see your therapist tomorrow," Stella told Candace, as she pulled back the covers on the twin bed shared by the girls, a bed Stella and Bernard had bought and assembled together with such a sense of purpose and family it felt like a daylong dream.

"Will you make sure she knows I really need those meds?" Candace asked. "Emmie too."

"Don't worry, sweetie." Stella stroked her little girl's chestnut hair, especially the thin white streak she bore as a souvenir of her brush with death—and an oddly poignant reminder, of her big brother. "No one will make you stop taking them, as long as you need them."

Candace's relief was visible. Stella knew the girl's real father, Aloysius, had withheld medical and emotional attention his children desperately needed. It was understandable that Candace would fear having it taken away. "Whatever it takes to keep you feeling safe," Stella added.

"*You* make us feel safe, Mom," Candace said, as Emmie crawled over and scrunched up against her on the wall side. "Thank you for taking care of us." The earnestness in Candace's eyes, the ferocity of her hug, swelled Stella's heart.

Emmie joined the hug, radiating the same gratitude.

Bernard stepped in with a storybook, smiling at the huddle. "Hey, me too!" He playfully covered Stella and the girls, mashing them into the bed and eliciting a chorus of giggles. He relinquished them quickly, careful not to make them feel trapped, or remind them of a closed bedroom with a terrible predator implacably tearing its way to them.

Bravo took his nightly post in the bedroom doorway, where he had a good view in all directions.

* * * *

Rushing into the barn, Yoshida met the glowing gaze of the werewolf Aura and felt a weird relief that she was safe. But he couldn't help feeling her howl had been meant for him. A summons—or a test of his will.

"Thank you, Deputy Yoshida." Ysabella said. "Just put them down anywhere."

"Matilda had quite a stock here." Maisie, wearing an expression of mild alarm, appeared from between two of the shelving units with an armful of bottles, decanters, and wooden boxes. "*No* one should have most of these things. For any reason."

"It cost her." Ysabella had McGlazer open her case on a scarred worktable.

"Reverend, there is a hand pump outside. Would you fill this?" Maisie handed McGlazer a tin bucket that had to be fifty years old. "And consecrate it?"

McGlazer considered telling her he was neither Catholic nor altogether certain that a blessing from him—or anyone—would "take." He decided to just do as asked, an act of politeness, if not faith.

Ysabella pointed to a row of bundled roots hanging from the rafters and asked Hudson to get them down. As he did, he discreetly watched Yoshida, sensing his friend's growing agitation. He also noticed that Aura had stopped moving. She pricked her ears toward any small sound—but never took her gaze off Yoshida.

The witches cast a circle—five white candles—around the cage at about a dozen feet from each other. In a well-rehearsed chorus of commanding tones, they called on spirits of the elements and directions.

"All right." Ysabella gave Hudson a look of dread. "Please open the cage."

* * * *

"That's a bad idea, lady," warned Yoshida, regarding Ysabella's order to open the cage.

"I'm afraid you'll like my next idea even less," Ysabella said, as she accepted a large clay jar from Maisie. "We need her brought out of the cage."

When she opened the jar, an alien odor hit their nostrils like a shock wave. Ysabella was the only one who did not show disgust as she took a sniff and handed it back to Maisie. "Her muzzle must be removed also."

Hudson and Yoshida exchanged a leery glance, as Hudson handed Reverend McGlazer the dart gun. "You can still shoot, right, Rev?"

McGlazer nodded and raised the weapon. As Hudson unlocked the cage hasp, Aura lowered her ears and issued a deep growl that rumbled in his bones. Judging by McGlazer's expression, it reached him as well.

Hudson and Yoshida took hold of the loop of chain around her shoulders and dragged her forward, halfway out of the cage. "She hasn't gotten any lighter."

Ysabella dowsed her own face, neck and arms from the bucket of blessed water, then stepped forward without hesitation, knelt, and slowly reached out with both hands. Aura growled stronger and deeper as Ysabella's fingers made contact just under the ears. "Remove the strap."

Though she didn't move at all, Aura continued to growl as Hudson unfastened the buckle of the makeshift muzzle. He kept the strap pulled taut, sure she would bite his hand the very instant he relinquished it.

"I won't be able to shoot her fast enough to keep her from biting," McGlazer told the witch. Realizing the rifle was trembling in his hands, the preacher felt admiration for Ysabella's steel nerves.

"Now, please," Ysabella whispered. Hudson unwrapped the strap and eased it off, relieved—and shocked—when the beast did not snap.

Ysabella remained poised and steady, her expression as placid as a pond. "You are ready to come out now," she whispered.

Aura peeled back her black lips to show teeth larger and sharper than any of them had ever seen. The vibration of her snarl had saliva drops dancing like moths on the ivory needlepoints.

As Ysabella's fingers and palms spread over the wolf's lean jowls, her growls grew louder, drowning out Ysabella's whispered litany.

Aura's eyes rolled in their sockets, then stopped on Yoshida.

"Come out, Aura." Ysabella dug her fingers into the wolf's fur. "Face your fate."

Yoshida felt righteous anger rise in his veins—on behalf of the she-wolf. *How dare this arrogant woman try to manipulate destiny.*

...What...?

Given his long-standing contempt of the murderous, very *human* criminal Aura, Yoshida was alarmed by his own sudden empathy for her.

"Come on," he mumbled. "Hurry it up..." Yoshida was betting and hoping that the reversal of Aura's transformation would sever whatever this link was that made him feel more under her control by the minute.

Hudson saw him trembling, wincing, mumbling.

Ysabella began to show signs of stress as well—shaking hands, fluttering eyelids. "The salve," whispered the petite elder witch.

Maisie already had it in her hands, rubbing them together vigorously. She leaned forward behind Ysabella and began working the strange-smelling concoction onto the monster's forehead. Aura snarled louder, her right eye wide-open and straining to focus on Yoshida with desperation and insistence.

Hudson checked on McGlazer. The minister's knuckles were white from his grip on the rifle.

"Pray for her," Maisie told the shocked minister. He blinked back at her, as if not understanding.

Ysabella's entire body now shook with the vibration of Aura's snarls. Still, she rubbed the salve into the wolf's face as Maisie continued to slather it around her fingers.

"Are you . . ?" Hudson didn't know how to finish the sentence.

"We have to pull her out of there," Maisie explained. "Quite literally."

Seeing McGlazer's shocked face and Yoshida sweating like a salad-hater in a sauna, Hudson felt a surreal kind of aloneness, like an out-of-body experience.

"Come here," Ysabella whispered like a midwife. "Come out."

Aura's savage snarls became more strident, pained instead of fearful and angry.

Yoshida subtly mirrored the wolf's distress. Hudson had the feeling that if something wasn't done about Yoshida soon...

"Unchain her," said Ysabella, her voice presenting strain that her expression did not.

"Um...have you lost your mind, lady?" Hudson asked.

"I have her immobilized," Ysabella said softly. "I think."

Keeping his weight on her thick back, Hudson drew the keys from his pocket and gingerly reached for the padlock connected to the chain over the blanket near her shoulder blades. "Say when."

Maisie leaned in over Ysabella's shoulder, a good-sized glob of the stinky ointment in each hand. Aura's howls suddenly became gurgling pants.

Yoshida reached for his sidearm, taking a step toward them.

"Yosh!" Hudson barked. "Stand down. Let them work."

Yoshida maintained eye contact with the beast, as his trembling hand hovered over his weapon.

"Yosh," mumbled Hudson. "What the hell are you doing?"

The deputy snapped his head sharply from the wolf's gaze once again, as her throat swelled like a bullfrog's.

Ysabella put her hand on this sudden growth and stroked it toward her. "Come out here, Aura." Ysabella's tone was soft yet commanding. Maisie raised her voice, chanting a series of strange old words, faster and louder with each repetition.

Ysabella raised her left hand for Maisie to generously coat with the balm. Then she formed a spearhead with her fingers—and thrust her hand into the wolf's mouth.

"Good *God*..." Hudson thought it was an internal exclamation, and maybe it was. But Maisie sharply shushed him.

As Ysabella forced her hand deeper and deeper, the werewolf made garbled, almost human sounds of anguish. Its eyes went full white.

Yoshida kept his head turned away, his eyelids crushed shut. He trembled and gnashed, his face distorting into a mask of agony that nearly matched the rolling-eyed wolf beast.

A gallon of blood burst and splashed out around Ysabella's arm, now fully a foot deep in the monster's maw. The crone remained calm, focused. "I have you."

Yoshida fell to his knees, violently convulsing.

Reverend McGlazer ran to the deputy, setting down the rifle.

"Hold her neck, Deputy Hudson!" stammered Maisie. "Tight as you can!"

Hudson wrapped his arms around the giant neck, keeping an eye on Yoshida. "He okay?"

"He might be having a seizure," Reverend McGlazer answered, prying at the deputy's steel-trap-clenched teeth.

"He'll be fine," murmured Maisie.

Ysabella's expression finally took on a hint of alarm, maybe even doubt.

Hudson tried to ignore the unreal sensation of writhing he felt beneath Aura's hide, so much like Leticia's belly in late-term pregnancy—writ much larger, and decidedly less poignant.

"Here we...are..." Ysabella said, as she began to withdraw her arm from the lycanthrope's gullet.

Slick-scarlet, Ysabella's dainty wrist and hand emerged. She had hold of something.

A hand. Hudson had the horrifying thought that Ysabella was dragging out the arm of someone Aura had eaten.

Ysabella clasped this larger hand with both of hers, straining to pull. "Come…out!"

"Come out!" repeated Maisie.

The pale hand, now connected to an arm streaked with blood, continued to issue from the monster's snout till it was just past the elbow.

The wolf's body shook so hard it blurred Hudson's vision. He was grateful for this.

The animal's gurgle suddenly became the scream of a woman violently giving birth. Fresh blood sprayed from the edges of the monster's mouth as the flesh ripped, spattering Hudson's face with blood and saliva. Looking away, he saw that McGlazer had gotten Yoshida on his back and was trying to straighten the deputy's legs. "How is he?"

McGlazer looked at the bloody wolf with disgust and horror. "Better than *that!"*

Maisie chanted words that sounded as old as language itself, louder with every word, as she held tight to Ysabella's wrists, helping her pull and pull.

The monster shifted forward—then set its four powerful legs in a strong stance and yanked Ysabella toward it. The monstrous maw stretched open further, impossibly, like a giant crocodile, to consume Ysabella. She screamed as her head disappeared within the tunnel of teeth and flesh. Maisie, caught off guard and off balance, shrieked in sheer terror.

Hudson held tight to the thing's undulating neck with his right arm as he reached for the makeshift muzzle on the floor, wishing he had thought to drop it closer.

"No!" Maisie's loss of control nearly broke Hudson, except that he didn't have a choice. It was up to him now.

Ysabella's petite form was sucked waist-deep into the werewolf's mouth and gullet. Maisie pulled at her legs without gaining an inch.

Hudson let his headlock grip slide away, snatching the loose skin of the wolf's neck before she could gain leverage.

With a great lunge, Hudson reached for the muzzle.

For an instant, it seemed the silver chain was going to fall away from the strap and render the restraint useless. But Hudson pulled the loose skin with him to gain the extra crucial inch.

He got both the strap and chain securely in his fist.

Hudson smashed himself chest-down across the skinwalker's back and whipped the belt over the upper jaw like a horse's bridle. The unnatural undulations of flesh beneath him became more disturbing and intense than before. Hudson cast away all thoughts of this, as he wrapped the ends of the belt in his fists and tugged like he was reining in a literal nightmare.

"Do your ritual!" he shouted to Maisie, shocking the young witch out of her panic.

She stood and raised her hands, shouting six syllables, faster and louder with each repetition.

Yoshida shook just like the wolf, foaming at the mouth. McGlazer hugged him tight.

Hudson pulled the silver-chained strap. The reverend's grunts of effort joined the distressing chorus of Yoshida's unnatural ululations, Maisie's chant and Hudson's roar of exertion.

Smoke rose from the beast's snout, which began to shrink.

Whatever suctioning force was dragging Ysabella into the beast now started to fail.

Hudson again recalled when Leticia gave birth, feeling as queasy as when he held her hand in the moment of delivery—then worse. Between the sounds of ripping flesh and cracking bones, the weird movement in the monster's flesh, the squeal of animal agony and the realization that Yoshida was approaching disintegration just a few feet away, Hudson was certain he would be spending this Halloween—and probably Thanksgiving and Christmas—in the loony bin.

Maisie wrapped her arms around Ysabella's waist and dragged her out of the terrible tunnel, gaining momentum until the elder witch rocketed away from the monster's mouth and landed hard, yards away. The naked, bloody and very human Aura came out along with her, falling atop Ysabella with a cry of shock and a splash of bloody mucus.

Hudson collapsed on his side. The skin he held was empty, more or less. The wolf's head, its eyes sunken into the blackness of its crumbled skull, lay stretched and torn open like latex, the split flesh rendered grotesquely opaque, the gray fur falling out in clumps.

The hide smoked and bubbled. Hudson realized it would soon be gone.

Yoshida had calmed by a few degrees, though he wasn't out of the woods yet. McGlazer had forced a handkerchief between his teeth to stop the distressing chatter.

The witches too had gone silent, their screaming replaced by Aura's infantile cries, underscored by the hiss of smoke rising from the wolf's dissolving carcass.

Barely conscious, Ysabella held Aura, rocking the biker-turned-baby as the thick coating of blood and wildness burned away from her skin like morning fog, leaving her as clean as a child baptized in a rushing river.

Hudson went to help the sobbing Maisie to her feet, not surprised that she seemed as traumatized as he was.

Chapter 7

Lust for Flesh

Standing in the cool air outside Matilda Saxon's "Barn of Wonders," as he and Yoshida had dubbed it, Hudson accepted the dented, extra-large coffee thermos from the other deputy. They had traded it off like a jar of moonshine since the end of Aura's rehumanizing twenty minutes ago. "Damn, what'd you do? Shotgun it?"

"I was thirsty," Yoshida said.

"We have plenty of water."

"I'm also exhausted, if it's okay with you."

Hudson took only a couple of gulps and gave the thermos back to Yoshida. "Relax, Yosh. It's you I'm worried about, not the java."

"Yeah." Yoshida wiped the thin sheen off his face. "Sorry."

"Wanna tell me what the hell happened to you in there?'

Yoshida looked in the barn to check on the minister and the witches, as they attended Aura. The biker was bundled in a blanket on the lawn chair, her expression the slack blank of a newborn.

"Chalk it up to stress," Yoshida said.

Hudson wasn't convinced. "I thought you were having a seizure."

"I don't think so. Never had one before." He offered Hudson the thermos. When it was refused, he emptied it in three large gulps.

"Still. Wouldn't hurt you to see a doctor."

Yoshida looked at his friend as if to protest, then saluted with the thermos, closed it up and went back in to help the others.

As McGlazer and the magic folk gently pulled Aura to her feet, the biker looked at them like they were aliens, her childlike expression far removed from the smug sneer she wore before she became a wolf.

Supported on either side, she took trembling steps, looking up from her feet to McGlazer and Maisie.

"Her memory is gone," murmured Ysabella. "Wiped clean."

"You don't think she's…?" Hudson warily began.

"She's not faking, Deputy."

"Will she regain it?" asked McGlazer.

"We don't know," said Ysabella, her tone that of a very tired woman. She looked and sounded like she had aged twenty years during the ritual.

Maisie continued for her. "We've never heard of a skinwalker who remained in animal form for this long. There is no precedent."

There were other questions: Would she change back? Was she still as strong?

"We have to study and consult with our coven."

"Not to be disrespectful," Hudson said, realizing he was falling into DeShaun mode, "I hope your coven has a good benefits package, because it looks like you ladies are going to be working overtime."

His humor served him well. Everyone relaxed and laughed, except Aura.

* * * *

"Dennis! How go the rehearsals?" Reverend McGlazer secretly hoped the singer, whom he sponsored through AA, hadn't come by for a sobriety pep talk.

Though McGlazer himself had stayed dry—a miracle itself—in the wake of his possession by the ghost of Conal O'Herlihy, he hardly felt qualified to offer strength, much less faith, to anyone lately.

"You got a few minutes?" Jill appeared beside Dennis in the Community Center office's doorway—but not too close. "For both of us?"

"Oh, sure!" McGlazer couldn't help but grin, assuming they were finally going to ask him to preside over their marriage ceremony.

He began the perfunctory and futile ritual of trying to straighten up the desk. The sagging particleboard furnishing was in use at any given time by any of at least eight people, from coaches to janitors. A wrinkled clutter of plans for the Devil's Night party, poor replacement for the Pumpkin Parade that it was, had spread like kudzu in the two weeks since Mayor Stuyvesant suggested it.

"Oh, please," said Jill. "We don't care about the mess."

McGlazer grew concerned. Jill's voice didn't carry the note of excitement he expected from a newly engaged young lady, even a cynical punker. "All right. Take a seat."

There was only one, made of hard plastic, and it was hosting a net bag full of dusty kickballs. Dennis moved the bag for Jill, then leaned against the wall, well outside of her contact range. "Which thing first, Jilly?"

She regarded McGlazer earnestly. "You know me and Denny are supposed to keep our filthy mitts off each other for a few months, while he readjusts to sobriety."

"It ain't easy," Dennis immediately added. "You gotta help us."

"Oh. I understand…" McGlazer scratched his ear. "Well, I doubt you're interested in…supportive bible verses."

Dennis gave a wan smile. "Here's where your counseling skills kick in, Padre."

"Let's hope. So—tell me how you were…handling it, before now?"

They both laughed. "I know you're not going for double entendre," Jill said. "You'll have to look past our childish preoccupation."

"I'll try to meet you halfway."

"We're always under adult supervision," Dennis began, "if you count Petey."

"I try to dress down," Jill offered.

"It don't help," said Dennis. "She's still…her."

"And he's still him." She locked eyes with him. The sexual tension was as palpable as they had said.

"How did you make it here today without…?"

"Pedro drove us. He's waiting for us outside," explained Jill. "Didn't want any part of this conversation,"

"It was his idea we talk to you."

"Says he wants to split the suffering with somebody else."

"Well, give him my thanks."

"So, you got anything for us?"

McGlazer took a deep breath, mostly as a stall, while he mulled an inventory of stratagems he might once have suggested. Praying with those struggling against temptation was usually the big go-to in the minister business. But McGlazer grimly realized that would be disingenuous these days. "I think I'm going to have to make a referral on this one."

"Huh? Who?"

McGlazer just stared at them for several seconds.

"A therapist is out of the question, man." Dennis's frustration was obvious. "You've always done me right as my sponsor. So what gives?"

McGlazer's inner dialogue made him feel like he was possessed by Conal O'Herlihy again, as if two minds were at war in his body. He fought his way back to the surface, past a rising tide of doubts he had been ignoring for months. "I know it's time-sensitive," he said, "but I think it's best if I give it some thought and check with said referral." He was thinking of the witches.

"I guess I can bite the bullet for one more day," said Jill, making Dennis shake his head at the vague innuendo. "What about you, Den-Den?"

He slid down the wall to hold his head in his hands, mumbling, "You know what that nickname does to me."

"*Everything* does that to you lately."

He looked up at her and bit his palm comically. "Let's move on."

When Jill turned back to McGlazer, it was with a graver expression.

"Uh oh. You kids aren't…the 'P' word, are you?"

"Not at present," said Dennis. "Right now, we need to ask another big favor, which is…access to the church's sublevels."

* * * *

McGlazer recalled last November 3, going back under the church, with the terror he had just lived still fresh on his mind and nerves.

First, there was a closed-door meeting in the same Community Center office where he now sat with Dennis and Jill. Hudson, Yoshida, Dennis and Pedro, all bandaged and scarred from their own battle with a pack of werewolves, crowded together to listen, as he and Stella gave their account of the nightmarish events in the church's hidden basement.

With his body under the control of Conal O'Herlihy, the reverend had taken DeShaun and Stella down into the subterranean chamber—unknown to him before then—where he force-fed them a rare mushroom that induced visions, mind control and a form of zombification.

Stella's engineer husband, Bernard, drafted by Stuart Barcroft, had thought ahead, bringing several strips of classroom-grade magnesium with him when he and Stuart set out to rescue their wife and friend. Once ignited, these simple chemist's wares vanquished O'Herlihy's army of mushroom-covered ghouls and gave Reverend McGlazer a chance to eject the malignant spirit of O'Herlihy.

After the meeting, Hudson and Yoshida collected some chemical hazard suits from the local fire department as protection from the mushroom's hallucinogenic spores. Bernard got his hands on more magnesium, and with Dennis along to keep him busy (not drinking), they entered the chambers. After a brief debate over preserving the stone caskets that contained O'Herlihy's fungus guardians, all agreed it was best to destroy everything; all traces of the mushroom, the caskets in the anterooms, even the symbols painted on the walls were blasted off with a high-pressure hose after Yoshida took pictures.

Once it was all over, there was nothing but stone rubble and empty space.

They decided to shutter the building and keep the mushroom monsters a secret while maintaining close watch to ensure the threat was truly over.

To be extra sure, they would wait through the coming Halloween, of course.

Hudson and Yoshida, though frequently griping about how much of their job was off the books these days, were nonetheless vigilant in making regular patrols of the chambers. McGlazer, always joining them, was nevertheless unsettled by those first few steps, even with the high-powered hunting lights the deputies used.

Dennis's request seemed reasonable enough on its surface.

"Why the catacombs?" McGlazer asked the musicians.

"I explained to you about the new sound…" Dennis began.

"For *now,* anyway," Jill contributed. She had made it clear she was far from sold on the idea of going pure death rock, as opposed to the punk/psychobilly fusion that was their basic sound.

"At least for this demo," conceded Dennis.

"Sure."

"It's gotta be deep. Dark. You know, foreboding."

Dennis produced a mini-recorder from his back pocket and played a snippet from "Is Everything Real?" by The Frozen Autumn, then fast-forwarded to Ghosting's "Disguised in Black."

McGlazer nodded. "Yes, I see what you mean."

"So what do you think?"

"It is close to Halloween, you know."

"I know," Dennis said, "and you wanted to wait till after to figure out whether to reopen or not. But the thing is, we're on a tight schedule to get this into the studio guy's hands. And with the joint's history and all…it would just be perfect."

Dennis's gaze was too imploring, so the minister looked to Jill—and immediately understood why Dennis was having such trouble keeping his hands off her.

"We'll make sure Hud, or Yosh, or somebody is there to babysit the whole time. Keep the doors opened, have Bernard stand by with his weird science."

"Well, you've given me a lot to consider," McGlazer said.

"Take the night, Rev," said Dennis. "Whatever you can do is great. On either deal."

"We better go," Jill said as she rose. "Or we're gonna have one hungrumpy meathead bassist on our hands."

"'Hungrumpy'," McGlazer repeated with a laugh.

"Feel free to work that into your next sermon."

* * * *

Stella parked in the Grand Illusion Cinemas' massive lot, which hadn't filled to anywhere near capacity for a year now. It was the most convenient spot for the Riesling family to meet after Candace's session. "We'll walk down Main Street," Bernard said as he took Emmie's little hand. "We'll find something fun."

A light, musky breeze caressed their hair as Stella and Candace walked the block to the little beige building that housed Dr. Lanton's office. Though the single-story structure was surrounded by azaleas through the summer, its autumn sparseness made it appear abandoned.

Stella watched Candace to see if she would raise her face into the wind, as she, Stella, did when she was the same age. But Candace only stared ahead.

"Candace, baby...are you nervous?"

"Not really. Doctor Lanton is nice. I like her."

"Is there anything you want me to bring up?"

"Just remember to tell her the pills are working. Okay?"

In the waiting room, Candace stared at the four placid abstract pastels on the wall, going from one to the other repeatedly until she was called.

"How are you sleeping, Candace?" asked the pixie-faced therapist.

"Well..."

Stella found Candace's uncertainty perplexing. The girl always made a point of saying how glad she was to be sleeping again, how grateful she was for her new life.

Dr. Lanton examined the girl's face closely, then asked a series of questions that were vague and pointless to Stella's ears. "How about just Candace and I talk for a few minutes? Would that be fine?"

Stella excused herself and returned to the waiting room, where she went over the exchange, fearing she had done something that might endanger her hopes of adoption or, worse, hurt Candace.

Chapter 8

Ghost Town

"Jakka-lannern!" called Emera, stopping her bunny-hop to point at the decoration in the window.

The pumpkin was only a sun-faded cardboard cutout taped to the window of Calloway's Exotic Pet Supply. Bernard wondered if it had been there, untouched, since last year. Or the year before.

The pet store was locked, blinds down, leaving him to wonder if, like so many local businesses and farms, the proprietors had up and left.

"Zat where the fishes an' turtles are?" asked Emmie.

Bernard's heart sank at the idea of letting his daughter down. "Well…I don't know."

Father and daughter went to the window. Bernard tried to peer between the blinds for a clue. The window decal was intact, and the business-hours sign, though coated in dust, remained in place.

"Maybe they had to go somewhere," Bernard told Emmie. "We'll check back in a few minutes."

"Okay!"

Bernard feared he was just delaying the little one's disappointment.

Bernard remembered walking along the sidewalk this time of year in previous autumns, even well into the evening hours, and finding himself jostled by people coming and going to prepare for Halloween at all the mom-and-pop shops that sold every conceivable kind of Halloween-related merchandise, often handmade.

Preparations for the annual Pumpkin Parade, Ember Hollow's long-standing claim to tourism fame, would be in full gear, with every shop sign, window and door, every fire hydrant, parking meter and bike stand subject to trick-or-treatment, as the town, and particularly Main Street, transformed into Haunted Hollow, a family-friendly, autumnal Mardi Gras.

It saddened him that Emera might never experience that infectious air of excitement and anticipation.

Now, memories of the parade two years past were inextricably tied to Ragdoll Ruth, the notorious demented doll-costumed domestic terrorist, raining on the parade with her tainted candy, distributing it indiscriminately to anyone unlucky enough to cross her path.

Thanks to her, the parade had quickly devolved to a full-scale riot that night, with costumed revelers becoming a horde of senseless, raging savages.

Many lives were lost. Some, like Bernard's friends Reverend McGlazer, the members of The Chalk Outlines, and his own Stella, somehow survived, with scars to show for it.

The next Halloween, last Halloween, was just as harrowing.

A gang of bikers, snarkily described by Chalk Outlines bassist Pedro Fuentes as "volunteer werewolves," arrived to avenge Ragdoll Ruth. Turned out she was the gang leader's "ol' lady."

At least half the businesses here on Main Street had since closed down, the owners moving on to greener, less "cursed" pastures.

Shops and offices on the outlying streets seemed to be shuttering at an even faster rate. Farther out in the county, many of the farmers whose pumpkin crops were intended to go out into all the world were cutting their losses and putting their land up for sale. The lucky ones had already sold. The others, it appeared, would soon be slashing their selling prices and applying for government relief.

The few folks who did walk past Bernard and Emera wore glum or disinterested faces. The only thing missing from this desolate picture was a rolling tumbleweed.

Bernard hoisted Emera and gave her a kiss. "How about some cookies for my pretty princess?"

"Yeah!"

Bernard internally scolded himself, realizing he should have made sure the Cookie Kitchen wasn't closed as well.

A sparkling-clean Cadillac XTS appeared, cruising toward them at well below even the city speed limit of 20 mph. Spotting the rental plate, Bernard tossed up a welcoming wave, which Emmie emulated.

The Caddie stopped beside them, the driver's window powering down. "Good afternoon!"

The strawberry-blond woman dressed in pricey casual wear was vivacious in a way that locals would describe as "uptown," very much like the record-company executive with the British accent who had come to check out The Chalk Outlines a couple of years ago, God rest her.

"Hello and welcome," Bernard said, and so did Emera.

"You two are the cutest couple in this town, I'd bet!" said the visitor.

Seeing their reflection elegantly framed in her Versace sunglasses, Bernard couldn't argue. "Well, Emmie here counts for at least seventy-five percent. Looking for someone?"

"The Blue Moon Inn."

Bernard always winced at the name, only because Stella had stayed there during their brief split right around the time of the werewolves on wheels. Bernard could not know how much this woman, Violina Malandra, could glean from his tiny wince, just as he would not have understood what *she* was doing if he'd seen her just fifteen minutes ago, looking out over a pumpkin field at the strange, charred trail left by Ysabella's vomiting episode.

Bernard pointed to the high hill at the far end of the street. "Just drive in the direction of that old church up there. A series of increasingly large signs will guide you right to it."

Emmie pointed too.

Violina smiled her thanks and waved two burgundy-gloved fingertips at Emera before motoring off.

Emmie wore a concerned look Bernard had never seen from her before. "Is she…another wolf monster, Daddy?"

"Hmm? Surely not. Why would you ask that?"

Emmie frowned deeper. "She feels kinda like one."

* * * *

"We can talk about anything you don't want your foster mom to hear."

"She's my *Mom*-mom. Not my foster mom."

"Right."

"It's just, well…the sleeping pills don't always work like they should."

Dr. Lanton was incredulous. Candace's dose should be doing the job well enough.

The doctor nodded and listened, remembering the girl's history. Like the fact that her previous foster parents, in debt to The Fireheads motorcycle gang, had given Candace too much or too few of her prescriptions, both to control the troubled girl to their own ends and to sell or use the surplus.

"Why haven't you told your fos—your mom and dad this?"

"I...I don't want to worry them. They have a lot to deal with. With Emmie and me both."

Candace's body language indicated this was not the reason, at least not entirely.

"They'll have to approve and oversee any med change, you know."

"Oh."

"You're okay with that?"

"I just want to sleep without the nightmares."

"What happens in the nightmares?"

Candace looked down at her shoes, turning her feet out and in.

"Why don't you want to say?" asked Dr. Lanton.

"Because the dreams mean I'm not really getting better."

"Maybe it's just taking longer than you would like."

"You don't understand. They're not just dreams."

Dr. Lanton felt her skin crawl. She already knew what the girl was going to say.

"Everett will never die," she said plainly. "And he'll never stop killing."

* * * *

When Maisie's jaw began to ache, she realized she had been tensing it since the moment Violina arrived at the Blue Moon Inn.

After the biker's de-transformation ritual, Maisie and Ysabella had plummeted into their beds and slept as deep as a sea, until Violina rang them from the lobby.

The wealthy witch had long been at odds with Ysabella. "Personal differences" was the cover Maisie had rehearsed in case any outsiders asked. The true reason behind their enmity would rightfully shake the confidence of everyone counting on them.

There was a coldness when they went down to greet Violina in the Blue Moon's lobby. Maisie noted a faint fog accompanying her speech and realized that the coldness was manifesting in a very literal sense.

Now, quietly alarmed by Ysabella's trembling, constant since the healing of Aura, Maisie held her mentor's hand and sent waves of vitality into her.

Though Violina and Ysabella were outwardly professional, the tension between them was worse than ever. Maisie was beginning to feel crushed between the conflicting energies.

As they walked to the Ember Hollow Community Center entrance, Violina maintained a default smile that seemed more like an imperious sneer.

"Ooh!" she lilted. "Maisie, what's another word for quaint?"

Maisie only gave her a quick smile. Violina had a stronger vocabulary than Maisie or anyone else she knew. She never needed anyone's help with antonyms or anything else. The query was an oblique dig at Ysabella and at this small-potatoes endeavor.

The coven queen did not dignify it, remaining as placid as a Zen monk.

On this summery-warm day, the Center's doors stood open, allowing in sunshine and errant leaves. With the Community Center serving as an ersatz church during Saint Saturn Unitarian's "mold" crisis, McGlazer maintained the same habit he had at Saint Saturn's, of staying available during daylight hours and leaving doors open for folks to come and go.

Stella appeared at the door to sweep out a cluster of leaves that would soon wander back. "Morning! Hope you all slept well! That was some adventure you had!"

As she regarded the guests, Stella had to hide her alarm at Ysabella's wan, almost sickly appearance. The elder witch clearly had not fully recovered from the exertion of taming Aura. The newcomer who accompanied them, attractive as she was, bore a smile that would shame a shark.

"Hello, dear," Ysabella grasped Stella's hand, skipping the small talk. "Is there a private room we could use?"

Stella felt a slight tremble in the witch's hand. As a wave of agitated energy washed over her, she looked at Maisie and saw a confirming tension in the girl's face.

The quartet made their way in absolute silence across the center and to the office where the door stood ajar. Stella stuck her head in. "Visitors!"

McGlazer stood up from behind a mountain of paper, ping-pong paddles in mid-repair and decorations for the center's Halloween lock-in, offering his gracious smile and hand to Violina. The way she extended hers was like a queen expecting a kiss upon her ring. The reverend returned only a kind pat upon it.

"Could they use the office?" Stella asked.

"It's a terrible mess..."

"Thank you," said Violina, patting the reverend's shoulder with what might be condescension as she breezed in and took the seat behind the desk.

Ysabella's gratitude, though strained, rang sincere.

In the echoing click of the closing door, McGlazer pivoted to Stella. "What's wrong here?"

* * * *

The plain, wooden office door was like a thick snow cloud, quiet yet pregnant, radiating cold.

Reverend McGlazer and Stella filled the silence by telling Maisie how they had adjusted to using the Community Center as a church. Then they made some small talk about planning the party. Both topics dried up quickly, leaving them all to glance around the basketball court for a new filler.

"Know what? We should introduce Maisie to Pedro," Stella told McGlazer, starting toward the closed door of the weight room at the other end of the wall from the office.

"He's the…bass player?" asked Maisie.

"Yes. They've been rehearsing h—"

Stella was interrupted by a resounding crack, like a long-dead pine succumbing to gravity and decay. The trio tensed with alarm as they realized it had come from the office door. They looked at it, just as it exploded.

Three large, jagged sections and a mist of splinters flew from the frame like a grenade had gone off.

McGlazer threw himself over both women and brought them to the floor. He covered them with as much of his body as he could, certain that the terrible and towering specter of raging murderess Ragdoll Ruth had escaped both the grave and his nightmares, to claim revenge.

He shot a look back at the now-empty door frame. To his relief, no cackling, doll-costumed harridan emerged to finish the job of killing him.

The weight room door swung open. "What the jumped-up jack-o'-lanterns is going on out here?"

Neither McGlazer nor the stunned ladies he sheltered had an answer for Pedro.

"Is everyone all right?" Ysabella asked from the office threshold. She looked pale and drawn before the skull session with Violina. Now she looked ashen and exhausted.

Pedro, in his sweaty, sleeveless, bloodstained Sex Pistols T-shirt, helped McGlazer and the ladies to stand.

Despite her alarm, Maisie found her appreciation for the male form well intact as she regarded the big bassist. The feel of his calloused fingertips and palms were an appealing contrast to her own well-kept hands.

“I’m Maisie,” she said before she was fully on her feet.

“Pedro.” His smile was as boyish as his arms were powerful. “But you might as well call me Petey.”

“Sorry about the door,” said Violina, flippant as ever. She strolled out of the office behind Ysabella, making a shooing gesture at the door fragments. “I’ll have it replaced.”

“What happened in there?” asked McGlazer.

“Let that stay between us,” Ysabella said.

Maisie scrutinized her mentor’s expression for signs of a resolution. What she found was despair and resignation, as if etched with acid.

Chapter 9

Beyond The Darkness

The post-midnight chill was like a fall from a great height, so violently did it shock Yoshida awake.

Awake?

He was surrounded by forest, under a haloed half-moon.

His feet stung and ached. They were bare and dirty, like the rest of him. "Just great," he grumbled. "Where the hell am I?"

Shivering, he did a quick three-sixty to find his sleep clothes, cursing when he didn't. Not that the boxer shorts and T-shirt would offer much warmth, but at least he'd feel less vulnerable.

Yoshida slapped himself, hoping to come out of this new dream level and find himself in his bed, with soft music playing at low volume on the nightstand as usual, his digital clock dimly reassuring him he had many hours of night left. But the slap changed nothing.

Yoshida searched his last memory. It was what it should be—lying in bed, whitewashing the day with some focused breathing to carry him off to slumber.

After that—dashing through the woods—on the hunt.

He didn't remember killing anything. Only wanting to. Hungering for the chance…

Naked and filthy, he could expect exactly no late travelers to stop and help, if he could even locate the road.

Then, rubbing his cold arms, he circled forty degrees and stared assuredly into darkness between trees. He saw something—but not with his eyes.

The way home.

He could not have given directions if asked, nor could he have seen his own footprints in the dark to retrace them. He could walk to his house, though, in a straight line, with no misgivings, no doubt that he would find his way.

Beginning the trek, Yoshida rubbed the place on his arm where Aura had bitten him but felt nothing.

A hot bath, a cold beer and back to the sack he'd go—hopefully to stay.

* * * *

"Thank goodness, the boys didn't jump the fence again." McGlazer said to Stella. He was not about to let anyone enter without him. Not even Hudson.

Though McGlazer's house was within walking distance of the church, Stella had picked him up, still accustomed to doting on him from when he was recovering from the crippling assault at the hands of Ragdoll Ruth.

"Oh, yeah." Stella gestured at the gate. "We all know how insistent you are that no one goes in without you."

She let him out right at the gate. "Did you get some sleep, officers?" he asked Hudson and Yoshida.

"Ten solid hours," Hudson said. "Leticia apparently threatened to murder anyone dumb enough to wake me."

Yoshida's haggard face was his answer.

The three witches gave their greetings. Ysabella looked little better than she had after the ritual to cure Aura. Maisie stood between her elders, a folded white cloth clutched to her chest.

Dennis Barcroft's flame-painted hearse rumbled around the corner of Ecard Street, loaded down with bodies: Pedro, Jill, DeShaun and Stuart.

"Hmm." Violina all but rolled her eyes at the cartoonish hearse, but smiled her appreciation for its lanky androgoth driver.

"Now it's a party," quipped Hudson.

"Damn right," said Dennis.

Stella unlocked the gate. "Who's driving up?"

"Looks like a nice walk, actually," Ysabella commented, and started doing just that. Only Maisie noted the slight wobble in her gait.

Yoshida issued a quiet, irked huff as he began to follow.

"Maybe you should head home," Hudson told him. "Pretty obvious you didn't sleep."

Yoshida waved him off.

"Something up?" Hudson asked.

"Insomnia, I guess."

As they trekked up the long hill, the others broke into groups as well.

Maisie looked to Ysabella, as if for permission, and received a knowing smile. The young witch dropped back to greet Pedro, presenting him with a proud smile and the tightly folded cloth she had been hugging.

"No way!" Letting the Sex Pistols T-shirt unfold, Pedro inspected the collar. "You got the blood out!"

"As promised."

"Don't tell me it was magic."

"Of a kind."

"And the logo ain't even faded!" He side-hugged her, gave her a kiss on top of the head. "You're the coolest, lady!"

"'Sex Pistols'..." She took the shirt from him to make one more inspection of the pristine white fabric. "So...should I give them a listen?"

"If you hear us—*old* us, that is—then you'll know." He flashed a smart-ass grin at Dennis.

Maisie watched him admire the shirt, remembering the day before when she met him at the Community Center and coaxed from him the story of how he had gotten blood on his favorite shirt.

"See, I got scratched during the, ya know, howl-a-baloo with The Fireheads...or Furheads, as it were."

She laughed so loud it made her instantly self-conscious, until he said "Ah, you ain't gotta sell it like that."

It seemed a wild contradiction that this well-muscled, overtly theatrical rock-and-roll personality was so modest, until she learned just a little more about his past. The muscles were more armor than decoration, and the music, escape. These had kept him alive during the kind of harrowing childhood only Candace could top.

"Maybe I could watch you rehearse then," she said. "Or even record, if we're around long enough."

"Maybe we could have a picnic or something first." He gave her a shy smile. "Believe it or not, I'm a little shy at first."

"Warm-up picnic, then rehearsals," Maisie said. "Sounds like a full day to me."

"It's a date then," Pedro said. "'Cause if you chicks are here to do what we're asking of you, you're gonna be staying a while."

* * * *

Dennis bumped against Jill. "Aww, ain't Petey cute over there snuggling up with Sabrina the Teenage Witch?"

She nudged him back. "Ain't *you* cute, though."

Dennis met her gaze and put both hands over his heart. "There goes all my focus for the day."

"Don't you worry, Sugar-Tits," Jill said. "We finish this demo, and I'll see you on the other side."

"You're moving quite well today," Violina told Ysabella, a curl of the lip betraying her sarcasm.

The crone returned a genuine smile. "Sensible shoes and simple living, Violina."

"Mmm. That's all it takes to make it so long?"

"That," Ysabella said, "and disregard for petty slights."

"You scared?" DeShaun asked Stuart, too quiet for the others to hear.

"Nope!" The answer came quickly. Stuart had expected the question. "But I swear, DeShaun, if you so much as goose me, jump out of the shadows, make creepy moan sounds"—Stuart counted off the many possibilities on his fingers—"do your Candyman impersonation, or your Pinhead impersonation, or your Pennywise…"

"Dude," DeShaun stopped, grabbing him by the arm, "you saved my life up there."

Stuart felt his face flush. "Yeah, well. I guess you owe me, huh?"

"Always will."

"Then you can talk your parental units into not moving, and we'll call it even."

"I'm trying like hell, man," DeShaun said, stone serious.

"Either way…" Stuart held out his hand and the little scar there, and DeShaun displayed its match on his hand.

* * * *

"Do me a favor and stay with them," Hudson said to Yoshida, nodding at McGlazer, Stella and the witches as he led the others around to the maintenance shack built against the church's least-seen side.

"I don't get why we can't start ahead," said Pedro.

"'Cause it ain't our place to come and go as we please, meathead," explained Dennis.

"Since when are you such a square?"

"Abe's the only one with a key anyway." Hudson yanked down the sign reading NO ENTRY BY ORDER OF CRONUS COUNTY HEALTH DEPARTMENT he had fudged when they locked it down. "Even Stella didn't get one."

"Anybody else freaking out a little bit?" asked DeShaun.

"Don't worry." Stuart opened his backpack and reverently withdrew from it something that looked like a slate-gray corndog.

"Mega-sparkler!" DeShaun exclaimed.

"You know those aren't even remotely legal," said Hudson.

"Sorry, sir." Stuart's apology was sincere.

"Just put it away," warned Hudson. "Unless you need it."

* * * *

As he entered, McGlazer looked around the stained-glass-filtered sanctuary wistfully. Stella gave him a gentle pat on the arm.

"Don't tell me you already miss the place." Violina's tone held understated mockery.

"I just hope I won't have to."

"We'll get your church back up and running," Ysabella said. "If that's what you really want."

McGlazer didn't ask her to elaborate. "This is where…Ruth beat the hell out of me with the gun."

"Oh, I'm so sorry," said Maisie. "Is it…painful to be here?"

"It will be if I…if we never hold services here again."

"Violina, would you be so kind as to sage?" asked Ysabella, subtly supporting herself against a pew. "Every room, please."

"Saging?" Violina gave a smug smile. "That's more of an apprentice task." She looked to Maisie, who was already drawing a bundle of the dried herb from her bag

"Our ghost loved to play this," Stella strode almost wistfully to the organ, "and scare the living daylights out of me."

Ysabella beheld the mahogany instrument dreamily, touching a D key but not quite playing it. "No longer?"

"Not since Halloween before last." Stella gave a self-conscious smile. "Sometimes I almost miss it."

The witch laughed. "I shouldn't promise to bring it back."

They proceeded to the hallway beyond the sanctuary's rear door, leaving Maisie to smudge the room with the smoking sage bundle.

Discreetly, Violina lingered.

In the hallway, McGlazer pointed to his office door. "Here is where I first became…possessed."

Ysabella opened it and stepped in, leaving the light switch untouched, remembering the power was off. "No windows."

"The place needs a lot of renovations. Modernization."

"And light," added Ysabella.

Chapter 10

Procession

Maisie, mostly a jeans-type girl, had worn an out-of-season floral skirt, as Ysabella sometimes did, once again in defiance of the black-garbed witch stereotype. Was the girl imitating her role model? Or was this in deference to the fundamentalist Christian directive against women wearing pants in a church?

Violina was sure it was one or the other, or both. The young enchantress was impressionable, malleable—and this would be useful.

"Maisie, sweetie." Violina placed a motherly hand on Maisie's arm as the girl waved her burning sage around the foyer. "Sorry to interrupt."

Maisie ceased her mumbled chant. "Oh, no, it's fine!"

"I feel bad about talking down to you the way I just did." Her face filled with shadow as she made a contrite expression. "As if…this was beneath me, and you were a lesser witch."

"No apology needed. I *am* still learning."

"We all are," Violina continued. "And I should know by now that no one is above doing good work. Can I help?" She took the smoldering bundle and divided it.

"I'd be honored!"

"Our rocker boys are handsome, aren't they? I see you're friendly with the bass player."

"Pedro. He's really nice."

"Nicely muscled, right?"

Maisie giggled. "That's a bonus."

"I think he's a good match for you. His energy syncs with yours."

"You can tell that?"

"Without a doubt." Violina leaned toward her and whispered. "I can help…encourage things along, if you like."

Maisie had to chase away her teen-girl grin.

"It's not cheating, you know," Violina persisted. "He's single, I hear."

"Thank you, but I sort of like the way it's progressing." Maisie's expression showed distrust.

"Oh, I did it again, didn't I? Overstepped."

Maisie stayed quiet.

"This tension between Ysabella and me…it must be stressful for you," offered Violina. "I don't want you to think I would ever hurt or undermine her. I love her, just like you do." Violina made a show of arcing the sage over the organ. "On the contrary, I'm afraid she's overextending herself. I'm worried about her health."

"She just needs a day or two to recover. The whole thing with the werewolf girl. God, it was stressful."

"She's stronger than any of us," Violina responded. "But she takes on too much. She's not good at delegating."

"What can we do to help her?" Maisie asked.

It was time to coax the rabbit further into the trap.

"Let me give it some thought." Violina exhibited an earnest expression, lowering her voice. "It's critical that we protect her at all costs. Even…if it's against her wishes, I'm afraid."

* * * *

Strength in numbers did not offer Reverend McGlazer the comfort promised by scripture. If anything, it only made him more leery of potential trouble. "You should have brought your spotlights, deputies."

"We left them in the hunter's blind," explained Hudson. "Had to move fast when we were transporting our furry friend."

McGlazer unlocked the heavy-duty padlock on the equipment-shed door. Reminding himself that the phantasmic fungus was gone and it was okay to breathe, he eased the simple plywood door open. The punkers, the witches, the two boys and the lawmen all warily stepped back from it with him.

Ysabella went first, hoping the darkness of the stairwell hid her need to steady herself against the wall.

Soon, they all stood in the basement's first room, waiting while McGlazer took the ancient candle lamp down from the door-side sconce and lit it.

"This is where you want to record your album?" Maisie asked Pedro.

"Our demo," he corrected. "The studio guys will decide about the album."

Dennis whistled a few notes and listened to their echoes. "So far, so good."

"What if I get scared?" teased Jill.

"Don't start!" from Stuart.

"I feel the residue of the malevolence that was here," said Ysabella. "But it has gone."

"Gone where?" Stella asked.

It was almost a minute before Ysabella, sliding her hand along the wall, stopped and faced her. "Somewhere in the ether."

"Somewhere in time," enjoined Maisie.

Ysabella went to the arched door at the far left from the entryway. "Beyond here, spirits once waited," she said. "But no longer."

They all watched her peer at the doorway in the dark, until Violina spoke. "Shall we cleanse it too, then?"

"Not now," said Ysabella. She looked at Maisie. "Years ago."

* * * *

The catacombs expedition party resurfaced to a bright sun reflecting off the yellow leaves of the nearby maple. A mantle of relief settled over veterans of the horror show it had once hosted.

"Not nearly as creepy as I remember it," said DeShaun.

"I definitely prefer its current non-mushroom-freak state," said Stuart, "and it looks like the rev is gonna let us work on the demo down there."

He yanked a thumb back at the happy trio of punkers exchanging fist bumps. Dennis and Jill even hugged, only to have Pedro get between them like a boxing referee.

"What about your dad?" Stuart asked.

"He's okay, but he's been awful hush-hush since the woods." DeShaun cast an inconspicuous glance at Yoshida. "And Yoshi's acting kinda weird, don't you think?"

* * * *

With everyone distracted and Violina finally in front of her, Ysabella held onto Maisie's arm. The girl slowed her pace and clutched Ysabella's hand. "Should we stop for a moment?"

"No," answered Ysabella. "Just help me look strong."

Violina overheard but said nothing. She was well aware of Ysabella's weakened condition. For months, she had been working to manifest it. "Boys?" she called, gesturing at Maisie to join her. "How would you like to have high tea with a couple of witches?"

The teens needed only a second of deliberation. "Make it milkshakes and you got a deal, lady."

Chapter 11

Before The Nightmare

"The religious freedom thing was touchy as all get out," DeShaun began, as their waitress breezed away. "Bennington had traveled the world and learned about all different religions."

"Somewhere along the way, Benny found connections between a bunch of 'em," said Stuart. "He settled on the idea that most so-called religions were really just the same thing with different names."

"That's where you get the Saturn connection. Our boy knew it wouldn't be an easy sell. He had to feel out his candidates to make sure they would at least accept his idea, if not necessarily toe the line on it."

"The way the math adds up, Conal got wind of Bennington's plan and tagged along on the trip to escape getting caught for a whole grocery list of nefarious deeds he had committed." Stuart frowned. "Not a good dude."

"What else can you tell us about Conal O'Herlihy?" asked Maisie.

"Conal was a butthole," said DeShaun. "He got on Bennington's good side, then came up with a cockamamie plan to take control of the whole deal."

"Told his crew the Lord was on their side," added Stuart. "But we're not so sure he was a bible believer either."

"Remember that mushroom we were talking about?" DeShaun explained about the hallucinogenic fungus from the Greek isle of Patmos that had been the main ingredient in murderous zealot Ragdoll Ruth's poisoned candy.

Stuart picked up the narrative. "He and his crew started digging a cave under the church foundation, to grow the stuff and—get this—preserve their own bodies for resurrection."

Violina gazed like a predator hungry for more.

"Yep. Pretty crazy." The boys told the tale of the mushroom men they had encountered the year before.

"Back to way-back-when," Stuart said, "Conal organized his coup." Having only ever read the word and not heard it, Stuart pronounced it "coop."

"Was he successful?"

"Yes and no," DeShaun said. "There's not much in the archives. It gets murky."

"But here's what's key," Stuart said. "The church is called Saint Saturn's. And this is Cronus County."

"My guess is, the factions eventually split. But what became of Conal and pals, nobody really knows."

"Physically, anyway," added DeShaun. "We're pretty sure it was his ghost that possessed Reverend McGlazer last Halloween—and his crew that wore the mushroom suits last year."

"You dear children," muttered Maisie. "You've seen and been through so much."

"Yeah, well, if you can help our town…" DeShaun began.

"It'll all be worth it," finished Stuart.

* * * *

Settlement era

By the time Friedrich Schroeder had driven his horse to the settlement's dusty main street, he'd had considerable time to regain the composure that bled from him like Hezekiah's blood when he found the poor man's corpse in place of his bootzaman minutes earlier. A measure of his special wine helped, of course. He slowed his horse as he pondered the circumstances of making a hysterical announcement to the entire settlement.

One of their own, slain and posed in such sadistic mockery, was certainly a matter of grave concern. But did it warrant the reaction it would cause?

Other questions came to him as he and the horse trotted, then ambled their way toward town.

Could the Tsalagi—or Cherokee, as many had taken to calling them—have learned about the enslavement of their young men? It seemed they would simply have come in the night with torches and arrows and burned as many homesteads as they could rather than killing one man and posing him in such a bizarre state.

Was it a warning from one of the other settlers? If so, was it meant for him specifically? Or for others in Conal O'Herlihy's growing contingent?

In any case, galloping into the middle of the settlement and screaming bloody murder, imploring all who would to follow him back to the horrific scene, would not do. At worst, he could find himself accused.

Schroeder steered his horse toward O'Herlihy's home on the big hill at the end of the settlement, wishing, for a mile, he had brought something to offer the Irishman to smooth things after Schroeder's failure to attend the previous night's meeting.

The only vice of any kind the Celt indulged in these days was the spotted mushroom he secretly grew beneath his house. Perhaps, with this show of loyalty, Conal would offer him another chance to ingest the life-changing fungus today.

After these months of refusing it, was he ready? If it would chase away the horror of seeing Hezekiah bled and crucified, the answer was yes.

* * * *

Schroeder took his place between two large men—Gregor Tiernan and Jonas Cooke, son of the town's constable, Adonijah—and issued a candlelit smile that the other settlers did not see. Eyes closed, they stood in a sort of trance.

The subterranean room was crowded now, where there had been only Schroeder and two others for the first gathering some years back.

Conal O'Herlihy presided at the far wall of the dank room, near the arched doorway that led to a kind of purgatory. The Irishman stood with his head bowed and his hands clasped, waiting.

Though he was late in arriving for the clandestine meeting, Schroeder knew what was happening even before hearing the panicked pounding on the arched door behind Conal.

Conal ignored this, raising his hands and head toward the low wood ceiling in supplication. "O Lord Jehovah, God of earth and altar, we praise Thee and thank Thee, on behalf of these, Your beloved sons, who now find wisdom in terror, salvation in suffering."

Muffled voices cried for help—or the relief of death—on the other side of the door.

The other men in the room called "Amen!" in robust harmony.

Schroeder knew the door was sturdy. But even in mere candlelight, the dust bursting from its cracks and the sound of desperate assault against it raised alarm.

"Let us out!" was the staggered chorus. "It…it's *rearranging* us!" one martyr clumsily explained.

Unlike the others present, Schroeder had pledged loyalty to Conal and his cause, even without experiencing the fungus-catalyzed visions. His curiosity was strong, his desire for spiritual enlightenment stronger, but his fear of going mad was strongest of all.

As a result, he often felt alone amid the other disciples, who seemed to view the trial-by-terror as simply a giant leap toward God.

When the cries and bellows began to wane, Conal nodded for help from Jonas and three other large devotees and opened the arched door to accept the saucer-eyed trippers in firm, reassuring embraces. They were eased to the masoned floor, where they all sat and wept or stuttered.

Conal knelt to put fatherly hands around the face of the nearest: Kemlin Farrady. "What did you see, brother?"

"The cock crowed! Its hens all fell dead!" Farrady gripped Conal's wrists. "Their eggs broke open and bled smoke!"

Farrady tried to stand. O'Herlihy wouldn't let him. "And then?"

"The smoke rained burning semen!" Farrady cried. "It spread like moss…it melted wood and burned stone!"

"Yes…" said Conal. "The cock is all of us! The men of Ember Hollow!"

He stared out into the barely visible faces of his attendees with doom. "The smoke and semen are our children, doomed to hell by our inaction—and destined to lead others to condemnation!"

The men nodded at the wisdom of the interpretation, given so quickly and forcefully it had to be true.

Conal moved on to the next of the three. "What came to you, brother?"

"A giant descended on our land, dressed the color of the new-world squash, its eyes aglow." Henry Gourlay could not have known he had seen into Ember Hollow's future and the night of the Pumpkin Parade. It was the whimsical character of the Night Mayor, a man on stilts who would lead the Pumpkin Parade down Main Street.

"It's Wilcott Bennington, asserting his will, controlling us all utterly," explained Conal. "If…we are not vigilant to stop him."

Grumbles of alarm and discontent echoed off the stone walls.

Chapter 12

A Wolf's Age

Modern day

"Unlike most of the other settlements and colonies, folks here in the Hollow didn't live practically on top of each other," Stuart took a draw from his pumpkin-spice milkshake. "The big selling point was, you could have your own field and homestead, and barter down here on Main Street for whatever you needed."

"Conal O'Herlihy, God rest his evil soul, took dibs on the big rocky hill nobody else wanted. He let folks bury their dead there—for a fee." DeShaun rubbed his fingers together.

"Started holding secret meetings with people who weren't totally on board with the idea of broad religious freedom. Told them about his mushroom trips and even shared the crap, once he started growing it."

Maisie and Violina were as amused by the boys' shorthand as by the details of their story.

"He got these dudes—plus some handy kidnapped Cherokees—to dig the church basement, which was really just a big cellar for growing his 'shrooms. But it was also his secret meeting hall. No one who didn't know about it could see them gathered down there."

"Anyone who wasn't totally on board usually fell in line once they sampled the fungus," Stuart continued. "It scared the crap out of 'em. Then Conal would conveniently interpret their visions for them—in a way that favored his little scheme."

* * * *

Most of the flight had been under an overcast sky that allowed few precious pockets of sunshine. As one such pocket made a dramatic appearance, Brinke Mercer raised her head from her photo album, one of dozens she kept, to soak it in. She smiled down at the patchwork of farm fields and the stretches of woodland broken only sporadically by towns and neighborhoods.

She dug into her carry-on, a handmade, papoose-like souvenir from South America given to her by a centuries-old shaman, and extracted a Polaroid camera.

The antique camera wasn't ideal for aerial photography, but she only wanted the link to the memory, not a reproduction. Memories, she had long ago realized, are fluid, and that's the way they should be.

Her seatmate, a middle-aged businessman named Herve, who had briefly experimented with chatting her up before concluding he was in over his head, raised a magazine over the Polaroid to reduce glare. "Does this help?"

"Let's try," she answered.

Passengers in the seats just in front turned around on hearing the camera click, as if annoyed.

Standing six-foot-two, the striking biracial anthropologist was used to being stared at and judged, subtly and less than subtly. Her kinky locks, grown into a foamy afro that naturally parted in the middle from its own weight, made her seem both taller and blacker. It was not an uncommon "compliment" for someone to tell her she must be great at basketball.

Brinke always smiled at commenters and gawkers, wished them well, and sent them silent blessings. They were staring at her, but she was studying them. It was a fair-enough trade.

She took four snaps and fanned them out like playing cards, casting a net of good wishes onto the people and crops below. Her persistent optimism was born of a lifetime of practice and mindfulness. She wondered if Ember Hollow would be its greatest test.

Ysabella had no idea Brinke was on the way, just as Brinke herself had not known until a day and a half ago, when she saw the scrawled message at her motel in Arizona. "We're going to Ember Hollow...Need you here! Maisie."

While Brinke was out on a ten-day wilderness excursion with the Cocopah tribe, without phone access, Maisie had diligently tracked her down, learning her location from her landlady in Oklahoma. Like Violina, Brinke found her interest piqued by the name Ember Hollow.

The North Carolina farm town was not far removed from the national news cycle, especially with Halloween approaching. Brinke had already done her own research into its history to try to nail down a theoretical supernatural origin for its strange troubles.

The message from Maisie came at exactly the right moment. The itinerant Brinke hadn't yet settled on her next destination for study and work.

She placed the Polaroids in the back of her photo album, to be organized later, and settled easily into a light meditation.

* * * *

The Cronus County Sheriff's Department, like many Ember Hollow institutions, was left shorthanded by the slow exodus. The department's two female officers had both vamoosed. Zero applicants had queried since.

It was a godsend when Elaine Barcroft had volunteered to help out as needed. Then again, like her sons Dennis and Stuart, Elaine had been toughened by recent hard times. A widow who has nearly lost her sons will either break down or power up—and this farmer's daughter was already nails-tough long before marrying and burying Jerome Barcroft.

Better, she was strangely nonplussed about coming in to help tend to the vacant-minded ex-werewolf Aura.

"She's been docile as a…I don't want to say puppy," Hudson told her. "You want this, just in case?"

Elaine took the canister of pepper spray from him, blinked at it, then handed it back. "I have a grown son and a teenager, Deputy."

"Right. I'll be just outside the cell with my back turned, like a proper gentleman."

They walked along the corridor between cells in an odd silence. Cronus County's criminals weren't generally the dangerous kind, but they were notoriously mouthy.

It was a prolonged whine, the sound of a woman imitating a forlorn canine, that not only made Hudson and Elaine halt, but brought out a low complaint from the cells. "Cain't you put her somewheres else, Shurf?"

"Yeah," enjoined frequent customer Bern Addison. "She's giving us the heebie-jeebies."

"I'll book you a suite at the Regis," deadpanned Hudson. "You want room service?"

The grievances ended there, except for Aura's. When they arrived at her cell, Hudson and Elaine found the biker chick cowering in the corner with her head held low like an abandoned German shepherd, the blanket they had draped over her bundled around her feet.

Hudson turned his head from her nakedness as he unlocked the cell. "You sure you want to do this?" Hudson handed her the bucket of bathwater he carried. "I can have one of the neighboring counties send a female."

"She seems harmless enough." Elaine entered, setting down the bucket of warm water at the door and extending a dish of mashed potatoes and chicken strips, atop a folded, county-issue orange jumpsuit. "Hi, there!" Instinctually mothering, Elaine might have been talking to little Wanda Lott.

Hudson closed the cell door, keeping his eyes averted but listening close, as Elaine went to work earning Aura's trust.

* * * *

Violina thanked the boys, paid everyone's tab, tipped ostentatiously, and effortlessly coerced Maisie into taking a walk with her along Main Street.

Beyond the looming smog of its troubles, Ember Hollow still offered beauty and tranquility. Watching poplar leaves breeze by, the witches smiled at the mystery. There was no poplar tree in sight. The recently liberated leaves might have traveled aloft for many miles.

"I'm amazed at how your gift has grown," flattered Violina. "Ysabella is teaching you so well. Frankly, I'm envious."

"How can you tell? We haven't…"

"I can feel it." Violina stopped and looked intently at the younger girl. "Your energy radiates like a sun."

"I still have so much to—"

"I do too, dear," interrupted Violina. "I see how you've grown, and it makes me realize…I've stunted myself."

"No! You have so much to offer, Violina. The battle took its toll, but we've gained something from it. I hope we'll all have a chance to grow closer here…"

Violina took Maisie's arm the way she had seen Ysabella do. "You're the apprentice Ysabella deserves, and I wish I had under me."

"Oh, please," said Maisie. "I'm privileged to learn anything you're willing to teach me."

Violina smiled wistfully as she started walking again.

"Did I say something wrong?" asked Maisie.

"Not at all. I just don't want to interfere with Ysabella's teachings."

"She's the one who told me every witch has something to teach."

Violina took on a hopeful expression. "Well, then, that would include me, wouldn't it?"

"Of course!"

"I would like to help you with your Akashic ritual," said the elder witch, beaming with enthusiasm. "I could be your apprentice!"

Maisie seemed stunned.

"Will you at least think about it?"

"No need. I'd be honored!"

Violina deftly switched the topic to Pedro, and they were soon giggling and bumping against each other like high school freshmen.

* * * *

At lunch, with most officers and personnel busy or out, Yoshida took the opportunity to put to the test a few of his concerns and suspicions.

Aura was scheduled for pickup by state mental-health personnel the next morning. He needed to face her before then.

She sat slumped on her bunk with her back against the graffiti-scratched cell wall, blinking away sleep. When she looked up at Yoshida, it was as if for the first time.

All traces of her lycanthropy had vanished, along with her power over him, real or imagined.

He had left his weapon and gear behind when he stepped away from his desk to make this trek. He wasn't about to tell anyone he was afraid she held some kind of psychic control over him, and certainly not that he had sleepwalked naked into the forest. Not till he had a chance to do this—to stand near her and make eye contact with her in human form, to see if he was affected in the same way as when she was caged in the murdered witch's barn.

Before settling down in Ember Hollow, Yoshida had spent four years with the Orange County Sheriff's Department, during which he had been in a couple of high-speed chases. On one such pursuit, he had made a curve too fast and skidded off the highway, down a thirty-foot bank. Fortunately, it was both shallow and scrubby enough to prevent a catastrophic nosedive. But he had not forgotten the terror of plummeting through a noisy tunnel of blur, unable to right his vehicle no matter how hard he clutched the wheel or mashed the brakes.

That was what he had felt back in the barn, watching the panicked wolf fight her forced transformation.

Now—nothing.

The tendrils of her wild mind burrowing into his, the tingling of the tiny bite wound she had given him, the ownership in her eyes—gone.

Hudson had expressed doubt that she was truly amnesiac. But Yoshida was now satisfied she was. A true clean slate, with only basic human function.

"Do you know me?"

She blinked. His words were just sounds, bereft of the kindness inflected in Elaine Barcroft's or the baritone authority of Hudson's. Yet nonthreatening. Neutral.

Yoshida looked at the place where she'd bitten him—or where he imagined she had?—and rubbed vigorously to see if the tingle would return. Like the wound itself, it did not.

Yoshida walked away from Aura's cell.

"What did you guys do to her?" asked inmate Buddy Sandstorm, as Yoshida walked past. "She stopped making them weird noises."

Yoshida didn't respond. He was too busy in the moment, the wave of relief washing over him.

Relief over what, though?

Rather than try to answer his own question, Yoshida considered his own strange behaviors and dismissed them as stress-induced.

Chapter 13

Storm In My Head

Violina was pleased to see the clouds gathering and condensing, as she had willed. Thunder, so subtle only she could hear it, grumbled inside the high, condensing mass. The storm was as devious as she was.

Thumbs hooked in his creaky belt, Officer Kebbler greeted her at the open door. "Yes indeed, ma'am! Hudson called over and said you'd be by!"

With his sun-spotted pate and deep crow's feet, Kebbler looked to be well past the age of retirement. Yet his brisk movements and snappy speech pattern gave the impression he would be better in the field, rather than overseeing this dusty former machine shop at the end of Ecard Street, which served as an annex to the Cronus County Sheriff's Department's evidence lockup.

"Right this way." He whistled a tune that seemed disjointed, as if he only needed to hear its reassuring echo in the plain-block building. They walked a while, passing locked cage rooms that housed everything from damaged Pumpkin Parade floats to one serious collection of armaments taken from a white-supremacist, militia-type group.

"This stuff's kinda funny, ain't it?" Kebbler asked as he unlocked the flimsy door to the small room, formerly the shop's office. A clipboard hung by the door held a list that was labeled SAXON FARM/DEVIL'S NIGHT.

"Funny?" asked Violina.

"Silly!" he elaborated, nodding his head in quick little jerks like a hyperactive teenager.

He swung the door open and flashed his coffee-browned teeth at her. "Hey, how about I keep you company?" Kebbler was shameless in his lack of subtlety given his age—and wedding ring.

"Aren't you kind?" Violina made plain her sarcasm. "But I wouldn't want your wife to get the wrong idea."

"Oh, she's passed." Kebbler folded his fingers to hide his ring and his lie, face flushing.

She patted him on the chest as she entered the room. "Heart attack?"

"Yes…ma'am"

"Condolences." Violina flipped the light switch and surveyed a simple table with folding chairs and a trio of steel shelving units not unlike those in Matilda's barn. Plain boxes marked with sequential numbers lined them neatly.

"Are y'all ladies with one of the colleges?" asked Kebbler.

Violina hadn't considered that Hudson and his circle were wisely keeping it quiet that witches were now involved in their town's ongoing struggle against the unknown. "Of course. Duke University." She said, naming the school not for its paranormal studies program but because it was the state's most prestigious.

"I love college girls!" Kebbler laughed and laughed.

As Violina tugged one of the boxes down and onto the table, Kebbler made to help.

"No, I've got it," she said. "Watch your heart!"

Kebbler seemed confused for a second. "No, that was my wife. Mine's fine."

"Surely it's still broken."

Kebbler was tongue-tied.

The box contained several sealed plastic bags. The top one, labeled FOOTPATH TO BARN, contained shards of glazed pottery. The footpath was where Jill had battled for her life against Everett Geelens. The shards had to be from the container the punker girl had smashed over the Trick-or-Treat Terror, the one that made him "vanish."

"I hope you don't think all of us around here believe in that hokey, horror-movie nonsense," said Kebbler, regaining momentum. "I think the Halloween parade got into a few empty heads around here."

The next bag contained a clay jar, about the size of a cold-cream container, engraved roughly with the letters LUP. This would be skinwalker salve, for either changing or restoring. Unimportant to Violina.

"Some kind of lube?" Kebbler giggled like a frat boy. Violina didn't look at him, but she could feel his gaze like a heat lamp on her legs and ass.

She took down another box and opened it, facing toward Kebbler this time. Inside was something of a knife collection: Aura's bone-handled balisong, Rhino's boot knife and Matilda's athame, still speckled with blood.

Beneath these smaller blades were Everett's toys: hedge clippers and the kidney-shaped bone saw he used to make real, live skull masks.

"Don't get yourself hurt with those, now," said Kebbler. "Be a shame if ya got blood on that nice blouse." His breathing had gotten heavier. "… And had to take it off."

Among a stack of Polaroids, she found several of sigils splashed onto a stone wall, possibly in blood. A notation at the bottom told her these were taken in the chamber under the church.

"I'll need to take some of this with me," Violina said.

"Oh, I'm sorry. Can't do that without the sheriff's say." Kebbler leaned out to look toward the front and make sure no one was there. "You can just take your time and…examine 'em here."

A third box yielded a find more mundane in appearance, yet infinitely intriguing to Violina. GIANT PUMPKIN FROM FIELD NEXT DOOR said its label. The contents were at least two handfuls of massive pumpkin seeds, about twice the normal size. Tiny brown dots on a few of them could only be blood.

"Are you all right, Deputy Kebbler?"

"Oh, I'm righter than rain right now, hun."

"Are you"—she cocked her head and stared at his chest—"certain?"

Kebbler cleared his throat. He raised his hand to his sternum. "Maybe a little heartburn."

"Some water might help," said Violina.

Kebbler wheezed, louder with each breath, as he stepped away from the little room and started toward his desk.

Violina rearranged the contents of the boxes, putting all she wanted to take in one. She carried it cradled in her arm like an infant as she left the room and made her way toward the exit.

Kebbler was at his desk, trying to move the dirty, clear-plastic rotary on the ancient telephone cradle with a quivering finger.

"Can I call someone for you, Officer?"

Neutered by distress, he could only look at her with suspicion. "I think I'll be all right. Just need to sit for a minute or two."

She patted his suddenly pale hand on her way to the door. "Thanks for all your help."

Before the door had clicked closed behind her, Kebbler's breathing had gotten so heavy and strident it echoed throughout the building, like his off-tune whistle.

* * * *

The Wolf fought to stay. Spurred by the shock of sharp pain, the Man eventually claimed the greater measure of control.

Yoshida snarled and snapped, but the violently wriggling cat was out of his paws—*hands*—and bolting through the clattering pet door before Yoshida could drop to all fours to pursue it.

Out of breath, his hands stinging from cat scratches, Yoshida rolled onto his back on the rough bark mulch around Mr. Campbell's Japanese maple and squinted in pain at the sky. Fast-growing clouds had covered the moon, but he knew, somehow, that it was at about three-quarters, and this seemed disappointing for some reason.

"What the hell is wrong with you, Purrf?" asked Mr. Campbell, smelling strongly of store-brand shampoo and a toasted bacon-and-cheese sandwich he'd eaten roughly twenty minutes ago.

Yoshida looked toward his neighbor's door, realizing he had never heard more than an indecipherable muffle from within before tonight. He rose from the mulch and shook to throw off the clinging chips.

Shook?

He reached back and slapped the mulch away, as he hunkered down to hide between some shrubs. A second later, the bathrobed Mr. Campbell flipped on his outside light and, opened the door, searching the yard with tired eyes. "Did you fight another kitty?"

Mr. Campbell went back inside and switched off the light. But Yoshida found that he could see just the same without it. He could trace the oozing trails of his cat scratches just as well as he could feel them, even in the deeper dark of the hedges.

How the hell did I piss off Mr. Purrfect? Yoshida asked himself.

Campbell's tuxedo cat had been friendly to him since the day Yoshida moved to Ember Hollow. Yoshida even allowed him into his home and petted him sometimes.

The cat must have gotten scared.

Yoshida realized he was naked again. And that his teeth ached from gnashing.

"Crap on a Chrysler!" Yoshida whispered. "Did I just try to eat Mr. Purrfect?"

Yoshida's heart sank. Taking the wolf out of Aura had not taken it out of him.

It didn't take a Harry D'Amour to figure out that he was drawing closer to full-on werewolf status as the moon grew fatter.

* * * *

Hudson set the phone on its cradle gently, as if out of respect for his fallen fellow officer, Kebbler. The relieving officer had found him face down on his desk, dead of a heart attack.

This should be a day of mourning. Unfortunately, as with the past two Octobers, that would have to wait.

* * * *

Deputy Yoshida signed out, changed into civvies and drove his personal car to Ember Hollow Recreational Grounds Park, sure he looked like an undercover rookie about to make his first drug buy.

He tried on a smile, checked his reflection and decided against it. It seemed predatory somehow, exactly the last thing he wanted, as he was going to meet the kids.

The sky was a Hitchcock film, heavy with suspense. Clouds were gathering like an angry flock of bloodthirsty birds.

The kids were out on the soccer field, passing a jack-o'-lantern-painted Frisbee between the three of them and the exuberant Bravo. Yoshida raised a hand to wave, but they were having too much fun to notice. He envied them and remembered how much they deserved it after the extremes of raw terror they had lived through.

He was within thirty feet before Bravo charged for a vigorous greeting rub—then stopped hard. Some troubling scent had him on edge.

"You don't seem so square in your regular clothes," quipped DeShaun.

Bravo issued a low growl.

"Bravo disagrees."

Yoshida slowed, extending his hand for the dog to sniff. "Hey, it's me, boy!"

Bravo remained leery.

"Jeez, what's wrong, Bravs?" asked Stuart.

Candace tossed the Frisbee to Yoshida and went to hug the dog. "You're trembling, fella!"

"Maybe he thinks you're a cat," said DeShaun.

Yoshida smiled, but it was not genuine. He was reminded of his skirmish with Mr. Purrfect.

"Sorry, kids. Not feeling very jocular."

"Yeah, well, my dad is gonna give you a major frowning-upon if he sees you sporting that scruffy samurai look, Lone Wolf."

Rubbing his chin, Yoshida had a disconcerting moment of paranoia that DeShaun knew his secret and was mocking it—then realized the boy was making reference to a Japanese manga and film character with that appellation. His point was well made; there was already gritty stubble where he had shaved just hours ago.

As DeShaun hoisted his backpack and started toward the nearest picnic shelter, Candace attached Bravo's leash. "Maybe I should hold onto him."

"Stay close, okay?" said Stuart.

Watching how the kids kept careful watch on one another drove home for Yoshida just how much they had been through together. He winced at the sound of distant thunder, which the kids did not seem to hear.

Candace laced Bravo's leash around a picnic bench at the next table and sat close to the dog.

"Did you bring the books?" the deputy asked, as he sat opposite the boys.

"Nah." Said DeShaun as he unzipped the backpack. "This is just full of heroin and whatnot."

"Didn't think anybody but us ever looked at these," said Stuart, helping DeShaun unload the books.

"Mrs. Washburn at the library must have thought the same. She said she was letting you guys hold onto them indefinitely."

"Friends in high places." DeShaun arranged the books, seven in all, side by side on the table.

* * * *

Modern day

Yoshida found himself avoiding eye contact with Bravo. The mastiff seemed to be studying him like a code, reading his darkest secrets and fears straight from his brain.

His eye caught the title of the book before him on the picnic table—*Men into Animals: A History of Magical Transformation.* "Is this a joke?"

Stuart opened the book to a page he had marked with a folded Chalk Outlines flyer. "Why don't you ask yourself from a year ago?"

With this, Yoshida realized how deep was his denial, that he was willing to ignore the battle with lycanthropes he had personally experienced, to avoid the idea of what he was becoming.

"Why'd you even want to see that stuff if you don't believe in it?" asked Candace.

"I'm curious about the biker girl."

"But that's a done deal."

"Is it a crime to be curious about something?" he snapped.

"Yeah, so arrest yourself, Deppidy Doofwad." The kids were as quick on the draw as ever.

"Sorry, guys. I haven't been sleeping well."

"Who has? We live in Scarytown, USA."

Yoshida skimmed over several passages in a couple of the books, wondering how he could pose his main question without giving himself away. "Is there anything about what happens when a skinwalker bites someone?"

The kids all blinked in alarm, having skipped to the end. "Oh, shit, Yosh."

"When?" asked DeShaun, in a low tone.

Yoshida sighed with resignation. "When we caught her."

"My dad…?"

"He didn't get bit, and he doesn't know," said Yoshida. "For now, I'd like to keep it that way."

The kids circulated a grim look. "All that stuff about the curse being passed on from a bite, that's just made up for Lon Chaney movies," said Stuart.

"*Werewolf of London* with Henry Hull was actually the first," added DeShaun.

Stuart raised a middle finger in his friend's face as he continued. "On the other hand, I didn't read anything about anybody being bitten by a skinwalker and actually surviving."

"Maybe you're the first," said Candace.

When Yoshida turned to look at her, Bravo gave a low growl, placing his big body in front of his girl.

"I've had some weird incidents," Yoshida said, giving details about losing control at Aura's transformation ceremony, sleepwalking, following the moon home—and apparently trying to eat Mr. Purrfect.

"Psychosomatic maybe?" DeShaun said.

"You see how Bravo is acting. And these cat scratches…" Yoshida rubbed the pink lines on his arms that looked a week old. "That was last night."

The kids gawped.

"I'm at a point where I can't take any chances." Yoshida said. "How long do we have till the full moon?"

"What's the moon like now?"

"Wait, you guys…" Candace began. "You already said it's not like the movies."

"Yeah?"

"He could be changing a little more every night."

"Which means..." Stuart did not want to finish.

"It means I might turn full-blown wolf one of these nights." Yoshida closed the book. "And...never turn back."

Chapter 14

Witchery

Violina had asked Maisie to meet her in the Blue Moon lobby.

"I want you to come here if you need." Violina pressed the slip of paper with the address into Maisie's hand like it was a precious gem. Before Maisie could ask—"I've rented a little house in Ember Meadows, just near the church."

Her brow furrowed as she slid her hand around Maisie's elbow and hugged her close. "I was afraid my being at the inn was too stressful for Ysabella, on top of all she's going through now. I want to do whatever I can to help her, and there's just too much raw emotion between us. I'm afraid…she resents me."

Maisie searched her memory for indications that would confirm Violina's assertions and felt insensitive that she couldn't find them. The elder witches had been wary of one another since the coven's war with a shadowy group that ended months ago. Their numbers reduced, the witches needed one another more than they ever had.

The rift between the coven's two most adept witches had to be healed. Maisie couldn't imagine her saintly mentor, Ysabella, being the one refusing to meet on common ground, rather than the narcissistic and self-indulgent Violina. Yet here was the latter, bending over backward to make concessions and ease the burdens of the former.

Perhaps Ysabella stubbornly clung to her personal issues with Violina, and it was clouding her judgment.

"Ysabella might need time to herself. Or you might. Or we can just spend time together," said Violina, embracing the girl like a daughter. "You're welcome here anytime,"

* * * *

"Are you cold, Ysabella?" Hugging her, Maisie felt the smaller woman shiver. "Can I make you some tea?"

"No, dear." Ysabella patted her arm. "I'll have a nice bath."

Maisie said good night and went to her room, next door to Ysabella's, wondering how long she should wait before calling Pedro.

Was that thunder she heard? All day, the cloud cover had been like a trap ceiling descending to crush them.

Just before stepping into her room, she took a last look to make sure her mentor got in all right. Ysabella's jacket hem disappeared past the door—which did not close.

"Ysabella?" Maisie called. "Are you all right?"

No answer.

Maisie stepped over to Ysabella's door—and saw her collapsed on the floor.

* * * *

Thunder was usually a comfort to Brinke.

While the pilots continued to circle the plane around the peculiar storm, she had laid her head back to relax and again engage in light meditation. But this thunder, this entire storm, in fact, was too strange, too disconcerting to foster relaxation.

With the latest rumble, several passengers expressed awe, like a primitive tribe witnessing the eruption of a volcano. Something was very, very off.

Brinke looked out toward the roiling gray blanket and waited for the next lightning burst. She did not have to wait long.

Bursts of red blossomed behind the billowing density in random sections, revealing what seemed like giant, cruel faces. It was easy to understand why the passengers were so agitated.

Then, stranger still, the gray plume went solid black, as if the near-insignificant light of the stars and lights from the ground were nonexistent for a split second. It was a negative, the opposite of a lightning burst.

The maelstrom was focused on, or from, Ember Hollow. The horror there was at its greatest—and growing furiously.

Brinke's mind raced. She had to get the plane down somehow—and asking nicely wasn't going to do it.

She realized she was looking around wildly when her seatmate, Herve, already nervous from the storm, gave her an alarmed look. "Miss, you're not about to get all hysterical, are you?"

"Not anymore," she retorted. "You're such a comfort."

"Well, I don't know how much more of this my heart can take," he said. "I gotta empty my tanks." He struggled out of his seat and stumbled toward the lavatory, unaware that he had unwittingly offered a solution, after all.

The only thing that would make the pilots and flight controllers put the plane down was a greater emergency than the storm. And failing a handy jihadist, what was there?

She waited for her seatmate to return, already improvising the affliction she would work on him, hating that it had come to that.

* * * *

After calling the church, Maisie sat and watched over Ysabella until Stella arrived, sending healing vibrations to the sleeping crone.

Self-recrimination set in, as Maisie realized Ysabella had been faltering, showing signs of illness before even the roadside vomiting incident.

Chapter 15

Magic Circle

The five-minute wait for Stella felt like a day.

"I'm so glad you were still at the church," said Maisie, her eyes swollen.

"You got her into bed?" Stella asked.

"I had to carry her. She hasn't moved at all."

Stella breezed through the suite to the bedroom, well familiar with the Blue Moon's room layout both from her work as an EMT and her brief separation from Bernard.

By the time she got to Ysabella, the old woman's eyes were open—barely. "Oh good…It's you."

"No one else knows except Abe."

Stella was relieved to feel some strength in Ysabella's hand when she clasped it. "You understand…It's crucial that I don't appear ineffectual."

"Your health is more important."

Ysabella's pulse felt normal, but her breathing was shallow.

Stella patted Maisie's hand. "Bring me some cool, wet washcloths, please."

"Maisie lacks experience," Ysabella said, taking a deep shuddery breath. "And…judgment. I'm so worried about her."

"She will rise to the occasion, if need be," reassured Stella.

"Can you?" whispered the crone. "Can Emera? Candace?"

Stella once again bristled at the thought of involving her little girls. "Is there…anyone else at all?"

Ysabella gave a small smile and a faint nod.

Twenty minutes later, Stella sat down with Maisie in the suite's front room and took her hands. "I understand why you don't want Ysabella in the hospital. If she gets worse, there won't be any other option."

"I can't lose her," said Maisie. "We can't."

"Does she have any kind of condition?"

"Other than obsessive micromanagement? Physically, she's healthier than any of us. When she brought that girl back from her skinwalk, it drained her reserves of power, which were still recovering after our previous mission. When this happens, a witch's vitality begins to drain."

"How long till she regains a normal level of...whatever it is that gives her power?"

"I'm afraid she's at a point where her sisters have to prime the pump, so to speak," said Maisie. "That's the purpose of a coven, to support one another and pick up the slack as needed. To feed our sisters from our own reserves."

"You and Violina could help her?"

Maisie considered her response. "Violina is the last person she would want to have find out she's weakened. There's a long-standing misunderstanding between them. But maybe I should tell her."

"If it will help heal Ysabella, you should," Stella said. "Is there anything I can do?"

"Maybe if you brought Reverend McGlazer here to offer prayer," Maisie answered. "Your little girls too, if you're comfortable with that."

"Is it that obvious that...I'm *not?*"

"What kind of mother would you be if all this didn't worry the hell out of you?"

As Stella rose to leave, Maisie clasped her hand tighter. "We all have to move fast now. Halloween is coming."

Maisie took the keys to the Mercedes and drove to Violina's rented house.

* * * *

Yoshida stared at his noisily working coffee maker like it was a crossroads.

He thought of the film DeShaun and Stuart had coaxed him into watching, the only horror film that had utterly scared the hell out of him—*The Exorcist*.

But it wasn't the demon Pazuzu that worried him. It was himself.

It hurt Yoshida to his core that he had caught himself trying to kill Mr. Purrfect.

The faces of his friends—Stuart, DeShaun, Hudson, The Outlines—appeared in his mind's eye as mangled corpses, a glimpse of the future and the victims of savage impulses he could not control.

A fist battered his door. "Open up, already!" Dennis Barcroft, polite as ever.

Yoshida found Dennis at the door holding his keyboard case, and Pedro with his bass, regarding Yoshi like he was the rudest host they had ever met. They entered without invitation, knowing they didn't need one.

"You look pretty hairless to me," said Pedro. "Like a twelve-year-old girl."

"What?"

"Stuart and DeShaun told us," explained Dennis. "But don't get sore. They were worried."

Pedro muscled past Yoshida on his way to the kitchen. "Yippee, it's a sleepover!"

"Took the liberty of calling in to work for you," Dennis continued. "Hud says for you to get some sleep, even if we gotta knock your ass out."

Yoshida followed Dennis to the kitchen, where Pedro was busy extracting beers from his refrigerator and emptying them down the drain. As with the invitation, no explanation or apology was needed.

"You guys are staying over?"

"Duh," answered Pedro. "You got any soft-core? Full penetration makes me squeamish."

"Some…Japanese pinku," answered Yoshida, catching on fast. "What are you dudes hoping to accomplish, exactly?"

"Keep an eye on your ass," said Dennis. "Figure out your malfunction."

Pedro tossed two empty bottles in the trash can. "You really think you're hulking out at night?"

"…I don't know."

"Let's find out together," said Dennis, handing Yoshida a bag of candy corn. "You'll have the privilege of hearing us practice our new tunes."

"Where'd you stash those silver chains?" Pedro asked. "'Cause you're about to get 'blinged,' as the young folks used to say."

* * * *

Reverend McGlazer's dream was frightening, distressing, confounding—but not surprising.

He was at the altar of Saint Saturn's, giving communion and tending his eager flock, like Jesus at the Mount, as they stood in line to receive his blessing.

First came Hudson with his family: Leticia, DeShaun, Wanda. They stood side by side and looked up at him with sad expressions. "We're leaving now," said Hudson. DeShaun extended his hand. "You come too. We'll drop you off."

When McGlazer did not take his hand, DeShaun smiled with understanding and withdrew it. Hudson patted the reverend on the shoulder, and they shuffled off.

Then came Dennis. McGlazer spun fast to take the silver tray of communion wine to the side exit, where Stella took it, opened the door and dashed away toward his office.

Dennis waved and walked away.

Next was Candace. She was holding Emera, who had regressed to infanthood. Candace pointed toward the wooden cross mounted on the back wall.

He faced front to find Elaine and Stuart Barcroft standing there. McGlazer held out his hands to touch them and found thick mud on his fingertips. The Barcrofts closed their eyes and waited. McGlazer gently rubbed the mud around their eyelids. The mud dried and fell off, then mother and son nodded their thanks. McGlazer started to make the sign of the Eucharist, but Elaine stopped his hand halfway through and kissed it.

"Abe," called Stella. When he turned toward her voice, he found himself sitting in his office, looking at his phone, which rang like church bells.

McGlazer woke from the dream in his parish bedroom and answered the telephone on his nightstand.

"Abe," Stella repeated. "Please come to the Blue Moon. Ysabella is very ill."

"Oh..."

"We need to form a prayer group for her, but...judiciously."

McGlazer understood the need for discretion, but..."Prayer group, you say?"

"I'm gathering the girls. Bernard too." McGlazer was relieved by this. He had wanted to speak with Bernard for some time. "I'll call the Lotts. Please get here quickly."

McGlazer hung up and stared at his coat and collar hanging on the closet doorknob, then left without them.

* * * *

Ever the gracious hostess, Violina mixed light drinks and raised brows of concern, directing Maisie to sit in the rental home's antique rocking chair. "Tell me what's wrong."

Doing so was going against Ysabella's wishes. But there was no other way. "Ysabella collapsed."

"Damn. I was afraid of something like this."

"Stella came to look her over. She's resting in her room."

Violina came back and knelt before Maisie on the rocking chair, taking the girl's hand.

"I need your help," Maisie said, her voice cracking. "We need to do something. We have to help her."

Violina hugged her, stroked her hair, commiserated. "She's too valuable to us. To the world."

"Will you come and help me chant over her?"

Violina considered. "She doesn't want me to know she's weakened. If she sees me—do you really think it will help her?"

"She'll see, like I do. She'll see that you care."

"And then what? She'll go to work trying to save the town. And she won't stop till it's done. Or *she's* done."

Maisie slumped with despair.

"We can't let our love for her cloud our judgment. We have a duty to this town. And to her."

When Maisie nodded her agreement, Violina continued. "Let's go to the church. Let's do what she would want us to do."

Violina raised her drink, coaxing Maisie to do the same. "Let's make Ysabella proud."

* * * *

The deputy found himself both annoyed that the rockers essentially had taken over his house and touched that they had come to help him. "You guys aren't gonna do anything kinky to me, are you?"

"You're awfully particular for a murderous monster." Dennis said. "Just count yourself lucky we don't sell you to the circus."

Pedro checked the tautness of the same silver-coated chain that had restrained Aura, now stretched over a quilt, handmade by Leticia Lott and Elaine Barcroft, that lay across the prone Yoshida and around the bed. "I bet you wish you were back in L.A. about now."

"Nah," answered Yoshida. "I never had any friends like you guys back there."

Pedro and Dennis both looked at Yoshida to see if he was being sarcastic. It was Dennis who broke the silence. "In case you forgot, you hung with me more times than you should have when I was balls-out blitzed. Even held my hair when I puked, like a true sorority sister."

Yoshida laughed for the first time since the night of Aura's ritual.

"Me, I'm just lookin' to get out of future speeding tickets," added Pedro. "And believe this—there's gonna be a lot."

Yoshida no longer felt alone—or doomed. He felt like whatever was happening to him, there were friends who cared, who would see him through to the other side. "So you think your magical girlfriend and her buds can help me?" he asked Pedro.

"Hey, I'm really into her, so don't jinx it, bro," answered Pedro. "They got that biker chick declawed, so I'm thinking you should be a cakewalk."

"Yeah, but…look how she wound up."

"Shut up and comb your face," said Dennis. "Sorry. Look, you might as well relax, 'cause, like Petey said, you ain't going nowhere."

"You want a lullaby, sweetie pie?" asked Pedro.

"Just promise me, you…won't let me hurt anybody."

Pedro reached for the tranquilizer rifle Yoshida had taught him to use. "Don't blame me if you wake up with a sore ass cheek and a hangover."

The Outlines stepped out of Yoshida's bedroom. Dennis gave a thumbs-up before easing the door nearly shut.

Yoshida closed his eyes—and felt a now-familiar tingling sensation radiate from the bite location and out though his body.

Chapter 16

Lupine Tooth

A short while later, Maisie stood behind Violina, watching her finagle the padlock to Saint Saturn Unitarian's landscaping shed with a lock-picking set, as she had the front gate, never asking herself why her elder would have such a thing. She followed her down into the catacombs, a battery-powered lamp held at eye level.

"How far back in time can you go?" Violina asked.

"Infinitely," explained Maisie, "but I have to align with the lunar cycle."

"It's a three-quarter moon now," whispered Violina. "Does that mean you can only travel to a time of the same cycle?"

Briefly, Maisie felt apprehensive about divulging such sensitive information. But she knew Violina could learn it easily enough on her own. "That's right. I just have to fall into the InBetween and search for early human contact with this region."

"How do I help you?"

Maisie's answer was simply to take Violina's hand. "Can you remember the things I describe?"

"Oh, I won't forget," Violina said. "I promise."

* * * *

With Yoshida's pantry and fridge well raided, Dennis and Pedro set up the keyboard, bass and a small amp in the living room, Pedro keeping the tranquilizer rifle close.

As Dennis presented Pedro with a fresh, clean copy of the new material, Pedro suggested "Let's try something by, say, Psyclon Nine or Rammstein, dude. Then we'll get, you know...dronier."

"Petey, my boy, I think you're starting to get it," praised Dennis. He cracked his knuckles and pinged the D on his new keyboard, cycling through several instrument settings before settling on musical saw. Pedro plugged in his bass, keeping the volume set at low, in consideration of their host.

They would not get a chance to play another note.

From Yoshida's bedroom a low growl alarmed them—then a violent crashing. Both leaped to their feet and bolted down the short hallway, Pedro grabbing the rifle.

Dennis yanked open the door—and ducked, pulling Pedro down with him. A piece of the headboard flew over their heads and smashed into the hallway wall behind them.

"Dart him!" shouted Dennis. Pedro didn't hear him, but he rose and tried to aim, nonetheless—a daunting task. The shadowy figure in the darkened room was fast, erratic and loud.

Dennis reached for the light switch. He was snatched into the dark before he could find it. As he cried out, Pedro fumbled around on the wall. Sensing the mêlée coming closer, he pointed the rifle at the murky movement but stopped short of aimlessly firing. There was only one dart.

The snarling and screaming painted a horrifying mental picture. When Pedro finally found the light switch, the reality was only mildly better—a wild-haired, fanged, misshapen mockery of Yoshida, straddling Dennis.

Not as wolflike as the bikers, not as man-like as Yoshida, the man-strosity snapped at Dennis's face with teeth too big for his mouth. His hook-clawed fingers stretched toward the singer's eyes.

The silver chain they had wrapped around Yoshida lay slack and meaningless in a heap of wood, cloth and foam that had been a bed. Pedro realized that they should not have wound the chain under the bed. It gave the beast a weak point, uncontacted by the chain, that allowed him to break free.

Pedro quickly raised the trank rifle and fired at center mass.

For a split second, Yoshida's head was a blur. Then he was facing Pedro with furious, feral eyes, the dart clenched between his teeth.

"Holy shit!" Dennis and Pedro locked eyes for a moment, exchanging a look of astonishment.

Yoshida tossed his head to the side, pitching the dart away. By the time it flew over his dresser, bounced off the wall and fell behind the dresser, the wolfman had resumed trying to tear Dennis apart.

"PeteeeEEEY!" cried Dennis, pushing against Yoshida's chin with one hand, blocking the killing claws with his leather-coated forearm.

Pedro snatched the chain and tried to jerk it away from the ruins of the bed. Hopelessly entangled, it yielded only two or three useless feet.

Pedro dropped it and launched himself to tackle Yoshida. The impact would have driven those nail-point teeth straight into Dennis's face if the singer hadn't bobbed to the side.

Pedro briefly felt bad about smashing Yoshida's face into the floor—until the beast wriggled and rolled like a fresh-caught trout, trapping him under its back. The monster scrambled, stomach-down, with agility more befitting the rounder physique of a wolf.

Now Petey was the prey.

Dennis tossed the torn sheet over the deputy's head and yanked it up and away from Pedro, who used the weight shift to shove him off.

In less time than Dennis had taken to ensnare him, Yoshida tore the sheet away like tissue and tossed the singer into the dresser.

Pedro glanced at the chain. In grabbing the sheet, Dennis had untangled some of the slack. Pedro lunged for the nearest section.

Shaking away the cobwebs, Dennis knew what his friend had in mind. Yoshida crouched to pounce on the bassist's back.

"Hey!" Dennis dove for the door. "Come and get me, boy!"

Hunter instincts drew the beast like a moth to a flame. He leaped across the room, as Dennis ducked and yanked the door in his path.

Yoshida smashed headfirst into the flimsy wooden panel with wrecking-ball force, blasting through it.

Pedro, knowing the monster would recover fast, slid the end of the chain across the floor to Dennis. As Yoshida started to charge, Dennis entwined his furry left wrist. Pedro grabbed the right. The boys butted shoulders as they met to switch ends, drawing Yoshida's wrists together.

Pedro bobbed his head to the side to avoid a snapping bite, while Dennis dropped to his knees to loop the chain around Yoshida's feet.

Pedro took the end from him and jerked hard, putting the beast on its back and bringing its razor-clawed hands and feet together. Hog-tied, Yoshida jerked hard, nearly sending Pedro headfirst into the hallway. Dennis, still kneeling, caught Pedro's leg and kept him steady.

They pulled in opposite directions, taking away all of Yoshida's leverage.

"Now what!?" called Pedro.

"I don't know!"

Yoshida's roars of rage pitched up, becoming squeals of pain. Smoke rose from the chain's contact points at his wrists and ankles.

"Ah, shit!" said Pedro. "We're hurting him bad!"

"You gotta hold him!" Dennis said, handing Pedro his end of the chain.

Pedro doubted he could, but he wasn't about to let go.

Dennis went to the dresser and yanked it to fall facedown to the floor.

Tears of blood ran from Yoshida's amber eyes. The chain was melting through his bones like hot steel.

Pedro coughed at the stench of burning flesh, feeling his gorge rise.

"There you are!" Dennis picked up the trank dart and dove over Pedro to land on Yoshida's chest. He plunged the dart into his friend's neck as hard and as fast as he could, hoping it was with enough force to open the plunger and release the sedative.

"Unwrap him," Dennis called as he rolled to the side.

Pedro did, his eyes stinging from the smoke of sizzling skin; then he leaped in front of Dennis with the chain held out, the first line of defense against the monster they had just caught—and released.

Yoshida tried to stand. His weakened ankle snapped at a sickening angle, drawing a deafening cry of pain.

"Dammit, what can we do?"

There wasn't much. The musicians took positions on either side of Yoshida to keep him from hurting himself any further, until, after two excruciating minutes, he finally fell still, panting hoarsely as a veil of forced slumber fell upon him.

* * * *

En route to the church, Maisie gave a crash course on her method of accessing the Akashic records.

"I know the Akashic records are literally the past, resonating through our collective consciousness, but I confess I've never tried to access them," Violina told Maisie.

"I'll feel better just knowing you're there," Maisie explained. "All you have to do is pay attention while I tell you what's happening…*did* happen."

"I'll be right beside you."

* * * *

Dennis, Pedro and Bernard had already run power cords into the basement from a generator and set up a string of lights, which switched on at the top of the stone stairway. The foreboding gloom of the witches' introductory visit was gone.

Nonetheless, Violina tensed with apprehension upon setting foot across the doorway. "Those poor people!" she almost whispered. "What it must have been like to face all those terrors down here."

"They are a brave bunch," said Maisie.

"You're just as brave, my dear." Violina touched her new protégé on the shoulder. "Lead the way."

They went through the archway, along the corridor and into the chamber where the stone coffins had lain. Their shadows stretched across the high ceiling. Their breath rode on wispy steam.

Near the farthest wall, they cast a circle with white chalk, lit candles, called on the directional spirits.

Maisie took Violina's hand. "Let's sit."

They took cross-legged positions facing each other. Maisie closed her eyes and slowed her breathing, while Violina waited for the flow of information.

Maisie visualized a book—thick, heavy and ancient—and saw on its dark brown leather face the title *Chronicles of Ember Hollow*, flaked gold paint filling the hand-tooled letters.

She looked up to envision the moon as she had seen it just before they stepped down the stairs, sending from the heart of her astral self a silver cord to attach to it and another to tie her to the earth. Spreading ethereal arms, she rose out through the ceiling of the basement, passing into the sanctuary, then out into the sky.

She opened the book to its first few pages and saw something in troubled script: the beginning of the settlement's problems.

A wild land from which rose pillars of chimney smoke and the vapory colors of various auras opened up far beneath her.

Descending, she saw cabins, fields, barns, streets of dirt, herds of livestock.

A dense stream of light off to her right shocked her. In her Akashic travels, Maisie had never seen such a vivid red. Stranger still were the dark brown streaks running through it.

It was the very hill where her physical body now sat. But it wasn't a church. It was Conal O'Herlihy's home.

Passing through the wood and clay walls, Maisie floated into the master bedroom, to the wellspring of the scarlet hatred—a mean Irishman who grimaced even in sleep.

Maisie sensed from this man, Conal O'Herlihy, an abiding understanding and resolve that his myopic self-service must eventually empty into a dark sea of despair. Yet he was committed to enjoying the benefits of his wicked acts without regret, and in their fullness, until that time.

In his coat, hanging by the bed, there smoldered a bone knife coated with the blood of a dead man.

He reminded her a bit of Violina, only she was more evolved. Wasn't she?

Below Conal's lonesome room lay the basement that, in this time, was secret from all but a few dozen confidants, dug for the propagation of the Patmos mushroom—and more.

Several objects carried the heavy energy of this devious commitment.

Implements used to enslave natives—whips and whiskey.

The corridor led to a larger chamber, the one where her body sat now. Here lay the stone coffins, affixed with some type of funnel. They were empty.

But someone was here…

There was something beyond the wall, a congestion of decay.

Where was the entrance? For Maisie, it was simply a matter of passing through.

…into despair.

A pit, recently filled in. It held dozens of corpses, tossed atop each other haphazardly like detritus. Natives. Tsalagi men and boys.

Maisie passed through them to learn more, tensing with despair and horror as she did. Conal and his men had abducted them, one at a time, plied them with alcohol, and enslaved them to dig the chambers. They were worked to death.

No wonder Ember Hollow wreaked of despair. These souls deserved the sanctified farewell of their culture. The town had been doomed to dark times since its inception. It was terrifying, alarming and draining.

Farther out from the town's center, lined with rough-hewn buildings, was another powerful emanation.

There was the thick sense of a man who presided over the estate like a benevolent dictator. It came as a relief.

A servant, a woman of hearty constitution, slept fitfully, her hands performing the work of sewing and cleaning. Chloris was her name.

Blackness fumed from the bed of a small room at the end of a corridor, where a candle burned near the window.

A man who was out of place, out of time, and…missing something.

A soul.

This was an automaton whose only gears were kill and live, in that order. Here it lay—he lay, wounded but healing fast. This being did not belong here, or anywhere.

If Conal was a vessel filled with undiluted hate, the wounded guest of Wilcott Bennington was a killing machine oblivious to morality.

As she reluctantly explored the strange pale man in Bennington's guest room, Maisie came to a devastating realization.

This de-man was Everett Geelens, the very killer who had plagued—would plague—Ember Hollow.

He had already interacted with the settlers, killing at least one—and would do so again, when able.

Maisie tried entering his dreams, tried filling him with love—but found there simply was no capacity. Everett existed as a flesh-and-blood reaper, and nothing else.

What if…he's the end of us all? Maisie wondered. It was the despair of this terrible thought that made her want to flee back to her own temporal terrain. Alarmed and despaired, Maisie was ready to give up on Akashic travel forever, then and there.

* * * *

In her lifetime of learning the craft, Violina had visited other realms, other sectors of consciousness; she had even skirted the InBetween, where dead and living souls commune. But astral travel in the Akashic realm was not her area of experience. Years of dedication were required for any branch of magic. Violina found her time and energy were better focused in other areas, such as controlling outcomes—and people.

Now it would have benefited her agenda, but without the expertise, she had to rely on Maisie.

Watching the girl intently, Violina cemented the details of the scheme she was improvising, an opportunity that would be sinful to waste.

When Maisie came out or trance, it was with a shocked gasp that startled Violina.

She touched Maisie's shoulder. "Are you all right?"

"The sorrows there began when the settlers arrived." She told Violina about Conal and Everett. "I couldn't be near those energies any longer," she finished. "So much…darkness."

"It's in the past, Maisie. Don't be troubled," said Violina. "It doesn't matter."

"I don't think you understand…"

"No, dear." Violina arced her hand—with Matilda's athame in it—across Maisie's throat. "I just don't care."

Maisie's scream emerged as a whistle, not from her mouth but her throat, on a stream of hot blood.

Violina reached into her Louis Vuitton purse and withdrew a gold goblet, thrusting it under Maisie's chin to catch the flow, holding the dying girl's head steady via a rough claw-hold in her hair.

Chapter 17

Spilt Blood

Answering the door to Ysabella's suite, Stella furrowed her brow on seeing McGlazer's expression. "You're not sick too, are you?"

"No. Just have something on my mind." He followed her to the bedroom entrance to look in on Ysabella. "How is she?"

"It's something more than just exhaustion."

"You have a theory?"

Stella grimly shook her head. "Judging by her temp, vitals—she's getting worse."

Another knock. As Stella moved to answer it, McGlazer stopped her. "Let me get it. It might be the only way I can be useful." Stella didn't ask what he meant.

"Here's your prayer circle, Reverend." At the door stood Bernard, surrounded by familiar faces—Candace at his side, Emera in his arms, Elaine Barcroft, Leticia Lott holding little Wanda and Jill Hawkins behind him, DeShaun and Stuart nearby with Bravo.

McGlazer let them in, well aware that his smile was far from genuine, and leaned close to Bernard. "Can we talk?"

Bernard blinked with surprise. "You and me?"

The new arrivals murmured their hellos, taking in Stella's gloomy update on Ysabella. Little Emera, sensing something wrong under the pall of low light and whispers, crept into the candlelit bedroom and saw her new friend. "Miss Iss?" the girl whispered.

When there was no answer, her little face grew alarmed. "Cannisss!" she stage-whispered and waved for her sister to come, as she crawled into bed and hugged close against Ysabella.

In the front room, McGlazer came to stand close to Bernard. "You're an atheist, right?"

"Well…yeah, sure."

"I'm…not so sure myself anymore," McGlazer confided.

"You mean, about God?"

"Lately…this job seems forced. Dishonest."

Bernard nodded knowingly. "What brought this on?"

"I don't know exactly. It just didn't feel true anymore, the prayers and scripture. It didn't feel like any of it was…making its way to a god."

"Yet here you are, saddled with the job of minister."

"I can't do this anymore, Bernard. And I know I'm going to disappoint a lot of people. As I have in the past."

"This isn't the same as alcoholism," Bernard said. "And it's not…a hat you lost somewhere, that you can find or replace."

"Any advice?"

Bernard thought for a minute, nodding with empathy. "One thing I've learned from Stella. Regardless of what's 'true' about spirituality, there's a lot of power in ritual and ceremony. I think it has something to do with focus and the subconscious—but I know it works."

"Where does that leave me and my sad little crisis of faith?"

Pondering, Bernard glanced toward the bedroom and raised an eyebrow. "Maybe it's not as big a problem as you think."

At Emera's insistence, the women, all except Jill, had gathered on and around the bed, all making contact with the crone, all holding hands.

Jill put her arms on the shoulders of DeShaun and Stuart. "That's a whole lot of what you call 'goddess power' there, boys."

"What about you?" Stuart asked.

"I'm on it." Jill whisked away to the kitchenette and returned with a deep pot. She smiled at the boys as she sat cross-legged near the bed and put her percussionist skills to work, pounding a soft steady rhythm that summoned ethereal feelings.

"Maybe we should go try to find Ysabella's friends," Bernard said.

* * * *

Violina absently wondered what tune it was that played incessantly inside her skull while she was prepping the church basement.

Lush and insistent, orchestral yet soothing, Violina knew it would come to her if she stopped thinking about it. Her subconscious would continue to dig, as it did now for the sigil in the Polaroids she had purloined from the Cronus County evidence tombs.

She cast a new circle for her new purpose. Ceremonial candles lit, she switched off the electric light at the stairwell and crept back to the rear chamber in the dim flicker.

Using a brush with bristles made from the hair of a black horse, Violina dipped into the bowl and repainted the sigils that had been so recently blasted away. She had studied the police Polaroids and repeatedly drawn them on a notepad until she could flawlessly reproduce them from memory.

Not that she couldn't wash away any mistakes and restart—but that was such a waste of blood.

Ideally, she would have had an assistant for all that she had to do next. But there hadn't been time to bend Maisie to her will properly, and even if there had been, that would leave the problem of finding a blood source. Still, she would need someone to do the messier work that lay ahead.

Humming the mystery music to warm up her vocal cords, Violina took a moment to admire the dead girl lying crumpled on the floor, even to mourn her a bit. Left pale by the draining of her blood, Maisie reminded Violina of the fairy-tale naïf Snow White, who had also fallen to the wiles of a wicked witch.

Violina grinned at the Disney image. Women of absolutes: good or evil, with no gray area. If not for that, it might be easier to recruit so-called baneful witches, and then to change the world.

She considered the incessant earworm for a moment, and it hit her, drawing a fittingly wicked laugh—"Orinoco Flow," by Enya.

She chased it away and began to chant something else from memory, a Latin rite of transmigration.

Hands upraised, she slowly spun left, calling out the incantation with purpose and echoing volume.

Counting seven revolutions, Violina stopped and faced the blood sigil, pleased to see an eldritch red glow cracking around the edges.

* * * *

The glow, which began at the edges of the sigil, quickly grew brighter until all detail was lost, leaving only an shimmering portal into the InBetween.

"I grant you, Conal O'Herlihy, earthly manifestation here! Now!" Violina made an insistent summoning gesture, her tone commanding and assured.

Soon a nebulous shape formed in the opening, growing in size and detail until cruel and wary eyes, set in hazy features, peered out on her. "What is this?"

"Pleased to meet you, Conal O'Herlihy. I've heard so much."

"Do not trifle, fool."

"Now, let's not be like that," Violina said. "I'm here to make you an offer."

"First, the price."

"That's the beauty, dear Conal. The price is part of the benefit."

The spirit began to fade away.

"You and your followers, back in this plane physically," Violina explained. "And quite immortal."

"Why would I wish to return to the limitations of the physical world?"

"No need to be coy, old boy," Violina laughed. "You wander aimlessly in the emptiness, lamenting your failures here. You miss the solidity, the definiteness of the living world."

Conal's silence was encouraging.

"Flesh is more easily controlled," she continued. "And more amusing."

"I worked to preserve our bodies in the fungus. But they were destroyed." Was O'Herlihy showing the regret of his failure?

"In this time, magic is no longer so well-suppressed. And I'm a more powerful witch than you can even imagine."

Again, Conal was silent.

"You've been tied to those flimsy old mushroom bodies and this musty ruin for so long. Imagine being something stronger."

"You do sing a siren song."

"No crashing against the rocky shores, Conal. I will make you powerful and terrifying, and you'll only grow stronger, feeding off your victims. You and all your poor, displaced followers."

"And in these great and terrible bodies, we'll be expected to serve you in some manner?"

"I want to share in your immortality. You'll show me how."

"And...?"

"You'll help me bring all other witches to heel."

The spirit's detail grew sharper than ever, until she could see the very pupils of his stony eyes—and his sinister smile.

"The secret is the fungus," Conal said. "So long as it grows, the soul of its partakers can travel in and through it."

"Then we have a problem," Violina said. "Your fungus is extinct."

"You're wrong. There is a scrap that needs but to be nourished."

"And you know where to find it?"

The edges of the sigil flared, and Violina was stunned to feel a powerful wind suddenly kicking up in the isolated chamber and then focusing around her, becoming a vacuum force.

She was drawn toward Conal's cruel countenance like steel filings to a magnet. Certain that Maisie's body and the other items in the room would be sucked by the tide and made to smash into her, Violina glanced behind her. Trying to shield her face with her arms, she raised them, only to have them pulled toward the portal as if lassoed and yanked.

The vortex affected only her.

She saw that Conal's visage was gone, replaced beyond the boundaries by a dark, modern-looking room.

She lost her footing and fell forward, headfirst, into the opening, only to be abruptly halted by the solid edges of the chamber wall, closed snuggly around her neck.

The room was quiet, spacious, unoccupied. As her eyes adjusted to the dark, she saw shelves, tables, a wall of windows and a tall metal cabinet. From the crack between the cabinet doors, a dim glow shone. To the right was a set of stairs set against a cinderblock wall.

Violina saw a flyer posted on the wall. It read EMBER HOLLOW LIBRARY FALL BOOK SALE!

The pull of the vortex relented, as the edges of the wall began to close. Violina quickly withdrew, stumbling backward until she tripped over Maisie's corpse.

Conal was back, framed once again by the eldritch opening. "We will wait for you. And anticipate these new bodies."

* * * *

Yoshida might have stayed unconscious for a much longer time, if not for the pain of his broken ankle.

Lying on the floor of his demolished bedroom, nearly naked and wrapped in chains wasn't the worst possible outcome he could imagine. He was relieved to see Dennis and Pedro squatting to look at his ankle, both okay other than a few scratches and contusions. "What happened?"

"You wolfed out hard-core, man." Dennis answered. "Not like the bikers, but you'll get there next time, or maybe the time after, if we don't do something."

Yoshida leaned forward to examine his throbbing foot, flexing it up and down gingerly. "Who cranked my ankle?"

Dennis and Pedro looked at each other with astonishment. "You did. And it was a lot worse just a minute ago."

"Must be part of the condition. You heal in record time."

"Did I bite you guys?"

"No, but not for lack of trying," said Pedro, cupping his hands around Yoshida's ankle, squeezing lightly. "That don't hurt?"

"A little."

"Screw the circus," said Dennis. "We're selling you to science."

"You have to go get those witches," Yoshida said. "Make them do their thing."

"They're not answering at the Blue Moon. Maybe I should try to track 'em down." He turned to Pedro. "Unless you want the excuse to see your new fan."

"Nah, you go," Pedro said. "Not feeling too smooth right now. But we should go to my place, try to get some rest."

Dennis shook his head grimly. "Another whacked-out Devil's Night."

"At least Yoshi smells better than those bikers."

"Depends on who you ask, I guess."

"Never thought I'd say this…" Yoshida stood to test his ankle. "Could we just focus on getting me neutered?"

Chapter 18

Beauty of Poison

Violina parked her Cadillac well out of range of the gas station's security cameras. As she walked, the dense gray sky seemed to query her. Violina nodded as if to say, *Not just yet…*

Armed with tailored, almost-tight Earnest Sewn jeans, a scent of her own design that called forth trust and lust, a smile emphasized by lipstick a shade lighter than blood and a tiny flask of "treated" whiskey, Violina entered Gas Giant, Ember Hollow's resident truck stop/gas station/Halloween shop.

She smiled to the new-wave-styled teen girl behind the counter. Engrossed in a Terry Pratchett novel, the girl ignored Violina.

She traipsed between an aisle of chips and crackers, grimacing at the rack of slogan-printed lingerie, and made her way past the eighty-nine-ounce soda fountain and a glass-faced warmer, where glossy hot dogs rolled on metal bars, to the rear dining room.

One man sat alone at the nearest plastic table, his arms crossed, a foam and mesh cap sitting high on his sun spotted head. He stared at his barbecue sandwich and fries as if working up the courage to eat them.

Violina took a seat across from him, beaming like a diva's spotlight. "Good evening!"

The bleary-eyed trucker gave the merest of nods. Violina was not discouraged in the least. "Is that your truck out in the rear lot?"

"Yes, ma'am, it is."

Violina's smile faded to an expression of deep sadness. "Dear Lord. So many memories."

"Ma'am?"

"My brother drove one that looked just like it. He died in an accident."

"Oh, my Lord. Condolences, ma'am."

"Thank you." She extended her hand. "I'm Violina."

"Steve." He took her hand in an indifferent grip.

"I hope you won't find this too…odd," Violina began. "I used to ride with him. I would love to just sit in the front for a minute."

"Well"—Steve shrugged and took a bite of his sandwich, making it bleed brown juice onto his glistening fries—"I don't see why not."

"Oh, bless you." She kept his hand for a moment, letting him feel its softness.

Steve finished his sandwich and fries quickly and stood to dump his tray. "Ready?"

Violina followed him, glad to see the counter girl still ignoring them as they exited and walked around to the rear parking lot, where Steve's idling rig sat. The only other vehicle was the counter girl's '78 Camaro.

Pulling his hat down against the rising wind, he stepped up on the running board and opened the door, then stepped off. "All yours, as long as you need it, ma'am."

Violina gave a gracious smile and stepped up, disappointed that Steve had not propositioned her—yet. Any footage picked up by security cameras would show what could only be a trucker and his conquest leaving for a tryst. And though she didn't plan to need the alibi, it was good to have a contingency plan.

"So much like his truck," she said wistfully.

Steve maintained a respectful silence and distance. Violina realized she would have to work harder than usual to dissolve his gallantry.

"Oh!" Violina leaped off the running board with a faux clumsiness, widening her eyes exaggeratedly for Steve to see in the weak light of the streetlamp. "There's…something…"

"What!?" Steve seemed excessively concerned about his traveling home.

Violina stammered "I—I…don't know, maybe a mouse." She took on a frightened expression. "No. A rat, as big as it was."

"What!?" Steve was embarrassed.

"Dear God!" Making her hands tremble, Violina drew the little glass flask she had prepared and pretended to take a draw, very careful that she didn't. "It dashed under the driver's seat," she said .

As Steve drew his flashlight keychain, Violina stepped toward and offered the flask. "You should have a sip. To calm your nerves."

Steve looked at the flask, then at Violina's crimson lips. "I'll have a bit afterward."

Steve leaped up on the running board, drawing his little keychain flashlight. "I'll find you, you little vermin," he threatened under his breath. "And I'll squeeze you flat."

Improvising, Violina went around to the passenger side and opened the door.

"Hold up, ma' am," Steve said. "Close that door so he don't get away!"

She stepped up, dumping the flask contents into her mouth.

"Ma'am? Did you hear what I…?"

Violina blew the liquid into Steve's face. He fell backward onto the pavement with a shocked cry.

Violina spat and coughed, miffed at having to engage in such low-class behavior. As she wiped her tongue and gums with a silk kerchief, she hurried to check on Steve.

"Stand up," she ordered.

Steve complied, staring at her with frightened eyes, one of only two physical functions he could control.

"What…did…?"

"Good," she said, checking the back of his head for damage. "There's a lot I need you to do tonight."

Steve shook with terror, fully understanding his body would not respond to his brain. "What did you…do to me!"

"Not what did I do, dear," Violina said. "What will I do."

She spat again, careful to flush out even the most minute remnants of the puffer-fish-poisoned whiskey. "And the answer is…use you up and throw you away."

* * * *

Herve must have already been feeling bad; he didn't come back to his seat for fifteen minutes. When he did, he looked like a wax figure.

"You okay?" asked Brinke. He nodded, wiping his brow with his tie, which he then loosened as he took a deep breath.

Well, she thought regretfully, *here goes nothing.*

She took out her notebook and a pencil and began to write, careful to obscure the words from Herve, though he was well occupied with his own internal turbulence.

Strange-sounding thunder rolled through the fuselage, underscored with a discomfiting low-frequency noise.

She scribbled quickly, raising a subtle chant that was meant to seem secret while calling attention to itself. Brinke hated to deceive. But she was willing to pay the price if her ploy succeeded.

"What are you...whispering about?" asked Herve between unsteady breaths.

"Just an old nursery rhyme," Brinke said. Then she lightly placed her hand on his chest, allowing the journal to fall open at the right angle for him to see the runes, which his subconscious would then absorb.

"Is your heart all right?' Brinke would have been horrified to know she had just employed the same spell Violina had, just the day before, on poor Officer Kebbler at the Cronus County Evidence Annex.

Herve put his hand on hers to push it away, and she felt how cold and clammy his palm was. "Please...don't..."

The man who had so lasciviously ogled her not long ago now couldn't stand her touch. Brinke's plan was working.

Brinke stood and called to a stewardess.

"May I help you?" Her name badge read Helene.

"I'm afraid he's having a heart attack."

Helene went through the usual motions and queries to be sure the problem was beyond her limited training and finally whisked away to consult with her superior.

Brinke patted the man's shoulder, regretfully restraining herself from projecting any healing intent into him. "You'll be okay," she told him.

Herve nodded minutely, clearly unconvinced. Brinke felt his terror and helplessness quickly becoming despair. Tears of shame and guilt came to Brinke as she withdrew her hand. Herve seemed baffled that a woman who barely knew him was practically mourning his imminent demise.

Captain Winchell, the practiced reserve of his voice beginning to falter, addressed the passengers. "Evening, fellow flyers. We have a possible medical emergency. If there's a doctor or cardiologist on board, please contact a stewardess immediately. Thank you."

"Oh, God..." Herve murmured. "I'm going to die up here."

* * * *

Hudson had not been in Pedro's apartment for more than five minutes when an urgent knock came at his door. It was Ophelia, his ten-year-old upstairs neighbor, wringing her hands. "Are you in trouble?"

"Huh?" Pedro saw her nervous glance at the lawmen. "Oh. Nah. Believe it or not, these doughnut addicts are my friends."

Hudson and Yoshida smiled and waved.

"Are you sure?" asked the little girl. "I can give you my allowance…"

She was interrupted by the call of her name from upstairs—her mother, Camilla.

"Don't she know you came down here?" Pedro asked.

"I snuck! She didn't want me to…bother you…" Ophelia gave the deputies the same jittery look—and Pedro understood. Ophelia's family either had questionable immigration statuses or feared that the deputies might make up some.

"I'm just signing autographs for these fanboys. Nothing to worry about." He smiled, and she relaxed. "Go back to your ma, before you get us both tuned up."

Ophelia waved and ran off.

"I help her with her music-class homework."

"Dude, we could use you for immigrant relations," noted Yoshida.

"Nah, I like wrecking my eardrums slash rescuing you losers from terrifying deities."

"'Entities' you mean."

Pedro kicked back in his dingy and ripped recliner, a gift, coincidentally from Ophelia's parents as a thank-you for his work with Ophelia, and settled the tranquilizer rifle across his lap. "But you should definitely give me a badge and uniform, Hudsy, as much sheriffin' as I do these days."

"Babysitting a grouchy mongrel-man doesn't show up in any of the sheriffin' scenarios I've ever seen," Hudson answered, absently thumbing through Pedro's vinyl record collection, which numbered well into the thousands. "But I can get you on as a dogcatcher."

Pedro's cat, Joan Effen Crawford, appeared from the bedroom. She halted on catching Yoshida's scent and ran behind the recliner.

"Sorry, Joanie," Yoshida said.

"Don't you worry, Yosh. We'll get our witch pals on the case and have you smelling like your old square self in no time."

"Sure," Yoshida responded. "Just keep that thing aimed right at me, if you don't mind. Every time I change, it seems to last longer and become more dangerous. You sure you don't want to put the chains on?"

"I'm a little concerned about this sudden chain fetish, weirdo," Hudson quipped. "You never changed twice in one night. With a little luck, we're good for at least twenty-four."

He put on his hat and went to the door. "I'll come back and relieve you at the end of my shift."

"Forget it. You need sleep too, tough guy," Pedro said. "Me and Yoshi'll just crash here and doze till Dennis gets back with the bruja babes."

Chapter 19

Psycho Magnet

"Passengers, it looks like we'll have to make an emergency landing. This is gonna be..." Captain Winchell searched for a word that balanced truthfulness with reassurance. Not finding it, he clicked off.

Herve, milky sweat dripping from his eyebrow, looked at Brinke, seeking more comfort. She patted his hand, trying to remember the words of a Tibetan spell that would stabilize his condition, hoping he was generally healthy enough to survive the stress of the attack on his heart.

Lightning pulsed, thunder cracked and the plane shook like an alarm bell, drawing panicked yelps from all around.

Herve gritted his teeth and clenched his eyelids shut. His breath came in abrupt rasps.

* * * *

Settlement era

"You were right to come only to me," praised Conal with a grin that was indistinguishable from his more common grimace. "This could shake our settlement to its soul."

Schroeder covered his nose against the stench, marveling that O'Herlihy seemed untroubled by it. He felt more relieved than sad that Hezekiah's corpse, worse for wear under the autumn sun and the pecking of crows, was at least still here.

"Who could be responsible?" he asked the Irishman.

"I gamble we'll soon know," Conal answered. "But that's not important now."

"It's not?"

O'Herlihy held out his ruddy hand. "Give me your knife."

Schroeder drew the bone knife from its sheath and handed it over without hesitation. Conal immediately set about stabbing Hezekiah's body several times, distributing more scent of decay.

"What are you doing!?"

O'Herlihy wrapped the knife in a handkerchief and stuffed it in his waistband, penetrating Schroeder with his fiery stare. "I need to know I can trust you."

"Well…of course, you can. But…"

"This is God-sent," whispered the big Celt, "our chance to do away with that blasphemous robber baron!"

Schroeder still did not understand why O'Herlihy had jabbed the corpse with his knife, but he was beginning to. As for the "robber baron," Schroeder had no doubts just who Conal meant.

"Now help me with this." O'Herlihy took a large oilcloth from his horse, and together the Dutchman and the Celt wrapped Hezekiah up. No words of mourning were spoken for him, only an oath of loyalty to Conal.

* * * *

"It appears we have a killer in our midst," Bennington said, examining the wounded guest. "Or someone who would be."

Once he and maidservant Chloris got the unconscious stranger into the guest-room bed, Bennington watched over him while Chloris fetched calming tea and an herb poultice. Once these took effect on the peculiar man and he began to doze, Bennington decided to remove the burlap hood.

Underneath was the strange face of a young man with unruly black hair matted around pale, gaunt features. Despite Everett Geelens's present placid state, Bennington and his maidservant remained ill at ease—there was something about him.

"He can be no more than twenty," said Chloris. "Where could he have come from?"

“Perhaps there’s another settlement nearby,” Bennington answered. “But there is still the matter of his dress.”

“Taken from Schroeder’s effigy, you say.”

“The boy could have found the figure and taken the clothes. But then…the wound.”

“Wild animal? Cherokee?” wondered Chloris, patting Everett’s face with a handkerchief.

“It’s too clean and deep a wound for bear or wildcat.” Bennington leaned close to peer at the gash between the shirtless guest’s rib. “And it’s unlike the Cherokee to leave a foe alive.”

“When he’s better, perhaps he’ll be more lucid.”

“Yes, delirium seems likely. Yet there’s something else about him. Something very odd.”

“He should sleep for many hours, and the medicines will rejuvenate him. Then we could query him?”

“I hope.” Bennington pulled the quilt up to Everett’s chin. “Don’t speak of this to anyone else, Chloris. Not yet.”

Chapter 20

The Bottle Called

Modern day

Ever genteel, Violina covered her yawn, looking at Steve with no concern for his bedraggled state. “You stand at the window and keep watch while I get my beauty rest.” She sipped her chamomile. “Come nightfall, we’ll be busier than ever.”

“We?” asked Steve, as his enslaved legs took him to the window for the coming hours of tortured vigilance.

“There’s still some dirty work, dear.”

Steve had no reason to think she was being anything but literal. The well-heeled witch had made him break into the library to steal the ancient cask containing the last of the mushrooms, bury Maisie’s body, scrub off the blood sigil and generally return the church’s underground chamber to its previous state.

He had to hide his rig in the depths of one of the abandoned cornfields, then drive her home in her Cadillac, where she showered and changed into silk pajamas, prattling on about her scheme the entire time.

She didn’t even bother to make her own tea, commanding his hands to do it while she sat three feet away and nitpicked.

“When can you...whatever you’re gonna do?” Steve asked. “Kill me, I guess.”

“Don’t be whiny, or I’ll have you do nasty things to your little family,” threatened Violina, as she applied her nightly cold cream laced with the powdered uterine flesh of a pregnant woman. "If anyone comes, tell them they have the wrong house. If they're persistent, either kill them or keep them busy until I can get away."

Violina dimmed the lights to a pleasant ambience and closed the bedroom door, leaving Steve to hate his already-aching feet and hope his family never learned of what he did.

* * * *

Brinke was initially relieved that medical professionals, undaunted by the storm, were on the ground waiting to take charge of Herve. As they rushed aboard with a stretcher and started preparing him, she realized she had a pitiably small window of time to undo the magic-induced heart attack.

She needed to touch and speak to him simultaneously, but the EMS workers strictly enforced their no-contact rule. As he was being transported out, Brinke had no choice but to hit full-on giant crazy bitch mode. She leaped up, shoved past the rearmost med tech and lunged across Herve, beginning the incantation as soon as her hand touched his hand.

"What the hell's wrong with you, lady!?" The forward tech grabbed her hand and tried to yank it away, forcing her to grasp Herve's hard enough to make him cry out in pain.

Then the other one grabbed her around the waist from behind and called to the shocked stewardess, Helene, to get an air marshal.

"I have to do this!" Brinke screamed, barely maintaining her grip as she continued the chant.

She did not look at anything but Herve. Even a witch of her skill could lose focus if highly distracted.

Three repetitions were in order—but given the circumstances, one would have to do, with hopes that Herve's system was strong enough to bridge the gap.

The tech behind her wrestled her off and tried to drag her away, but Brinke stopped his spin with her foot against a seat, an inch from the face of the wispy teen girl sitting there judging her.

"I'm sorry, Herve!" she called. The apology added nothing to the reversal chant, but Brinke's conscience demanded nothing less.

"Calm down, lady!" said the restraining tech, but she already had.

Brinke relaxed so abruptly the EMS worker released her for fear she had passed out, or worse. She took her seat—Herve's, actually—and looked up at the confused tech. "I'm okay. You should get going."

* * * *

Violina had just closed her eyes, gratified and calmed by the sounds of the growing storm she had raised. A different rumble disturbed her relaxation: a powerful motor coming into the drive.

Recognizing the roar of The Chalk Outlines' hearse, she went to the living room, where Steve was trying to stop himself from taking up the fireplace poker he would use to kill the newcomer.

"Stop!" Violina ordered. "He could be useful."

"Are you going to take over his body too?"

"'Too' is not accurate," Violina answered. "He's going to replace you. Now get in the closet."

Dennis took a closer look at the Caddie in the drive to be sure it was Violina's, then went to the door and knocked softly.

In less time than he expected, Violina answered, smiling graciously as she pulled her red satin robe around her. "Dennis, isn't it?"

"Sorry to bother you this late."

"Come in." She stepped to the side and raised the lights by a degree. "Tell me what's the matter."

"There's not a lot of time." She moved to take his jacket, but he didn't give it up.

"Oh," she went to the kitchen, "let me at least get us drinks."

"Just water."

"I didn't take you for a teetotaler."

"These days, yeah."

"Ah," she nodded. "Say no more. Surely, I can find you something more interesting than water though."

"Got any Drenal-Ade?"

Violina laughed. "Sounds like this might take a while." Her smile bore the tiniest hint of innuendo. She took a bottle of organic cherry cola from the refrigerator and poured it over ice.

"I was looking for Maisie too. Seen her?"

"Hmm. Not since yesterday. Isn't your bandmate interested in her?"

"It's about our deputy buddy." Dennis gave the short strokes about Yoshida's unusual strain of lycanthropy.

Violina distracted him with a pair of vaguely pertinent questions, while prepping his beverage.

As she returned with the potion-infused cola, a muffled bustle sounded from the closet, where Steve had been made to hide. Amusing as it was to make the hapless trucker stand in place for hours, she cursed his occasional involuntary muscle reaction.

"What's that? You got somebody else here?"

"No, I…propped my bag rather precariously in the closet," she said.

"Your witch gear? Shouldn't we check on that?"

"It's fine." She glanced at his cola, mentally urging him to drink.

"Look, I don't wanna keep you. I just need you to help my buddy. He gets worse every night."

"Of course, I will. But I'll need assistance."

Dennis stood and went to the house phone. "I'll try the Blue Moon again for Maisie and Ysabella. If that's a bust, I'll get Hudson to swing by."

"No, don't." Violina stood and took the phone receiver out of his hand. "Shouldn't you…kiss me?"

Dennis stepped back from her. "What gives, lady? You on somethin'?" He yanked the phone back. "This is an emergency."

"You need release, Dennis." Violina put her hand on his groin. "I can feel it."

Dennis slapped her hand away. "Only reason I don't slug you is 'cause Jill's gonna want first crack. I'm leaving."

"Steve!" she shrieked. "Come out and knock this man unconscious!"

Dennis laughed at the clunky exclamation, shaking his head. If he had known that she had to be very specific in her commands, he would not have so easily dismissed Violina as out of her mind.

The closet door swung open.

The man who lunged at Dennis bore an incongruous look of such regret, dread and sheer terror that it slowed the singer's reflexes. The fireplace tool arced across his head and sent him straight down.

"You'd better not have damaged his motor functions, you imbecile!" Violina took the poker from Steve and swatted him across the back of his legs with it. "Now put him in my car."

"And then…you're going to kill me?" His throbbing legs already carrying him to the door, he asked her with less dread this time, more hope.

"Shut up!" she yelled. "I'm trying to think!"

* * * *

Just inside the arrival entrance, there was some back-and-forth with the air marshal, but Brinke's poise and compassion gave the officer no reason to pursue the matter further than a stern reprimand.

That done, she went to the nearest airport directory to find a rental-car office. Gathering her bearings, she felt a strange presence—something…tortured.

A man in a long, brown trench coat stood in the dimmest section of the airport bar's low light, staring toward the arrival entrance. As if his personal energy wasn't troubling enough, the man wore large-lensed, dark sunglasses and a black scarf around the lower part of his face. The overall effect was of a man painfully aware he was conspicuous and wishing not to be seen.

There was a pain as deep as a canyon residing in him.

If the storm was any indication, Brinke was arriving late to the game already. Ember Hollow, not to mention her witch colleagues, needed help. This man could not be her problem right now.

Brinke hurried to the rental-car area, not overly surprised to find that the offices were all immobilized by computer issues from the storm. The lights flickered and died throughout the airport for nearly a minute; time enough for a moderate panic to set in.

She stepped outside to check for waiting taxis or driver services. There were none in sight.

Back inside, she saw the covered man again, issuing a shy wave, like a toddler, as a middle-aged woman approached. The woman hugged him and spoke animatedly for a few seconds. He raised a tracheal amplifier to his throat and responded, then they went to the luggage conveyer.

Brinke found herself striding toward the couple, perhaps more determinedly than was prudent, for the covered man visibly recoiled as she came within a few feet.

Undaunted, and desperate, Brinke shone her blazing smile. "Pardon me, folks…"

The lady turned, also wary, yet receptive. "Yes?"

"Are you going to Ember Hollow?"

"Hmm, I'd better, I suppose," said the woman. "I'm the mayor. Would you like a ride?"

The covered man tugged at Doris's sleeve, as if imploring her to withdraw the invitation.

Chapter 21

The Sky's Gone Out

The Stuyvesants led Brinke to a light brown Audi A8 with heavily tinted windows—the "Mayor Mobile."

Kerwin, incapable of whispering or subtle speech, continued to tug at Doris's sleeve every few yards.

"Kerwin, stop it!" answered Doris. "What kind of mayor would I be if I didn't help our visitors?"

Brinke got in the back seat, impressed by the immaculate new-car smell and showroom interior.

Once they were all seated, Doris gave her brother a look of rebuke tempered with love. "This is my brother, Kerwin. Please forgive him; he's very self-conscious."

"Hi, Kerwin! I'm Brinke."

Taking off his sunglasses, Kerwin merely stared out the darkened glass as Doris started the Audi.

Stopping at the exit gate, Doris looked at Brinke in the rearview. "Where can we take you, young lady?"

"The Blue Moon Inn, please."

"You've come at a less than optimal time, I'm afraid," said the mayor. "Our town, and my brother…we've had some recent downturns. But you'll find we're a friendly and optimistic bunch."

"I'm sure."

Though it seemed to get darker and more oppressive by the minute, Brinke felt sad to see the stark confirmation of the reason her fellow witches had come here.

In about half of the fields to either side, beautiful plump specimens of the hearty Jericho's Wall Super-squash breed, unique to Cronus County's famed pumpkin fields, still grew, yet most of them would never be harvested. They were untended this season, save for those of a handful of stubborn, or optionless, farmers.

"What brings you to Ember Hollow, if I may ask?"

Brinke sensed wariness in the question, which was perfectly understandable given there was little reason for anyone to visit Ember Hollow anymore, unless you were into murder sites.

"I have friends here." There was no point in sidetracking the issue. The mayor should know if she didn't already. "We're going to try and help your town heal."

A minute head movement showed that Kerwin's interest had been piqued.

"Oh?" Doris said.

"Something's wrong here. We want to help."

"Are you with the, uh..." Doris wound her hand, as if drawing out the appropriate word from Brinke.

Brinke smiled. "The word I like is 'co-creators.' But 'witches' is fine too."

Kerwin looked at her. Remembering that he meant to be hiding, he sharply spun his face away. In that moment of eye contact, Brinke saw to the core of his deep regret, shame and self-loathing.

Doris explained that, in addition to being mayor, she owned a good deal of Ember Hollow's real estate, along with Kerwin. She was sincere in expressing that her stake went deeper than political responsibility.

"I have to admit," said Doris, "that we don't know quite what to think of this witch business."

Brinke's laugh was genuine, though she knew how very charming and disarming it was. "I don't either, if it helps."

Did Kerwin chuckle to himself a little?

"This must be disconcerting." Doris put a loving hand on her brother's shoulder.

"I just hope I'm not imposing," Brinke said.

"I trick Kerwin into coming out however I can." Doris looked over at Kerwin. "Like picking me up at the airport."

He stared out the window.

"He was disfigured by Everett Geelens two years ago."

Kerwin trembled at the name.

"But he's getting better. One of these days, he'll let someone besides me see how he looks. He'll realize it's not as bad as he thinks. And he won't be so withdrawn anymore."

Kerwin pushed his sister's hand away.

Doris drove in silence for a full minute. Then, as if prompted by a rumble of thunder, she softly apologized to her sibling. He did not respond.

Brinke gathered her courage, not a difficult task, and leaned forward. "Would it be all right for me to take a look?"

Kerwin spun toward her, his reddened eyes filled with shock and anger.

Brinke smiled. "I'm mixed race and six-foot-two, with a giant afro. I've been stared at a few times too."

Kerwin raised his voice device halfway, then set it back down and returned to staring out the window.

"Would you pull over please, Doris?" Brinke asked.

The pelting rain seemed to slow with the Audi. The mayor maneuvered onto a tractor road at the edge of a pumpkin field. Kerwin glowered at his sister as though she had betrayed him.

Brinke reached up to pat him on the back, then opened her door. "Come on."

She stretched her arms and took several splashy steps into the darkened, muddy field, raising her face to the pouring sky. Behind her, Kerwin opened his door.

As she walked to him, she brushed back the thick curls already plastered to her face. Four inches shorter than she was, Kerwin shivered worse than ever, looking at her with the frightened eyes of a feral kitten.

Standing up from the driver's side, Doris popped open her umbrella and offered Brinke an expression that was meant to be reassuring but was closer to doubtful.

Brinke reached up to take Kerwin's scarf. His hand shot to her wrist, clutching with a painful tightness. Brinke did not express fear or anger. She simply drew her hand away.

A moment later, Kerwin reached for the scarf and balled it in his fists as he pulled it away from his face, closing his eyes tight as a submarine hatch, squeezing out tears. He yanked it all the way off. He opened his eyes to see Brinke's reaction.

Brinke put her hands on the prosthesis, a heavy plastic lower jawbone that was screwed into his skull just under his ears. Brinke thought of the Hanna-Barbera cartoon *Frankenstein Jr.*, a pleasant childhood memory of lazy Saturday mornings.

"Oh, honey," she put both hands on the dripping, cold prosthesis. In the Audi's interior light, its flesh tone was darker than Kerwin's face, no doubt due to months of miserable indoor isolation. "A lot of dudes would kill for a jaw that square."

Doris beamed. Kerwin gingerly touched her hand to be sure Brinke was really touching him, as his eyes made the smile his mouth could not.

* * * *

Though he knew Violina held total power over his body, Steve was no less ashamed of his own actions.

Dressed in a purple, hooded robe, tailored to fit her waist and bust, Violina set about casting her circle.

Steve could only watch, feeling the odd stress of paralysis, as she placed red votives inside pentacle-etched sconces to protect their flames from the steadily rising wind. The ritual made Steve's skin crawl, yet another involuntary action.

Finished, she went to the body that lay across a mossy grave. "Wakey!" she sang, and Dennis sat up like a plank, shocked and confused.

"Hi, there, cutie," she mocked. "Thank you for joining my team."

"What the hell…?" Dennis stared at the flask shaking in Steve's hand.

"This evil piss makes your body do what she says," explained the tortured trucker, pointing his eyes toward the flask. "Sorry."

"Lady," Dennis tried to raise his voice but could only manage a strained monotone like Steve's. "Whatever you did to me, you better undo it right-the-fuck-now."

"My dear puerile poet," Violina began, "threats are the luxury of those who hold power."

Dennis intended to lunge at her but only stood still and helpless, his muscles and nerves bypassed by Violina's will and the poisoned whiskey.

"Don't make it worse for yourself, man," said Steve.

To emphasize her point, Violina went to Dennis and stroked his hair. "Kiss me."

"Hell no!" But he did, wishing and hoping to bite, or retch, or at least scream.

Violina released him and went to the towering obelisk gravestone of Wilcott Bennington that pierced a leaf-blown sky going black as midnight because of the wool-dense blanket of clouds she had summoned. "I think it would be fitting to start here."

"Start what?" Dennis asked.

"The annihilation of your sweet little town." She stooped to dig through her bag, coming up with the athame.

"Steve, come stand on this platform." She pointed to the base of the massive tombstone with the athame.

As Steve strode briskly to the grave, his expression of constant dread morphed into one of utter terror.

"Dennis, my dear"—Violina extended the knife toward him—"take this, please."

"Come on, lady. Please don't do this." Steve begged.

Dennis grunted with fruitless exertion as he obeyed.

Violina held up the photograph of the gateway sigil. "See this?"

Dennis tried to close his eyes.

"Damn you, boy. Stab yourself in the eye," ordered Violina.

Dennis beheld the knife point that flew up in his hand—

"Stop!"

—and halted a mere centimeter from his eye. "Jesus!" he murmured.

Violina theatrically addressed the obelisk. "Or Saturn, right, Mr. Bennington?"

"Lady, let me go right now, or…I'll haunt you for the rest of your life!" Steve threatened.

Violina cackled like an alpha coyote. "That's not for you to decide, I'm afraid, little man."

She went to Dennis. "Cut Steve open. Then paint this on the face of the beloved town father's monument with his blood."

"No way!" shouted Dennis, but his arm yanked the blade away from his face and pointed it at Steve.

"Don't do it, man!" cried Steve.

"I won't!" His right foot took a step toward Steve.

"You will," said Violina.

Dennis's left foot moved—and stumble-stopped halfway. "Lady, you gotta stop this now."

His right foot rose and stepped.

"Fight it, man!" Steve's face squeezed in on itself so tight he appeared to age twenty years, as premature night filled his wrinkles.

"So help me, bitch, I will kill you." Dennis held himself still for a full second.

But Violina did not show her alarm at his strength "Obey me, boy."

Dennis lurched forward.

Steve squeaked and grunted.

Dennis's stiff arm suddenly arced around toward Violina. Stunned, she took a step back.

"You kill him now, Dennis Barcroft!" she ordered.

Dennis's muscles ached as his arm rotated back toward the doomed trucker.

"You can beat this, dude!" Steve whispered.

"Hush, Steve," Violina ordered.

The truck driver's mouth obeyed, and Dennis took another unsteady step, despair replacing anger on his face. "Goddammit. I'm...sorry..."

Steve shook his head minutely, as tears streamed from his eyes.

Dennis closed his, as his body lunged behind his arm. Steve didn't even have the pitiable release of a death cry.

For some reason, Violina allowed Dennis to make it for him.

* * * *

"That was not the kind of magic I expected," Doris said, "though I'm not complaining."

Kerwin had pulled down his collar and removed his hat. He even glanced at himself occasionally in the visor mirror, still unsure, but well on the other side of his immobilization. Every few minutes, he used his scarf to wipe his eyes.

"He once managed a rock band, you know," Doris bragged. "Mister Personality—and I do believe he's back!"

Kerwin looked almost panicked as he raised the larynx speaker. "I was a dick."

Both women laughed at the strange abruptness of the statement as filtered through the prosthesis. Kerwin's body rocked. He too realized the humor.

"Maybe you should fix that next," asserted Brinke.

Kerwin looked needfully to Doris, as he had done for two years now, finding a spark of courage and inspiration to ignite his own. "I can try."

Thunder, only an insinuation before now, sounded low, loud and close, an instant after the lightning.

It was red, just as it had been behind the thick cloud cover. But seeing these sharp, jagged bolts only a few dozen yards away was far more alarming.

* * * *

It only took about three minutes of watching the witches, piled around Ysabella's bed and deep in whispering trance, for the males—McGlazer, Bernard, Stuart and DeShaun—to realize they were nonessential personnel.

"Perhaps we should drop by the party at the Community Center."

Stuart and DeShaun perked up at McGlazer's suggestion, then Stuart glanced forlornly at Candace.

"Maybe she'll make it later, dude," said DeShaun. "She won't be mad at you for going without her."

Stuart looked at his friend, inviting further encouragement.

"It'll be us two Halloween hell-raisers one more time." DeShaun extended a fist for Stuart to bump. "The life and death of the party."

Stuart smiled and knuckled up. Both gestures carried a note of sadness.

"We need costumes," Bernard said.

McGlazer looked at Bernard like he was a stranger. "Who possessed you?"

"Come on, I can be fun."

McGlazer led the way to the door. "I suppose we can thank Candace and Emera for that."

"Yeah." Bernard smiled at his womenfolk.

"Keep an eye on her, boy," Stuart told Bravo.

Chapter 22

(Stop Me) At The Edge

Dennis dragged Steve's hitching, pulsing body out of the way, looking at the dying trucker with all the sorrow and regret his enslaved face muscles would allow, refusing to close his eyes.

"That wasn't so hard, was it?" Violina inspected the dripping blood sigil Dennis had just completed, dabbing a droplet with her pinkie.

Dennis stood a couple of feet away. Close enough to kill her—if only he could—and sobbed. He wanted a drink of Diamante's more desperately than he had in nearly a year.

Violina took a roll of duct tape and a folded sheet of clear plastic from her bag. "Tape this over your beautiful work of art there." She looked up at the sky. "It's going to rain."

As Dennis performed the task, Violina drew the robe over her head and laid it across the nearest gravestone. She stepped to the center of her circle and raised her hands to the sky.

Still in control of his eyes, at least, Dennis could have looked at her shapely naked form but didn't.

Violina spoke magic words, projecting her voice like a seasoned stage actor. Instantly, the wind whipped up, blowing the plastic cover of the sigil wildly, along with Dennis and Violina's hair.

Violina slowly spun to the left, repeating the words.

Thunder rumbled. The lightning came in prolonged crescendos, diffused by the thick clouds that enveloped it.

Violina thrust her left hand toward the bloody symbol. Its edges began to brim with a sinister, scarlet glow.

Dennis closed his eyes and thought of McGlazer's account of being possessed, how it felt and how he had fought it, to no avail.

Violina screamed the old words at the sky, then balled herself up in a kneeling fetal position, rocking and whispering.

"You're a shitty interpretive dancer," said Dennis.

Violina's concentration did not waver. She lifted the wooden bowl in one hand, its phallic pestle in the other. "Conal O'Herlihy, I open for you and your followers a gateway to this world!"

She spat in the bowl and squatted to pour Steve's blood in it from the goblet, then stirred in the powdered pumpkin seeds and mushroom. "Come as flesh. Come as death. Come as demon."

She thrust the bowl toward the sky to meet the rain.

The lightning behind the clouds formed a sky-wide face of gleeful wickedness. Its rumble was a laugh of triumph.

"Come now!" Violina lifted the bowl again in her left hand, while extending her palm toward the sigil. "Come through me!"

On Bennington's monument, the sigil's glow flared, then shrunk to a million bright pinpoints that made Dennis's eyes hurt. Intertwining streams of void-black and crimson-red lightning shot forth, entering Violina's palm. The witch herself radiated pulses of blackness, her eyes like red spotlights.

The rain increased, pounding the grass and gravestones like falling glass. The wind blasted at an angle, driving the stinging droplets harder still.

The sky fired an identical stream of dark energy that hit Violina's bowl. Some sinister circuit was completed. Violina screamed in pain, then laughed like mad, vibrating with the clash of opposing and complementary energies.

The surge ended, leaving Violina steaming from head to toe. The bowl's contents burned with a white flame.

"Come now!" Violina spun fast, swinging the bowl like a discus to spread its flaming mixture into the air, just as a hurricane gust descended to spread it across the land like a malignant pollen.

Violina fell onto her back, and Dennis was glad to see that she hit her head. Yet the ground was little more than grass and slush at this point, hardly solid enough to hurt the witch, as evidenced by her grinning, naked delight. She spread her limbs as if to soak every inch of her flesh in the unrighteous rain and graveyard muck.

Dennis realized Violina had gained control of him only after forcing the odd whiskey down his throat. He remembered drinking a lot of water back when he was detoxing. He opened his mouth, letting the driving rain drizzle down his face and find its way inside.

Under the remnants of its raggedly flapping plastic cover, the sigil pulsed with a cold glow.

* * * *

Stopping off at the drugstore, McGlazer and Bernard ran in to pick up masks. Returning to the car, they tried for a quick jump scare, hunkering low to pop up at the windows with monster growls.

DeShaun and Stuart just looked at each other. "Our reflexes are officially dead."

"Maybe it's just the masks," noted Stuart. McGlazer had selected a badly painted knockoff of the robot kaiju Jet Jaguar, while Bernard had a child-size mask of a graciously smiling beauty queen. Framed by his wide head, it looked ridiculous. He had bought if for Emera, after all.

"Maybe these are better?" McGlazer handed a plastic bag back to the boys with their masks—Spider-Man villains: the Green Goblin and the Lizard.

The boys fist-bumped and smiled at each other, but just placed the masks on the tops of their heads.

Ten minutes later, they dashed though the rain across the Community Center's sparsely occupied parking lot, leaving Bernard and McGlazer in their splashy wake.

The muffled sound of Johnny Cash performing "Ghost Riders in the Sky" wafted out from the high windows, triggering wispy memories of Halloweens past—better Halloweens.

Low light, a sputtery, twenty-year-old fog machine and a spinning sphere projecting witches and ghosts across the rafters and bleachers was the closest to an enthusiastic greeting the quartet would receive. There was no deejay, just a portable stereo tuned to WICH with the center's PA microphone propped against it, as hurriedly assembled by Timbo Linger, the center's volunteer maintenance engineer and father to two of the dozen small children present. A dusty speaker bearing a cardboard cutout of an owl taped to the side completed the sound array's sad circuit.

The only other adult present—Kyle Trainor, a recent divorcé desperate for human companionship of any kind—smiled at the arrivals, though he barely knew any of them.

The underwhelmed children, primary schoolers whose parents saw the event as an evening of free babysitting, peppered the mostly empty bleachers and folding chairs, their costumes and makeup little more than afterthoughts.

"Whoop-a-dee-doo," deadpanned DeShaun.

The trio went to the office, and McGlazer opened the spiffy new door, which the boys expected would be the most exciting thing about the party.

"Let's get some punch," Stuart suggested, "and count yawns."

The boys dropped off their backpacks and moped out.

Leaving the light off, the reverend went behind the desk, dropping his mask to the side.

"Still pondering your place in the universe?" Bernard asked, clearing out the other chair.

"That and much more," answered the minister.

* * * *

"The settlers' first autumn here was hard-core. Even worse than Bennington's trapper buddy had said." DeShaun drew an ovoid shape on his napkin with a pen.

Stuart took over the napkin, adding a spiraling stem to the top of the ovoid. "Somebody remembered about putting candles in turnips during the end of harvest back in Ye Merry Old Tea Town. Some enterprising genius tried it out on these spiffy new orange melons. Worked out pretty well, so everybody started carving jackos in the fall."

"Stands to reason that this led to the town's name and, eventually, the parade." Stuart took the pen and started drawing curved lines from top to bottom to give the pumpkin depth.

"Don't forget to leave room for the eyes, nose and mouth," Stuart told him.

"Yeah." DeShaun looked up at the witches. "You ladies don't have an orange marker, do you?"

* * * *

Settlement era

Chloris knocked twice before entering the tiny guest room at the end of the corridor. She found its odd occupant much the same, pale and unmoving. She put her hand near his mouth. It was several seconds before she was sure he was still breathing.

"Would you rise for me, sir?" she whispered, taking away the napkin she had placed over the soup she had made. Pumpkin seeds, sprouts and bits of wild poultry made up the meal, designed to replenish the blood he'd lost.

She waved the soup steam toward him, hoping the strange man's appetite would do the job of rousing him so she wouldn't have to get closer. He gave little more than a whimper.

"Let's help you, then," she reluctantly offered. Chloris's physical strength, from years of servitude starting when she was still a child, served her well enough, even in her late thirties. Though tall, this odd lodger was leaner and lighter than many of the settlement men, certainly more so than any of the livestock she wrangled.

She got him to sit up, supporting his back with one arm while deftly raising the bowl to his lips with the other.

Stirring, he sipped a few drops. Chloris held him till she felt her arm would give out. As she eased him back, the strange-eyed young man sat up and rested against the headboard.

Chloris pulled a stool close and sat patiently while he moved his wobbly head around, trying to grasp where he was. His gaze fell on Chloris and remained fixed there. He raised his shaking arm halfway to horizontal, where it shook with effort. He pointed.

Chloris's skin crawled. It was like he was pointing through her.

"Jacko?" he rasped.

Chloris realized with relief that he was pointing to the candle on the windowsill behind her. Using the spoon this time, she raised more soup to his lips. "Let's have a bit more so we can feel better. Then we'll have a look at that nasty stab, and you can tell me about your friend Jacko."

Everett accepted the soup, smacking his lips as he stared at her with an intensity incongruous with his weakened state. "Treat?"

Chloris smiled. "Thank you, I suppose."

He sipped more soup as he again raised his trembling finger. "Trick."

"I don't..."

Everett opened his hand. It resembled the taloned foot of an owl, outstretched to snatch a field mouse and take it away to kill. He leaned toward her, shaking as his strength quickly drained away.

"What is it, dear boy?"

Everett finally reached her. He placed his hand on her throat. His fingertips hooked into her esophagus.

Chloris pried and swatted at his wrist, but her vaunted strength failed. "Nnnnoooo!" she sought to say, but Everett choked harder.

Chloris tried to stand and back away from him, but he held her fast. The room, already dark, faded to a uniform gray.

Then she was falling—backward, onto her butt.

The man had fainted from his own effort.

Chloris ran out of the room, anxious to tell her employer of the danger under his roof, praying he would get the man-demon far enough away from the settlement that it could never find its way back.

* * * *

Conal glanced up at his bed, as was long his habit, to see if Sibil was sleeping.

A year and a half hence, Sibil O'Herlihy, a light sleeper on the best of nights since coming to the new world, would have emitted another uneasy moan as she raised her wispy head to find Conal still at the table with the lamp burning too bright.

Now the bed only lay cold and empty.

It had been over a year since her passing, yet Conal still found himself searching for his wife in dark and quiet moments like this. It was often a brutish place, this so-called new world. Thus, her death the winter before last was not shocking. For someone like Conal, who thought of wives as little more than indentured servants, at best, it wasn't even all that sorrowful.

Yet her company had been some comfort. Left to himself, Conal had no one to punish for his sins.

Conal had no patience for that piece of the past. For there was more significant history to be recalled.

Meeting with the wealthy Wilcott Bennington and a few others in the back room of a cavernous pub those years past, Conal was one of a few men privy to the Englishman's explanation, concise yet meticulous, of his evolving beliefs about spirituality, society and destiny. At the time, Conal had neither agreed with nor cared about Bennington's thoughts, which qualified as blasphemy to many. His interest was in a new beginning or, more accurately, an escape.

In his two short years as a sailor for hire during his adolescence, Conal had lived as carefree a life as there could be. Amassing gambling debts, achieving unwilling sexual conquests and committing theft kept him busier than any honest man. Not surprisingly, vindictive men eventually hired brutal men to find him.

Conal had little religious inclination. But he did have a taste for new experiences. When one of his shipmates, seeking closeness with God, acquired the very mushroom that Saint John the Revelator himself had ingested, Conal reasoned that he could take the fungus and convince God to save him from his past before it caught up with him.

Though reasonably literate, Conal was infected with the impulsiveness and impatience of youth and didn't bother to read a single verse of the Book of Revelation before indulging. He could not have known that the visions experienced by the exiled scribe, John, did not always amount to blissful communion with Jehovah Himself, but more often resulted in incomprehensible and horrific visions of monsters, suffering and apocalypse.

These were the kind of visions that drove a man either to spiritual asceticism or unbridled hedonism. Only Conal O'Herlihy could find a rationale for both.

Several weeks removed from his first experience with the spotted mushroom, Conal O'Herlihy had become a man of purpose, with an eye toward serving both himself and the god of his visions—regardless of whether that truly was Jehovah, or some other deity—and thus reserving for himself a place at the right hand of...Whomever.

This god, via random followers, whispered to him word of the man organizing a mass exodus to the fabled new world of virgin milk and honey, where debt collectors and angry spouses had no cause to venture.

Bennington had his growing troop of followers, all ripe to be shaped and molded by a strong leader. While the wealthy entrepreneur Bennington would suffice for them in the short term, they would eventually need a man who carried the Wisdom of the Fungus.

This was the Irishman's quandary. Each of the settler families had received or had read to them a copy of Bennington's charter. Signing on was the same as acknowledging and accepting his beliefs.

And while Bennington had confided to Conal and other potential community leaders his conclusions that the Christ myth was derived from Saturn, he also made it clear he would not force this belief on any of the settlers. He only hoped he could share and discuss it openly, as everyone could their respective beliefs.

Conal saw his opening when Bennington suggested that he take charge of designing the community's worship center. In exchange for a claim to the high hill, Conal promised to build it there at the top "as a beacon to all the town."

The charter simply touted religious freedom, an equal community, a commitment to a shining future of prosperity hewn by the hands of the brave and the daring. Not a word about Saturn worship or anything else that could cast doubt in the settlers' minds or sway them to upend Bennington.

Bennington's charter was frustratingly flawless. It promised liberty of religion—and therefrom, a completely unheard-of concept back in England. The document offered nothing that could be counted on to rouse the rabble.

For Conal, an appeal to fundamentalist fears was the only answer.

The corpse of poor Hezekiah Hardison might be the very miracle that would change the landscape for O'Herlihy. He needed only to compose the perfect time and place to reveal it, once a few seeds of doubt were planted.

Rolling up his copy of the document, Conal sat back at his table and searched the candle-smudged darkness for details to add to his plan.

Chapter 23

Pumpkin Faces in the Night

Modern day

Her visibility reduced to a few yards by the downpour, Doris drove the Audi at a snail's pace.

When lightning crashed—every thirty seconds or so now—it had them all jumping.

"This isn't any normal storm," Doris remarked, looking along the side of the road for a pull-off. "Maybe we should stop for a few minutes."

Though she was accustomed to Kerwin relying on body language for much of his communication, Doris was not prepared for his abrupt, scrambling recoil.

When she followed his gaze, her eyes went wide as silver dollars. She slammed on the brakes.

Brinke caught herself as she pitched forward. What she saw beyond the windshield was beyond even the realm of her strangest experiences.

Three pumpkins, big around as dinner tables, clambered across the road some twenty yards ahead, on viney spider-legs that sprouted from their crowns.

"Good God in heaven…" whispered Doris.

Brinke spun to check behind them. In the harsh red of the Audi's taillights, raindrops veiled another of the horticultural horrors.

Then two more crawled out from behind it.

* * * *

Speeding up his windshield wipers, Hudson impulsively reached for his big orange travel mug, forgetting, for the fifth time, that it was already empty. Leticia only filled it half full these days.

"You worry enough," she had said, as she stopped him from topping it off. "Ember Hollow doesn't need a jittery sheriff."

"Still just deputy, 'Teesh."

"You heard me."

Further micromanaging, she had gone by the sheriff's offices and informed his coworkers of Hudson's coffee-cutback protocol. No one dared defy her polite request to keep an eye on him.

Hudson tried to make do with the radio—tuned to WICH, of course—playing something by the Japanese band Balzac. He had to resort to cracking the window an inch, which was enough to allow in a few chilly, invigorating drops.

The weird lightning and loud thunder certainly helped, but they didn't change the fact that he was going on very little sleep.

Patrolling the eastern part of the county as usual seemed unnecessary, given the storm. These pumpkin fields and cornfields were as quiet as ever. He would turn around at the next—

Hudson hit the brakes, as something rolled out into the road, casting a long shadow away from the headlights.

Luckily, he wasn't going fast enough to slide. But after two Halloweens under the threat of a serial killer who wasn't shy about performing decapitations, seeing a head-sized object tumble into his path was all the stimulant he would need for a few hours.

It was just a pumpkin, but that offered little reassurance. Surely no Devil's Night tricksters were dedicated enough to wait out here in the rainy woods on the outskirts of town just to toss a pumpkin in front of a county cruiser.

Still—Everett Geelens.

On this section of road, fields lay to the left, while woods lined the right side. The pumpkin had come from the right.

Putting his car in PARK, Hudson drew his revolver. After a moment's thought, he reholstered it and took the shotgun from its bracket. Opening his door, he stood up and shone his spotlight all around the vehicle's perimeter and into the woods from which the pumpkin had tumbled, then back to the squash. It was as far as the beam, diffused by fat raindrops and haze, would reach.

Hudson stepped out. "Sheriff's Department! Who's up there?"

Only the sound of rain answered.

"I'm armed!"

"Somebody's gonna come up on this and brake too hard," Hudson mumbled to himself. "Have themselves an accident."

Hudson went to the pumpkin. Thinking again of Everett Geelens, he prayed it was not, say, hollowed out and filled with intestines.

Kicking it gently, Hudson was, despite his preparedness, shocked when it rolled over. He reflexively stepped back with a yelp, keeping his eyes on it to be sure he wasn't imagining what he saw.

Human features—distorted and devious.

The pumpkin had a face. And it grinned at him, spreading lumpy lips to show ghost-white baby teeth.

Brown eyes, complete with sclera, iris and pupil, blinked.

Tendrils extended from its stem, working to move the abomination.

Hudson raised his shotgun and fired. The pellets sparked off the pavement as the pumpkin leaped out of the way, deft as a black widow.

"Dammit!" Hudson shouted.

There was no sign of the thing anywhere, yet his instincts told him it was just out of sight, in the dark beyond the headlight beam. He swiveled and took one step toward his cruiser, then realized the thing could have crawled underneath it, where it waited to ensnare him with those viney tentacles.

Hudson cradled his shotgun and leaned to shine his flashlight under the cruiser. The beam danced madly as the little demon leaped from the dark and bit into him.

Hudson dropped the shotgun, stunned by the stinging, sharp pain of tiny incisors sinking into his forearm. He wildly shook and swung his arm to throw it off, realizing quickly it wasn't going anywhere.

Hudson punched the orange goblin in the "face," landing three solid blows before it dropped off. Hudson spun to find the shotgun. It lay steaming at the edge of his headlight beam. The bugger could be just a foot beyond, and he wouldn't be able to see it.

Hudson drew his handgun and pressed it side by side with the flashlight, listening for any scrabbling or scratching sounds or…

"Hell with it." Hudson decided to leave the shotgun. He got in the cruiser and reverse-turned hard. His heart sank along with the car's rear end, as it slid violently into the deep ditch at the road's edge.

"Son of a bitch!"

Though he knew it was pointless, Hudson pushed the gas, then tried alternately gunning and letting off to try and rock it out, cursing when he felt the rear sink deeper than before.

He lifted the scanner radio microphone, preparing to call dispatch, when a sibilance—scrabbling, scratching, skittering—passed across the roof, barely louder than the rain.

Hudson moved to power up the window, too late. Gnarled brownish-green tendrils jabbed through the tiny opening like fast-growing cancer, finding Hudson's face and hand.

"Get off!" he shouted. He tugged up the power-window button hard enough to hurt his finger, trapping the legs.

But not the smaller vines that immediately followed.

The first slipped around his neck. It felt like a barbed-wire noose. A soft thump on the windshield drew Hudson's attention to the subhuman face set in squash flesh, leering and blinking at him, upside down.

Hudson felt the rain intensify on his face and heard the window glide back down; the goddamned monster-fruit had seen how he operated it and learned.

Hudson had to lean to his left, into the pull of the tentacle cluster, but that gave him just enough room to quickdraw his sidearm with his gloriously free hand.

Though the windshield was bulletproof, Hudson always carried his .44 these days. Nothing would withstand its force at point-blank range.

He covered his face, pressed his .44 against the windscreen and blasted the smirking aberration, sending it flying like a missile into the rainy dark as the glass noisily disintegrated.

Torn away from their source, the choking tendrils went limp. Hudson yanked the scratchy cords away from his neck and tossed them out. Then he found the spotlight and beamed it into the darkness.

"You…have got…to be…yanking my chain…" he murmured.

The thing, though the upper quarter of its head was gone, crawled toward the cruiser on its broken limbs. The two or three thinner vines that were still intact were wrapped around the shotgun—and aiming it toward him.

Hudson ducked as the twelve-gauge burped flame and thunder. The pellets finished off the windshield and pinged the hood.

Hudson thought of what would come next. The little freak would come around to the door and rise up on those insectile limbs. It would grin at him, and it would blow him away.

Hudson didn't wait for that. He yanked his door latch, kicked it open and rolled out into the road, firing off the rest of his ammo in his sidearm.

The horror was closer than he expected, which worked in Hudson's favor. Chunks of pulpy rind erupted from it.

The pumpkin went rolling backward, leaving behind the shotgun and a half-dozen encircling vines.

Hudson got up and dove for the shotgun, wishing he had the breath for a cry of relief when his palms fell on its smooth, wet grip and pump stock.

Ignoring the pain of the landing, Hudson hopped up and ran straight to the pumpkin thing.

Little more than a third of it was still intact. Yet, just above the massive hole where its mouth had been, its remaining eye rolled toward him, bloodshot and wet. Though most of it was gone, the atrocity projected no less perversity.

Hudson raised the shotgun and blasted it to a thousand pieces. He shot the largest chunks again, disintegrating them utterly.

Then he realized the cruiser was still stuck, and it was a long way back to town. Chances are, he would need the shotgun again.

At least the radio still worked—he hoped.

* * * *

"They're coming, Dennis," said Violina, allowing the corners of her lips to rise. "You can hear them over the rain now."

Dennis stood just behind her in the vestibule of Saint Saturn Unitarian, his arms aching to reach toward her, his fingers itching to squeeze her neck.

Since he could not, he peered past the rain at his town as it, once again, fell under the siege of evil. Low electrical bursts beyond the town's industrial border told him Violina's conjured army had come in past the fields and were now wreaking havoc, severing power lines.

"Call 'em off," he ordered.

Her laughter punctuated his helplessness, her control over him. "It's the fault of your gender, you know."

Dennis grunted with intention. His arms remained at his sides, the muscles not even tensing any longer.

"Men suppressed magic because it made women not only equal, but superior to you."

"Bitch," Dennis began. "I'm a suicidal loser alcoholic with a mom who's a widow and a girlfriend who saved this town. You ain't gotta sell me on girl power. But you couldn't carry water for either one of 'em."

Violina laughed again, almost a cackle, then leaned in to kiss him. "You don't know how aroused that makes me, Dennis." She returned to the doorway. "Maybe I won't feed you to them, if you can keep up this interesting banter."

Dennis wanted to get under the rain, to let it run down his face so he could swallow as much of it as possible to dilute the potion she had forced on him. That wasn't going to happen as long as they both stood in the shelter of the church vestibule.

"Feed me to 'em?" Dennis laughed. "I'm betting that Conal douche is gonna double-cross you bigger than hell."

Violina remained uncharacteristically silent as she peered down at the town.

"No telling what's really going on down there," Dennis said cryptically.

"Don't make me have you bite off your own tongue, lover boy."

"Hey, I'm worried too," Dennis continued. "He's probably gonna be a lot worse than you."

Violina contemplated for a long time before she spoke again. "Be a good worker bee and go get the car."

As Dennis felt himself walk through the building, he shouted a litany of curses that would shock a drill instructor.

"Oh, my goodness, what a mouth!" Violina mocked. "For that, you can take the long way."

Dennis felt a modicum of triumph as his body about-faced and went to exit through the front door, into the rain.

"And take your time," Violina purred. "Half speed, let's say."

Dennis felt the shock of cold water bashing into his face. He began to sing The Chalk Outlines' club hit "Rumble at Castle Frankenstein," reasoning that its fast pace would allow him to swallow more water.

Chapter 24

Return to the Living

The healing ceremony for Ysabella, ranging from rocking whispers to childish, off-key singing to focused stillness, never wavered as the storm grew more and more violent.

Only Jill, accustomed to watching out for trouble at the band's gigs, kept her eyes open. Catching sight of the lightning flashes, she knew instantly that this was far from natural. Stella intuitively opened her eyes to meet Jill's gaze.

Jill nodded toward the window.

The next flash sent a chill through Stella. She felt Ysabella's pulse and despaired that it was weaker than ever.

* * * *

As the rain-slickened orange goblins approached the Audi, Kerwin tried screaming "Go!" but forgot he needed his amplifier. Brinke said the same. Doris was already flooring it before she finished the single syllable.

The Audi's bumper banged into the closest pumpkin thing's sapling-thick leg and fishtailed on the wet road. Doris never stopped, regaining control with admirable dexterity.

The thing had toppled forward on its broken limb. But it still had three legs to keep it moving—and fast.

"Hang on!" Doris called, as she maneuvered around the biggest one yet, a Volkswagen-sized specimen. It skittered toward them with unnatural speed. When it got within a few yards, they all saw its "face"—a wicked countenance with all the nuance of a human being, including a sinister smile and blue eyes alight with an eagerness to shed blood.

Kerwin stared at Brinke. He didn't even try to say it, but she knew; he expected her to do some "magic."

Brinke tried to gather her pinballing thoughts to find a general protection charm that might apply. But all those she knew were to be done well in advance.

For now, Doris's driving prowess would have to do the job. "We'll get to town," she exclaimed, as she rocketed right between the spidery legs of a fresh-risen pumpkin demon. "Find Hudson."

"What can he do?" Kerwin asked, strangely calm through the monotone of the vocal enhancer.

Doris couldn't answer. She was busy veering hard away from a pair of the things, as they stalked toward the car in perfect unison, like the Martian killing machines of H. G. Wells.

Brinke saw the nearest of the demonic duo open its mouth, viewed the stringy innards hanging before the black cave inside, and saw the tiny, yet deadly incisors.

The pumpkin beasts were evolving—taking on more and more human attributes—by the second.

"We can at least warn the town," Doris said without optimism, "if we can beat these things there."

* * * *

Yoshida was usually lulled by thunderstorms. Exhausted as he was from all that had already happened this night, he was sure he would fall into a deep sleep within minutes. Yet the terror remained that he would transform again.

There was no precedent for that. Yet every night's change had been more intense, making him wilder and more unpredictable. The fear that he would become a wolf, and remain that way, left him in a constant state of alarm. He had already considered ending it all, via a delicious mouthful of gun barrel. But he didn't have any silver bullets, and if he was anything like his "wolf mother," Aura, it would be a useless gesture, serving only to drive home the extent of his dilemma.

There was a grenade launcher in the evidence annex. That would surely do it.

He both envied and enjoyed the sound of Pedro snoring on the recliner across from him. His friend deserved a good rest, after all he had done. He, Dennis, McGlazer, Hudson, the boys too—all had gone the extra mile as friends. If it was to be the end, the best consolation he could think of was that he would be well-mourned.

Someone, a woman or child, cried out in panic from the apartment next door.

"God, what n…?" Yoshida went to the window.

No detective work was required.

Under a flash that briefly painted the parking lot a foggy crimson, he saw three van-sized creatures moving toward the apartment complex.

They moved on uneven limbs, some jointed, like locust legs, others more flexible, like the tentacles of a squid.

Another scream—a man's voice this time.

Pedro stood up, dropping the trank rifle. "Whut the blue hades…?"

Yoshida shushed Pedro, then waved him over, as more terrified exclamations rose all around the building.

Pedro almost cried out when he saw one of the pumpkin-spiders clamber over a car.

"Wake me up outta this sick dream, Yoshi." Pedro gripped his shoulders. "Right the hell now."

Through the window, the rain and darkness smeared the pumpkins to moving blobs of orange, but it was clear they were coming closer to the building, drawn by the screams.

"Where's your sawed-off ten-gauge!?" Yoshida asked.

"You guys made me turn it in!"

Nearby, a window crashed. Then another. Through the rain-pelted window, they saw that one of the things was just a few feet away, moving toward Pedro's screaming neighbors.

"What about your revolver?" Pedro whispered.

"I locked it up when my super puberty hit."

"All I got is a spiked bracelet and some butter knives."

Lightning flashed again, engraving a savage photograph on their minds, of two spider-pumpkin-demons carrying flailing, pajama-clad apartment dwellers, one suspended in a viney tendril, the other quickly disappearing into a grinning mouth.

They physically recoiled from the window, falling over each other and the recliner. The crashing thump of the falling chair came just before the thunder. Pedro and Yoshida lay awkwardly frozen, waiting to see if the shapes would come to their window.

Other noises caught the beasts' attention, though. Someone had a gun. It popped like either a cap pistol or a .22. Hardly heavy artillery.

"We gotta do something," Pedro said, pointing at the ceiling. "Ophelia's up there."

* * * *

As "The Cat Came Back" played over the speaker, McGlazer made the rounds, passing out candy that was meant for later to the kids trapped inside by the raging storm. He was met with mostly troubled faces and pleas for their parents.

As for the adults, the thunder might as well have been pulses of direct current, with each clap jolting everyone deeper into a collective state of unease.

McGlazer heard the door latch echo and frowned. It didn't help that the boys were at the exit, holding it open.

"Sure is weird!" said DeShaun, shouting over the roar of the rain.

"There's no explanation for lightning to be red like that," added Stuart. The boys gave each other the look that had long ago become shorthand between them for "just another Ember Hollow Halloween nightmare."

Bernard wandered toward them. "What are you boys doing over here? Letting all the excitement out?"

"This storm's more interesting. Red lightning."

Bernard watched, silently counting between flash and thunder. "And it's coming closer." He stepped out under the aluminum eaves and put his hand over his glasses, as if shielding them from the sun, squinting toward the fringe tree rising from a grassy island in the middle of the parking lot.

There was a split second of total darkness in the sky. Then another angry rumble that seemed almost like the grumble of a giant.

"Did you see that blackness?" Bernard asked, too quietly under the squall for the boys to hear. But they got the gist. "That was no power outage."

Headlights appeared at the far end of Main Street, moving toward them fast.

"I think...here we go," said DeShaun.

"Whatever it is, whatever happens..."

Stuart did not need to finish. DeShaun was ready to defend his friend, just as Stuart had fought for him the year before.

"Watch out!" Bernard ran inside, past the boys, as the car slid into the lot at speed and careened straight toward them.

Chapter 25

Yet Not Human

Settlement era

"You must understand." Standing outside the guest room, Bennington patted Chloris's sturdy shoulder to reassure her. "He must be delirious from blood loss. He surely believed you were his assailant."

"Perhaps," Chloris said. "Yet there's…blackness rising from him. If he's gone mad…I don't expect that he'll return from it."

Staring at the door, Bennington nodded. "I want to try something."

Minutes later, Bennington entered Everett's room, wearing the scarecrow hood he had taken off the mop-haired man. Behind him came Chloris, clutching the matchlock pistol in a two-handed grip as steady as the settlement's best marksman, whom, if she wished to be indiscreet, she could decisively best in any shooting contest.

Everett stirred immediately from a stream of welcome nightmares and sat up like a corpse that had gone into rigor mortis. He regarded the man in the doorway wearing his mask, and blinked, as if he had found himself in yet another beautiful bad dream.

Slowly he formed a grin. "Trick?"

Bennington came to his side. "It's a trick, yes." He pulled the hood off. "It's me. We want to help you heal."

He handed the scarecrow mask to Everett. "We are your friends."

Everett took the mask and quickly put it on. Bennington helped him adjust it.

"I am Wilcott. That is Chloris."

Everett waved.

"And your name?"

Everett was confounded. He could not remember anyone ever asking him his name.

His father had tried to take Halloween away from him. Then the church men came to his room and took everything else.

He eyed Chloris, who had brought him treats, soup that tasted like pumpkins and sweet bread. She…smiled at him.

Then his gaze traveled back to the big man who had put him on his horse and brought him here to rest. But Everett felt he knew him from before that.

No. He knew his ghost.

"Eh…Everett…"

"Everett," said his host.

"Everett," repeated Chloris.

The two grown-ups smiled at him again. His Mamalee used to smile at him and speak kind words too, but she also let his father lock him up. She did nothing when the church men came. Mamalee did not love Halloween.

This man and this woman gave him Halloween.

Everett tried to stand, to hug his friends. The man put his hand on Everett's shoulder and stopped him. "You're wounded yet, dear boy." He pointed at Everett's stomach, where Glory Brightwell had stabbed him. "This must heal."

Everett knew what these words meant, and he did feel some hurt there, though he didn't mind it. But he reasoned that if the blood came out again, he might feel weak, like before.

The nice man had given him his mask back. Maybe the man and his lady friend liked Halloween too.

Everett lay on his back and closed his eyes. He would trust these people for now.

Later, when he was better, they would all probably decorate the town for Halloween together. Everett hoped so. He didn't want to make them die.

He would surprise them by starting early.

* * * *

Modern day

"I don't think I'd have even seen you without your rain slicker," said Deputy Astin as Hudson plopped into the passenger seat. "Did you really see some kind of monster out here?"

"I'm not out in this storm for my health, Astin." Hudson worked his way out of the reflective county-issue rain gear. "And I'm guessing there are more of them out here, heading into town. Did dispatch radio the National Guard?"

"Yessir. But they said they can't send choppers in this." The young deputy frowned up at the cruiser's roof like he was checking the clouds. "They're gonna be on wheels—and it's gonna take a while."

"Did you get ahold of all the off-duty boys and neighboring counties?"

"Well…get ready for bad news," Astin said. "The phone lines are fubar."

"Orange bastards must have taken 'em out…" Hudson stiffened as they passed a sign that read:

YOU ARE NOW ENTERING EMBER HOLLOW—
PUMPKIN-GROWING CAPITAL OF THE WORLD!

"Head to the evidence building, then the station. And step on it."

* * * *

"Class B," whispered Yoshida, as he examined the fire extinguisher under Pedro's kitchen sink.

"Is that the recommended type for fighting devil pumpkins?" asked Pedro.

"Do you have hair spray or anything like that?"

"I think Jill left a can when they crashed here one night after a gig."

"Grab it."

Seconds later, Pedro met Yoshida at the door. He didn't see the pumpkin things moving around outside the window. Thumping and cries of terror from the other apartments told him why.

"Spray them in the eyes," Yoshida muttered.

"Right. Think they'll wait while I get a ladder?"

"You're gonna have to be a little more creative than that, smart-ass." Yoshida opened the door and dashed out into the rain with the fire extinguisher, Pedro hot on his tail.

Two of the demons scrabbled on the side of the building, poking murderous tendrils into broken windows. The third crept along the edge of the roof.

"Hey!" Pedro grabbed a handful of gravel and began pelting the nearest demon. It swung its bulbous body to glare at him, giving the deputy and the death rocker their first decent look at its bizarrely human face, briefly rendered in unsettling detail by a red flash.

"Crap on a kickball..."

The thing leaped off the wall like a cricket, landing atop a car behind Pedro. Its mouth opened to issue a hissing scream, revealing its human teeth and orange gullet.

Pedro threw another rock as it lunged toward him, then raised the can of hair spray, waiting to push the button until the damned thing was nearly face-to-face with him.

The burst of aerosol drew another shrill hiss from the creature and made it scuttle backward. One gnarled limb punched through the sunroof of an SUV, trapping it for the moment.

Yoshida had more range with the fire extinguisher. He sent a ropy stream ten feet with one burst. Perhaps owing to the deputy's marksmanship, the fluid met the second creature directly in the eyes before it could pounce off the wall. The foam expanded, thoroughly blinding the creature.

"Come on!" Pedro and Yoshida ran into the breezeway and up the stairs to the second floor. Pedro kicked the door to Ophelia's apartment off the hinges and dashed into the darkened dwelling with the hair-spray can raised like a flamethrower.

Two thick forelimbs, invading through the window, crashed around the living room in search of prey. A broken body lay near the door, the tiny handgun they had heard lying nearby.

"Pedro?" The little girl peeked out from her hiding place, a lower cabinet in the kitchen.

Yoshida flip-rolled across the living-room floor and came up with a blast of the fire extinguisher, right down the monster's maw.

"Where's your ma?"

"It got her!" cried Ophelia.

Pedro pushed her back into the cabinet and ran to help Yoshida. The deputy lay pressed flat against the wall under the window, too close for its long, sweeping limbs.

Pedro charged, grabbing the extinguisher to bash the monster.

Screeching, it fell away from the wall, crashing onto a car with a distressed squeal.

"The one on the roof!" called Pedro, as he pulled the crying Ophelia out of the cabinet and held her. "It's gotta have her mom!"

"How do we get up there?"

Pedro stood and set Ophelia on the floor. "We're going to get your mom."

Ophelia crawled back into the cabinet as they ran out to the breezeway. "We gotta hurry. The rain is washing that shit outta their eyes."

Pedro arced the spray can over his head and onto the roof, then pulled himself up on the walkway's iron rail and deftly leaped up to grab the lip of the gutter and hoist himself up.

Yoshida did the same, raising his head over the roof's edge just in time to see the plump orange spider slashing down at him. He moved his head just in time.

Pedro tackled one of its appendages and tried to drag the thing away so Yoshida could finish his climb. It spun and plucked Pedro up with two whip-quick tentacles.

Yoshida pulled himself up onto the roof and dove for the fire extinguisher. Hearing a scream, he followed it—to see Ophelia's mother, Camilla, hanging from the end of a jagged leg out over the edge of the roof. With her eyes closed and lips mashed tightly closed, it was clear she needed to scream. Yosh understood that the only reason she didn't was Ophelia.

Pedro's dropped his spray can—just before a thorny-clawed limb descended to crush it.

Yoshida tried a blast of the fire extinguisher, but the monster moved too fast, darting away from the stream. At least, it also brought Ophelia's mother back across the edge.

Ducking behind an air-conditioning unit, Yoshida found a collection of spare pipe lengths lying haphazardly around the base, the longest around five feet.

Pedro briefly tried to power out of the rope-like tentacle but lost heart when the gourd focused its maleficent stare on him, an uncanny snarl blooming from its lips. It opened its mouth to engulf his head.

Then it projected a stinger from its tongue.

No, not a stinger…

A pipe, penetrating from below. Shocked by the sudden pain, the thing dropped Pedro—and Camilla.

Pedro landed on his hands and legs, splashing into a shallow puddle. A quick glance told him Yoshida had thought one move ahead, leaping to catch Camilla after stabbing the demon.

The horror wrapped a tentacle around the pipe and pulled it out. It swung the weapon at Pedro's head.

"Let's go!" he called as he ducked. They dashed back to the roof's edge. He grabbed the gutter and swung himself down to the walkway, waiting there to help Yoshida and then Camilla.

As she began to lower her feet, a gnarled vine-tacle whipped down and belted Pedro in the side, sending him rolling away—and Camilla dangling like a ragdoll, soon to fall, and likely smashing across the iron rail en route. Pedro picked himself up and lunged, catching her around the waist and spinning her away from the rail. "Get inside!"

"Yoshi!" he called, watching the edge. Just as he decided to climb back up to help, Yoshida was there, reaching for Pedro's hand as he made the awkward leap.

"Move!" Yoshida pulled Pedro along as he ran away from the thick leg hooking toward them.

A split second later, they were back in Ophelia's apartment. Mother and child had their rushed reunion as Yoshida went to check the man on the floor, while Pedro up-righted the front door and pushed it into the frame, leaning heavily against it.

Yoshida's expression told him that Ophelia's father was dead. "Better get away from that window, dude."

Yoshida went to Ophelia and Camilla. "Lost the extinguisher. You folks have one?" Opening the cabinet under the sink, he found it.

"Fire extinguishers and hair spray ain't cuttin' it, Yosh."

"Yeah? What's your big strategy, Sun-Effing-Tzu?"

"You ain't gonna like it."

"...I already don't."

Chapter 26

Too Fast for Blood

"If we live through this," Yoshida began, "I'm having you committed."

"I don't know if you noticed, genius, but they're growing," said Pedro. "I think it's the rain."

"Your point?"

"Desperate times call for blah blah blah."

"What are you talking about?" asked Camilla.

"You tell her," Yoshida insisted.

"Okay…Yoshi here got bit by a biker chick and now it makes him go all Monster on the Campus every night when he falls asleep."

Yoshida face-palmed.

The squash demons called to each other, their spine-shocking cries hitting an unpleasant frequency.

"They're making plans, bro," said Pedro. "Or arguing over pie recipes."

"Just what the hell do you propose, Petey?"

Pedro shrugged. "You wolf-out and dig up the garden."

"What!?" Yoshida looked like he had been betrayed. "How? Sleeping pills?"

"No, man," Pedro said. "I'd have to K.O. you."

"You think I'm gonna let you punch me, you beefed-up butthole?"

"Not punch, man," said Pedro. "The sleeper hold. From wrestling."

Yoshida blinked at both the insanity and the soundness of the stratagem.

"What if you put me out and I don't change? Then I'm a useless limp body for you to deal with. What if I do change…and go after you?"

"They ain't gonna just ignore you."

Yoshida stared at him, the dark making him appear half-transformed already.

"I just wanna get those chicks clear," Pedro whispered. "Then I'll come back and do whatever I gotta do to help you."

"But I'll probably attack you, man."

"Wolves are smart, and you are too, Yoshi. I'm guessing you'll make those things a priority."

The pumpkin's multi-jointed limb, notably thicker since they had last seen it, punched through what was left of the living-room window.

"Back bedroom!" said Yoshi, sweeping up Ophelia as Pedro huddled her mother close.

* * * *

McGlazer leaned into the Community Center's oily old drill until the screw caught and pulled the plywood flush against the door frame. It felt strange that Kerwin Stuyvesant, who, before being mutilated, had never been a fan of manual labor, was so quick to hand him the next screw and press his body against the plywood.

The drill died in McGlazer's hands, along with the lights.

Kerwin raised his voice modulator. "They took out the power."

"Are they capable of…?"

"Much worse." Kerwin knelt to grope for a hammer in the toolbox.

The silence was filled by the unearthly call of one of the pumpkin demons, all too close.

Another one answered, nearer.

"There's a deer rifle in my truck," said Timbo Linger, still dutifully adorned with a red foam nose and tiny derby hat.

"Get it now," said McGlazer.

Kerwin patted Timbo's shoulder twice and raised the hammer, nodding to say, "I'll cover you," then they were out in the blasting rain.

"He'll be right back, don't worry." McGlazer told son and daughter.

"Can we pray for him?" asked the girl.

McGlazer didn't stop for a dramatic pause. "Yes, let's pray."

* * * *

Timbo's GMC Sierra was parked halfway across the lot. With rain pelting them so hard it was painful and scarlet flashes rolling across the skyline, Timbo and Kerwin felt like they were on another planet. "Hop in!" Timbo called over the roar. "I'll drive us back!"

As Kerwin slid in, he realized his false chin was fully exposed under the truck's interior light. Timbo glanced at him, his gaze drawn to the prosthesis.

Kerwin raised his amplifier, prepared to apologize for the offense of his appearance.

Timbo waited for him to speak. Kerwin decided to stay silent.

"Check the glove box for the shells, will ya?" Timbo said, starting the engine.

* * * *

Across the gym, Bernard cursed at the sudden darkness but did not slow as he raised a folding table and considered what would be the strongest angle to brace it against the center's doors. Perhaps he had expected this, things getting worse. As they did every Halloween.

Bernard also considered how he had battled the mushroom monsters a year before. These…sentient pumpkin arachnid things the mayor had described would be operating under different rules. And he didn't have any of the magnesium strips he'd used against the fungus fiends.

Brinke appeared at his side, startling a cry out of him.

"Sorry."

"Well, it's not like I wasn't already scared, so…"

"I need a ride," said the witch.

"What? Are you…?"

"The boys said Ysabella is at the inn, and not doing well."

"Yeah, true."

"If it was closer, I would go there on foot."

"I'll take you," said Bernard. "I need to check on my girls anyway."

Chapter 27

Night Time Crawling

Settlement era

"We have visitors, sir!" Chloris called. Having heard the horses from her bedroom, she was out of bed and at the door before the knock came.

"Where's Bennington?" asked Adonijah Cooke without greeting. "I need to speak to him." The second of his four sons, Jonas, coaxed his mount to the corner of the house where he would keep watch.

"He'll be along in a minute," Chloris told him calmly. "Hello, Adonijah. Boys."

Cooke and his grown boys had long served as a police force for the settlement, due to their strapping size and legendary ruggedness. The oldest, Phineas, was considered Ember Hollow's best marksman, given that Chloris had never challenged him for the title. Their gruff demeanor was part of the job, a necessary emotional distance they could take on and toss off like a garment.

Their visit meant they suspected Bennington of something. Chloris immediately thought of their gaunt visitor and patient. He had, after all, been found bleeding—and then tried to kill her.

Initial panic told her to tell the Cookes about Everett here and now, before Bennington came. They would take the oddball away, and what a relief that would be.

But this was not what her employer had instructed.

"Gentlemen," came his booming voice as he entered, ending her inner deliberation. "It's late."

"Go with Jonas," Adonijah told Elias. "Stables and barn." He summoned Rufus to follow him inside. They brushed past Chloris, holding their matchlocks low.

"Have you seen Hezekiah Hardison?"

"Not in quite a few days, I'm afraid," Bennington answered. "He's friendlier with Conal these days."

Chloris glanced toward the short corridor that ended in the guest room, where Everett lay recovering, and realized her hands were trembling.

"Glory Brightwell is missing as well." Adonijah surveyed the room. "Their cabin is in shambles."

"Forgive me, sir," Chloris said. "Perhaps she and Hezekiah…"

Adonijah spun to glower at her in rebuke. "Bennington, kindly instruct your servant to be silent unless questions are asked of her." He directed his son toward the corridor.

"Chloris may speak as she wishes in her home."

Adonijah glowered at Bennington. "You may be the town's governor, sir, but I am its law."

"What law are you upholding tonight, Adonijah?" asked Bennington. "And at the behest of whom?"

Chloris watched Rufus go into the first room—hers. Where she kept her diary. Which told of their visitor.

"I don't favor Conal or anyone in my work," said Adonijah.

"I'm relieved."

Adonijah went to the corridor and met Rufus coming out. He hadn't stayed long enough to have picked up the diary. Adonijah stepped into the room across from hers, a sewing room, while Rufus moved along.

Chloris whispered, "What will we tell them about the young man?"

"The truth. Adonijah can decide for himself if he wants that boy on the back of a horse behind him or his sons."

Adonijah ambled back into the corridor. "When last you met with Hezekiah, were there words?"

"Of greeting, perhaps. Nothing more."

Rufus reached the door at the end.

"You, ma'am?" Cooke asked Chloris.

"Me? No." Her voice quaked as Rufus stepped into the guest room.

"And what of Glory Brightwell?"

"No."

Cooke regarded them like he would a sheep or cow, judging. "Are you well, ma'am?"

He had sensed Chloris's terror. She dared not speak, sure her voice would…

Rufus stepped out of the guest room, more bored than ever. "You should keep your windows closed, sir, as winter approaches."

Bennington winked at Chloris. "What have I told you, Chloris?"

"I'm sorry, sir."

"You keep an undeniably tidy house," said the elder Cooke, perhaps accusingly, as he walked to the door, no longer scanning about.

"Please visit anytime," said Bennington.

The sense of relief was short-lived. Urgent hoofbeats stopped just outside.

Adonijah swung open the door to find his other sons swinging down from their mounts. "We found Hezekiah, Father!"

"Yes?"

"In the barn." Jonas drew his matchlock and raised it toward Bennington. "Torn utterly asunder."

* * * *

Less than an hour after the Cooke boys locked her in the pillory, Chloris was aching from head to toe.

At least the rain, pouring earlier in the day, was only a fragrant memory—for now. Come the dawn and the rise of most Ember Hollowites, she would undoubtedly be pelted with everything from vegetables to mud to stones. She could only hope for a cool day or a quick resolution to the mystery of Hezekiah Hardison's slaying.

The pillory, meant as both punishment and interrogatory torture, stood only four feet high, forcing suspects into a miserable stooped position with head and hands locked in circles cut out of the two planks that fitted together. The stress on her legs and waist could only be relieved by letting her throat and wrists bear the weight. It made her think of a guillotine, which seemed nearly humane compared to however long she would suffer in this position.

She had wept when the Cooke men arrested Bennington and her, mostly from fear. She felt the need to weep now from the pain, yet recognized the need to conserve fluids. Bennington was locked in jail. No one would be obliged to bring her water.

From off to her side, Chloris detected a muted shuffling sound.

Just a few yards beyond the rear of the street's businesses and homes was the forest, carpeted with recently fallen foliage, and darkness. If she strained, Chloris could see the edge and the closest trees, but that was a waste of energy. She feared the thick, dark woods of the new world more than she ever had the sparse forest of her hovel back in England.

Though wolves, bears and other predators never ventured this close to the settlement, something had.

Her throat tightened with the recollection of Everett's crushing grasp. He was loose now.

She thought of calling out to Jonas, currently standing watch over her master in the jail two buildings away. Of the Cooke clan, he had been roughest with her, to the point that even the hard-hearted Adonijah had to admonish him. If he were to come without his father here to restrain him…

The soft shuffling on the leaves became softer steps on the street, still muddy from the afternoon's shower. The time had come to scream.

A hand smacked over her mouth; polished shoes fell just within her sight line. Then an insidiously sharp edge pressed against her neck. "Stay quiet, woman."

Despite its whispered tone, Chloris recognized the voice of Conal O'Herlihy.

He removed his hand. "This is a sad state for such a loyal servant. And your master sheltered and safe over there in the jailhouse."

She was helpless to stop the tears now.

"You need my help. No one can else can save you." Conal allowed a scoff. "Not even the great Wilcott Bennington."

She tried to raise her head to glower at him, wanting to show him some measure of defiance, even as her tears told a different tale. But she simply could not.

Conal showed her the bone knife he had taken from Schroeder, waving it near her eye line. "You declare that he killed Hezekiah, and I'll see to it you are freed and held blameless."

Chloris inhaled mightily to utter one word. "No."

Conal pressed the blade, harder. "No hurry, dear. You can just stay right here like this until you've come to the right decision."

The blade eased, the shoes disappeared, and Chloris was alone, more distressed and terrified than ever before.

* * * *

Modern day

Reaching the top of the ladder, Kyle Trainor leaned down to reach for a board from the dismantled pallet to brace the Community Center's upper windows. It was a precarious task at best. He would never complete it.

The window shattered inward, pierced by a dripping wet vine-leg. Smaller tendrils writhing at its end wrapped around Kyle and yanked him through the window in a blur.

Inhuman screeches of varying pitches echoed around the brick walls and wood floors, as driving rain blew in.

Another tentacle whipped in and found the ladder, scooting it noisily around the floor and banging it against the wall, before the demon realized it did not have hold of anything useful.

"Get them into the weight room!" McGlazer told Stuart and DeShaun, motioning to the children.

A hissing roar came through the window and echoed about the high walls and rafters like a swarm of bats. Then another, as several of the twisted appendages cast for prey.

"In here, you guys!" DeShaun and Stuart spread their arms wide as they rushed the kids into the weight room, relieved that none of them saw Kyle's demise.

Timbo backed against the rear wall and pointed the rifle toward the window. Kerwin opened the box of shells and stood by to hand them off.

"Get in the office!" McGlazer ordered Mayor Stuyvesant.

"I'm the mayor, not the messiah," Doris told him. "We all fight together."

* * * *

No sooner had Pedro pushed Ophelia's bedroom door closed than a crack appeared in it, the pumpkin demon's angry warbling cry signaling its intention to get in.

"Dammit, do it if you're going to!" Yoshida said, presenting his back to Pedro and pointing at his neck. "Are you sure you even know how?"

"I've seen all of Ed 'Strangler' Lewis's matches on *Golden Classics of Wrestling*. Paid close attention." Pedro wrapped his big arms around Yoshida's head and neck. "You ready?"

Yoshida nodded. Pedro began to apply pressure, wary of breaking his friend's neck if the thing battered at the door again and startled him.

Yoshida reflexively grabbed at Pedro's forearm, issuing a distressing gurgle.

"Just relax, bro," Pedro said. "Only takes about four sec—"

Yoshida's back and neck grew in mass and density so fast Pedro thought he was exploding. The gurgle became a growl just as quickly.

Pedro released and shoved Yoshida away. "Get in that closet!" he called to Ophelia and her mother.

Pedro charged to open the bedroom door, ducking as soon as it swung open.

He had guessed that the beast Yoshida became would pounce right for his back—and he was right. But his quick move caused the werewolf to smash fangs-first into the pumpkin demon.

Two otherworldly, yet wildly different bellowing reverberations blew out from the entangled monsters, like a sonic mushroom cloud.

Pedro rolled away from the action and toward the closet, glancing at the blur of fur and fangs and vine and rind, relieved the jumble was moving away from the door.

He grabbed the hands of mother and daughter and pulled them out. "Stay behind me!"

When they ran out into the dark demolition of the living room, Ophelia stopped stock-still and screamed at the sight of Yoshida clawing into the pumpkin thing's face. It sprayed very red blood several yards in all directions.

Pedro picked her up in his arms and ran to the door.

As the first demon collapsed, the second smashed its face through the battered window frame and bit into Yoshida's shoulder. The werewolf emitted a high-pitched howl of pain that felt like needles in Pedro's ears.

He ran with the women to the breezeway and pushed them toward the stairway. "Stay at the top!"

As they did, Pedro ran back to the edge of the walkway and once again hauled himself onto the roof.

Peering over the far edge, he saw the bulbous end of the crab-like goblin, Yoshida's opponent, sticking out of the window of Ophelia's apartment. Yoshida's continued shriek of pain told Pedro all he needed to know about what it was doing. "Dammit!"

He glanced around and found the length of pipe Yoshida had used as a weapon, those eternal seconds ago when the lawman was human.

Barely slowing to spot where the damned thing was, Pedro leaped off the edge with the pipe pointing straight down. He buried the pipe into that big, evil orange ass with the force of muscle and momentum, and tore it open from top to bottom. Blood cascaded over his head and shoulders as he hit the ground, flip-rolled forward and came to his feet—which stung like hell.

The creature made a cry of raging pain as it fell apart, spilling intestines, seeds and buckets of blood.

Pedro looked back up just in time to dive away from a twelve-foot-long, segmented leg falling toward him.

"Crap!" he called, checking to see if there was anything else coming at him.

There was—a roaring, toothy, blood-covered nightmare dog-man.

Yoshida smashed into Pedro and drove him onto his back on the muddy ground, knocking him breathless. The musician opened his eyes to see a vortex of teeth and bloody blackness beyond.

"Leave him alone!" called Ophelia.

Pedro felt the briefest instant of relief when Yoshida stopped mid-bite—and then the most despairing of horrors, as he realized the man-beast was now focused on Ophelia.

Yoshida leaped off Pedro, focused on his new easy prey. Pedro lunged to grab his foot. He was dragged face-forward a yard or so, and then left behind in his terrifying failure.

Except Yoshida slipped in the mud as he crouched on his hinds to leap. He fell to his back but immediately scrambled to all fours. As he coiled for another leap, Pedro crashed onto his back and once again sank the sleeper hold.

Yoshida squirmed and twisted and kicked like no rodeo bull ever had. Pedro clinched his legs around the monster's bony hips and held on, yelling, "Get going, Ophelia!"

Yoshida-wolf rolled stomach-up, putting Pedro on his back against the ground. Its instincts did not tell it this only helped to deepen the hold.

Just as he was sure Yoshida was about to peel his arms away from his neck—and his body—the werewolf went limp.

Pedro shook the rain off his face and saw the eyes of the wolfman roll to white, its bloody tongue hanging from slack jaws.

He released his friend, relieved to see him shrinking—becoming human.

"You okay?" he called up to Ophelia, but the little girl and her mother were already on the way down.

Chapter 28

Unfinished Business

The impromptu healing session for Ysabella had begun optimistically enough. Little Emera's innocent belief that closeness and love would heal her new friend was infectious among the women.

But Stella, keeping constant check on the elder woman's pulse and breathing, soon grew gloomy. Her frequent glances toward the phone, the door and the rain-smudged windows gave her away, first to Jill, then to Leticia and Elaine, who each raised their grim faces from the rocking and whispering circle to look at each other.

"She needs a hospital," Stella mouthed.

Jill stopped drumming the pot for a second, shocked still by the dread of sadness. This broke the concentration of the others.

When she picked the rhythm back up, it was too late. Whatever trance the younger girls had been in disintegrated. "Why'd we stop?" asked Candace.

"We need to do something else," Stella explained. "Soon."

"No!" Emera hugged close to the old woman, squeezing a breath from her that was too close to a death rattle. "Miss Iss hassa stay here till she gets better!"

Stella rubbed the child's quivering back. "Honey…"

With an excited bark, Bravo dashed to the door.

"Open up!" Bernard shouted, as he pounded the door like a raiding SWAT captain. "Hurry!"

Jill went to the door and was nearly knocked to the floor by the giant woman who rushed through.

"Where is she?" asked Brinke.

Bravo did not bristle, and no one asked who she was. Her urgency and self-assurance told them all they needed to know.

"Keep doing what you're doing, everyone." Brinke pulled Ysabella's blankets away and lay atop her like a lover, hugging Ysabella's lolling head in her arms. "Stay close, sugar," she told the confused Emera. The little girl reacted quickly, reclaiming her spot against Ysabella, like a cat seeking warmth.

"Okkala Boro-Tah Cam-Ura Tahn!" Brinke said in a tone that commanded attention.

She repeated the incantation, rocking restlessly.

"Hit it, everybody," said Jill, and the other women joined in the chant as best they could until they had the hang of it. As their voices rose, so did their assurance, and soon Elaine, Leticia, Candace, Stella and Bernard had formed a pentagon around the bed with their hands linked, their heads held high, and their wills rocketing into the universe.

* * * *

Staring expectantly at Timbo, Kerwin raised his voice-box amplifier in a shaking hand. "What are you waiting for?"

"No use shooting their legs," Timbo answered. "I'm waiting for one of 'em to show its face."

"At least the barricades are holding," Mayor Stuyvesant said.

The heavy double doors at both ends shook, as if the monsters had heard and sought to prove her wrong.

"For how much longer?" asked McGlazer.

In the weight room, each unearthly roar, every echoing crash drew ever more strident and frightened cries from the children huddled in the farthest corner.

"What's happening!?" asked a six-year-old boy whom Stuart and DeShaun only knew as Pockets.

The older boys grimaced at one another to pass the buck. Finally, DeShaun tried, "The storm's knocking down trees or something."

Stuart peered through the rectangular pane set high to the side of the door.

The tentacles had withdrawn, leaving a tense stillness, and leaving McGlazer, the mayor, Bernard, Timbo and Kerwin out in the open.

"Are the trees gonna fall on us?" asked Pockets.

"We won't let them."

"Why can't we have the lights on? I'm scared!"

"Hey, let's play a game, you guys," DeShaun suggested, peering around the room for some kind of prop.

A chorus of sibilant roars rendered the ruse ineffective. The kids broke into a chorus of their own, sobbing pleas for their parents, for the lights to be on, to be taken home.

The pounding at the Community Center's doors devolved to eerie scratching sounds, then to nothing, which was worse.

The monsters had stopped blindly thrashing with their tentacles and their scratchy-voiced screaming.

"Could they have left?" whispered Doris.

Their incredulity was apparent even in the darkness.

"No science-based defense this time?" McGlazer asked Bernard.

Bernard shook his head.

One of the high windows went black, filled by something from a bad Halloween acid trip.

"Good God. It's…a pumpkin…something…"

Timbo was quick to aim and fire, hitting a sickly eye. There was a burst of pulpy blood, then a cry of almost human agony. The thing quickly disappeared, leaving only the sounds of rain and lightning.

"Good shooting!" praised McGlazer.

"They must be too large to get in through those windows, maybe even the doors," noted Bernard.

"Maybe we can wait them out," wondered Timbo.

"But there's still the rest of the town," the mayor grimly added.

"How many can there—"

Timbo's question was cut short by the crashing of the flimsy pallet boards covering the windows above them as a six-inch-thick spider leg punched through. The boards fell across Kerwin's back, drawing a weird grunt.

"Are you o—?"

Six viney appendages flew in after the boards, moving as fast as the lightning that cracked at the same time. McGlazer and crew dashed to the opposite side to dodge the flailing killer cables. Timbo fell to his back as he aimed the rifle up at the newly broken window.

He got off a shot as another of the evil orange faces peered in, shrieking loudly enough to shatter nerves. The bullet missed, sparking the cinder-block edge of the window.

The quintet rolled and crawled back toward the middle, just beyond the reach of the vines on either side. "Dammit!" shouted McGlazer.

They huddled closer and closer, as the grappling root-ropes stretched to ensnare them. Awful orange faces filled the windows now, grimacing and grinning down at their prey, reducing the meager sodium lights of the parking lot to a dim suggestion.

"If they get any bigger, they'll be able to reach us," said Bernard.

"I don't think we'll have to worry about that." Pointing up at one of the demons with a trembling finger, the mayor spoke with more pessimism than anyone had ever heard from her.

It opened its mouth wide, squinting, as if in the pain of giving birth.

* * * *

"I should probably tell you now, dear boy," Violina began, patting Dennis's arm. "I know what you're trying to do with the sneaky, silly water scheme."

Dennis didn't react in even the minimal fashion he was allowed. He just stared ahead into the rainy road and drove, seething.

"That's why I'll let you have a little drink of your old favorite soon." She raised her flask in thumb and forefinger, shaking it a little to make it slosh. "Diamante's with a dash of magic motor-control potion!" She tucked it back into her cleavage. "A little something for both of us."

A crash of lightning startled her. "Ooh!" She tittered at herself. "That one got even me!"

She lowered her window a crack and listened to the thunder. "Something strange going on. Somewhere close."

She scanned the sky until lightning flashed again. "Behind us, wasn't it? My storm seems to sense a contingency."

She drew the flask. "Turn us around, and I'll give you a little sip."

Chapter 29

Anatomy of Despair

Settlement era

Bennington went to the tiny, wooden-barred window and tried to peer out. It was too high, even for a man of his height, to see much more than the roofs of the main street's other structures.

Turning to Jonas Cooke, stationed at a chair beside the door, he said "Can't you let me take her place? Poor Chloris doesn't deserve such abhorrent treatment."

"And you do, good sir?" Jonas lit his pipe. "Is that a confession?"

Bennington knew it was pointless to answer. "Tell me then, Jonas. Was Hezekiah's corpse there in my barn when you first searched? Or did you place it just before 'finding' it?"

Jonas approached without hiding his smugness. "Perhaps your false God will arrange your release, hmm?"

"Our God is the same." Bennington went to the window wall and sat on the floor. "How deeply is your father involved with Conal's scheme?"

"Don't speak of my father," warned Jonas.

"Only you then?"

"Best not to speak at all, perhaps." Jonas placed the candle lantern closer to the holding cell but well outside of Bennington's reach and settled in his seat.

* * * *

Chloris couldn't imagine trying to sleep like this, stooped in the pillory. But some time had passed, perhaps an hour, during which she had not been so aware of her predicament. The air had grown cooler, the blue-gray cast of the moon upon the ground, brighter.

Her agony, deeper.

After a lifetime of labor-caused aches and pains, Chloris had never hurt this much. Her back, wrists, ankles and neck all bore a dull burn she couldn't have imagined.

Relief was only a call—and a false confession—away. She shook her head violently, and instantly regretted it.

She wondered if she could somehow do herself in. Death seemed not like a terrifying plunge into the unknown but rather a sweet respite from the ever-increasing misery of her circumstances.

God forbade it—or so claimed the church.

Trying to conceive some method of suicide, if only as a distraction for now, Chloris suddenly had a sense that Death was already close. With its proximity came the sudden return of its inherent terror.

She would not betray Master Bennington. But she would call for Jonas and gladly accept his abuse if it forestalled this sudden certainty of imminent doom.

"Jonaaass!" she called, and again, louder.

* * * *

Bennington woke and stood from the floor, his joints crackling. For a moment, he was confused to find himself in this strange…

He was in the town jail, and it was his maid he heard, shouting as if the devil himself was upon her. His horror escalated when he recalled she was in the pillory

"Jonas!" he called. But the Cooke boy, whose father should have known was too deep a sleeper for night-watch duty, had his head back, dozing.

Chloris called again, more stridently than Bennington had ever heard.

He went to the wall of bars and used his own rumbling voice. "Ho!" Jonas popped up as if on a spring. "What is it!?"

"Chloris is calling for you!" said Bennington. "She's in danger!"

"This best not be some scheme of escape," warned Jonas, taking up his rifle. "My father and brothers are more vigilant than I."

* * * *

It was at Sloane's dry goods store, just behind her and to her right, that Death was, in the dark under the overhang.

"Come nowww, Jonas!" she screamed. Chloris could not see, hear or even smell anything unusual. She felt it. It was familiar, and terrible.

She was relieved to hear Bennington bellowing too. Soon the shopkeepers would rise and come to see. She had considered how much like a guillotine was this infernal device. Now it seemed like that exactly, a brace to hold her head still for removal. Chloris feared the curious would not arrive soon enough.

Sounds of movement from the jail eased her terror only a little. Jonas was coming, but in no hurry.

"Hush, woman!" he called. She did not obey.

His dirty boots appeared in her periphery, but reassurance did not accompany his appearance.

"Something's there!" She tried pointing to it.

"If you want release, you may start confessing." His voice carried groggy disdain. "Do you?"

"Yes. I will tell all."

"And all means what?"

A scraping of wood from Sloane's store sent her heart plunging into terror.

Jonas heard it too and spun fast. "Who's there?"

"Halloween in you?" asked the shadow in a raspy voice.

Jonas's rifle clashed with something heavy and fell away. Twisting her head to the point of near-unbearable pain, Chloris made out a silhouette against the dark blue sky.

An axe.

A fleshy thunk-crunch hinted to Chloris what had just happened. The two cloven halves of Jonas Cooke, falling messily to either side of her eye line, told her more.

"Yes!" said Everett Geelens. "There's Halloween!"

Voices rose from nearby. The townsfolk, finally starting to rouse.

The familiar, burlap-clad face nearly touched Chloris's. A groan of dismay came from behind it.

The axe rose again, then the sound of metal striking metal. A split second later, the chains closing the pillory fell to the ground.

Chloris pushed up the top board and fell to her knees, keeping her hands smashed against her eyes, certain the axe would fall on her next.

“Chloris!” called Bennington from his cell, the only other sound besides that of something heavy being dragged.

The moment of silence before shopkeeper John-David Sloane himself arrived seemed to Chloris longer than the hours she had spent in the pillory.

“Who’s making the disturbance h—?” Sloane’s complaint was cut short by his stunned shout.

Chloris finally opened her eyes.

His lamp held high, Sloane backed away from the corpse. But before the dark settled where the lamp had withdrawn, the dim candlelight revealed Everett’s handiwork: the two halves of Jonas Cooke, propped opposite each other on the bench, holding hands in some demented fraternal display.

Chapter 30

Cover My Eyes

Ten minutes later, anyone within earshot had thrown on a coat and made their way to the town square. Bennington continued to call out and demand to be freed. Given that the key to his cell was somewhere on one of the halves of Jonas Cooke, no one was making his release a priority.

John-David Sloane had covered Jonas's body halves with a horse blanket. It was instantly soaked through with blood.

The townsfolk gathered in a three-quarter circle around the pillory, staying well clear of the bloody, blanketed lump in front of Sloane's store. Someone had ridden hard to the Cooke house a mile away. Now they were riding back just as hard, with the Cooke men well in front.

"Someone come here and release me now!" Bennington called. Chloris felt guilty to be glad her master was going ignored by the muttering crowd. His integrity would dig graves for both of them.

Luckily, the clamor of Adonijah's horses drew their attention. The people crowded together to make room for the remaining Cookes, who rode their horses right up to Sloan's shop, hopping off the instant they stopped.

"What is that?" asked Adonijah, already teary-eyed.

"Jonas." Sloane gestured grimly toward his bench. When Adonijah lunged to pull the blanket away, Sloane seized him in a tight embrace. "It's better you don't, Adoni."

The patriarch pushed Sloane away and snatched hold of the blood-glossed horse blanket. He stopped himself from yanking it away at the last instant, instead drawing it carefully.

Cries of shock and horror emerged from everyone—except Adonijah. He stood as if frozen, holding the edge of the blanket in fingers going bone-white.

Conal O'Herlihy pushed through the cowering bystanders. "What is th…?"

With Conal suddenly shocked silent, clever Chloris saw her moment. She screamed, pointing at Conal's feet. "I saw them!"

Their silence was promising. "Those feet! Those are the shoes of the man who killed Jonas!" She pointed at where Conal had stood to threaten her, where his footprints remained.

Adonijah knelt to examine Conal's shoes.

"No! She's…" Conal didn't finish.

Elias lowered his lamp to the shoe print. "Have him to stand here, Father!"

Phineas and Rufus grabbed Conal's arms and dragged him to the print.

"Careful!" Chloris cried. "He has a knife!"

Phineas made a quick search of the folds of Conal's coat and found the bone knife Conal had taken from Schroeder—the one with which Conal had stabbed the corpse of Hezekiah Hardison. Rufus forced Conal's feet into the footprints.

"Conal came and threatened me to make me say my master was guilty!" Chloris continued. "When Jonas came to confront him, they fought. Conal took up the axe, and…" Her sobbing was both calculated and genuine.

Adonijah had glowered at Conal since her first exclamation. Now, satisfied by the paltry evidence, the elder Cooke snarled as he charged Conal. "I'll kill you here and now, bastard!"

The Cooke sons held the Irishman still to allow their father whatever vengeful act he wished.

"Adonijah Cooke, you listen to me!" From the jail, Bennington's thundering voice finally cut through the rising discord.

"Say your piece later, Bennington!" Adonijah took the bone knife from Phineas.

Conal's panicked pleading was silenced by Rufus's meaty hand, as he yanked the Celt's head back to expose his throat.

"Are we no longer men of law, Adoni?" Bennington shouted. "How will you serve this community and your Lord if you murder the man?"

Adonijah shook with rage. Everyone was silent for a terrible time. Then he released Conal. "Get Bennington out of that cell and put this filth in his stead."

As the boys shoved him toward the jail, Conal caught the eyes of a handful of his followers and gave a subtle nod. They all slipped away, as the citizens remained to share their shock.

* * * *

Modern day

The rains increased, the scarlet lightning flashed longer and brighter, the animalistic growl of thunder sounded deeper and louder as the vigil for Ysabella progressed.

Though there was some flinching among the chanters, no one broke contact or concentration. Bernard squeezed the hands of his wife and daughter as if they might float away, articulating the strange words with the same intent he applied to complex chemistry problems, remembering what he had learned—and said to McGlazer—about the power of ceremony and focus.

"Okkala Boro-Tah Cam-Ura Taaaaaahn!" Brinke's incantation was now a shout trumpeted to the heavens on the voice of one of its own warrior angels, insistent to the point of godliness.

"Okkala Boro-Tah Cam-Ura Tahn!" the chorus of well-witchers enjoined.

The sentience of Violina's storm grew as well, the thunder becoming angrier, more disturbingly alive in response to every repetition. The roars funneled to every ear as if from mere inches away—yet all eyes remained closed, all hands remained joined, all voices continued in perfect rhythm.

"I pass this piece of my life into you, Ysabella!" cried Brinke. "This piece of my essence!"

The others were unsure whether to repeat these words. They continued with the earlier words, their insistence, if not the same elements Brinke gave, moving and passing into the crone.

"I pass THIS PIECE of my BEING into Ysabella Escher! My queen mother! My Self!"

The storm's thunderous protest was wasted.

Ysabella rose from the bed and floated into the air on wings of Will, eyes, mouth and hands opening to unleash orbs of pure white light that warmed the faces of her attendants.

Brinke had anticipated the sudden power surge. As she was tossed from Ysabella, she grabbed Emera in a protective shell. The child giggled against her breast as they rolled onto the floor and away from the shaking bed, its sheets billowing as if from hurricane winds.

As the expulsion of light dimmed, Ysabella floated down to stand on the mattress, smiling at everyone around with joy and gratitude. Her eyes fell on Brinke and Emera.

"Oh, my beautiful girls!" she called "Thank you!"

* * * *

"Whoo!" said Violina. "'Tis a night not fit for man nor beast, aye, Kenny Killmore?"

Her use of Dennis's stage name was as infuriating as the kisses she kept giving his cheeks.

"We should see my little pumpkin pets soon. The ones that are going to eat your friends and family, I mean. Including your petite little punker girl."

She whirled toward him in a sudden flourish, with mock-imploring eyes. "Oh, Dennis! Could you? Would you...have me as your bride then?"

She giggled like a coyote and patted his groin. "Of course you would. But first, the inn. To see my old friend Ysabella. Should be fun, no?"

She drew the flask and raised it to Dennis's mouth. "Take a sip, lover."

He did, hating and loving the taste of alcohol spreading across his tongue.

"There we are." She lidded it and tucked it back in her cleavage. "If you need more, just reach right in and take it."

Dennis remained silent, knowing any threat would be meaningless without a physical will to enforce it. But he did not give up hope, even as he felt his arms turn the wheel to take the hearse into the Blue Moon Inn's parking lot.

"I want you to go up there to Ysabella's room and kill her," Violina said, thinking. "But I can't decide how...Any suggestions?"

Dennis could not resist. "I bet if you had me tear you limb from limb, she would just be heartbroken."

"That is good," Violina began. "But only half of it, really. Hey! What if I had you kill all of her little friends right in front of her!?"

Dennis now regretted his satisfying burst of sarcasm.

"Let's do that!" She opened the door and donned a raincoat over her robe, then popped up her umbrella. "Use this!" She handed him Matilda Saxon's athame.

Dennis didn't bother trying to swallow the rainwater this time, feeling more than a little foolish for ever thinking such a desperately contrived scheme would work in the first place.

Something told him Jill was up in that room, with Ysabella.

He tried to drop the knife, then to raise it to stab himself anywhere he could, preferably a vital organ or artery.

Violina sashayed into the lobby and rang the desk bell for service. "Should I do the talking, or…?"

Inn proprietor Lonnie Duckworth eventually appeared from the room behind the desk, his pristine blue oxford-cloth shirt wildly contrasting with his rumpled and stained, ill-fitting khakis.

"Hi, Lon," charmed Violina. "We're here to check on poor Ysabella."

"She's pretty sick, I think," Lonnie said. "You sure you want to risk catching it?"

"I'm just afraid she might not be around much longer," said Violina. "I…want to make sure I get my goodbyes out."

"Oh, yeah," Lonnie said. "Go on up."

"Call the sheriff," Dennis said.

"Huh?"

"Dennis has the worst sense of humor," Violina explained. "Now, Dennis, don't say another word to our host, naughty boy."

He didn't, because he couldn't. But he stared pure intention at Lonnie, who stared back in confusion.

"Come along, Dennis," Violina sang.

Dennis issued a strange grunt as he followed her to the elevator, further confusing the innkeeper.

Once inside, Ysabella raised a rebuking finger to his face. "You are testing the very limits of my patience, punk boy."

She glowered at him like a cruel mother, and he was helpless to fire back with his Johnny Rotten–style sneer.

"You just take that little knife out of your pocket, mister."

He did.

"Now. Let's see you get all emo. Jab yourself right in the tummy with it," she mocked. "Slowly."

Dennis pressed the point against his stomach, hoping the elevator would open before he could pierce his leather jacket, that someone would be there when it did, so she would be forced to make him stop.

Better yet, if only he could trick her into making him stab *her.*

Alas, the elevator opened onto an empty hallway gently washed with ambient lighting.

"You can speak now," she allowed. "Or cry. Whatever."

She said he "could," not "must." He stoically resisted doing either. The point of Matilda's athame finally pushed through the leather and pierced his lower stomach a half inch deep.

"All right, stop and pull it out, little boy." She waved him forward as she stepped from the elevator. "Save the real stabbing for…"

A door opened at the end of the carpeted hall…and out stepped his mother. "Dennis?"

"Ma!"

"Your mother? Oh, my dark gods, this simply could not be better!" Violina clasped her hands together like an excited child preparing to blow out a birthday candle. "Run down there and stab her in the heart. Be sure and look her in the eyes until she stops moving."

Dennis ran toward his mother, tears bursting from his eyes the way his stomach wound bled. "Run, Ma!" he shouted.

She stood there, perplexed. Bravo appeared, raising his ears in confusion at Dennis's strange behavior.

Dennis raised the knife high, just as his mother was pushed against the far wall.

By Jill. The drummer covered her boyfriend's mother, her petite back the only shield against the athame.

Someone else was at the door, with her hand extended toward Dennis. He stopped running so abruptly he pitched over Jill and Elaine like a triple-run hitter gunning for home. He landed directly on his face and lay still, bleeding from his nose into the patterned carpet.

Violina hadn't the breath for a gasp. She had stopped laughing as abruptly as Dennis had stopped running, and it made her choke.

Ysabella stood strong and fierce, just outside her door, wearing an expression of such rage her eyes physically glowed like fire, her hair blowing back from a sudden hot wind.

Brinke stepped out beside Ysabella, sporting a decade's worth of fresh crow's feet and a streak of gray in her hair that matched Candace's. "Go inside and rest, Ysabella. Let me deal with her."

"Together, Brinke." Ysabella grabbed her hand. "As we should have done from the start."

Stella emerged and took Brinke's other hand, but addressed Violina directly. "You should never have come to Ember Hollow, bitch."

Violina quickly got over her shock and regained her imperious smile. "How sweet! The crone, the matron, and…the hippy."

She clasped her hands together as if pleading. "I do hope you won't hit me with an expelliarmus!"

She swept her hands sideways, unleashing an arc of hurricane wind that peeled the wallpaper and knocked the women off their feet.

Bravo barked with rage.

Jill got Elaine back into the suite, grabbing Bravo by the collar as well.

Brinke recovered first, rising to a knee and extending her thumb and little finger. Twin beams of pink energy flowed as though from a high-pressure hose.

Violina blew like she was dousing a match, making the pink light disperse into harmless, quick-fading sparks.

Brinke stood and helped Ysabella to a stand, from which she continued forward, flying like a rocket with glowing hands outstretched.

"Des Irtix!" Violina shouted. The words turned to a black net that opened to entwine Ysabella. It burned away on contact, but Ysabella continued forward, her hands a battering ram to Violina's chest, knocking her back into the elevator doors.

Ysabella, momentarily spent, fell to her hands and knees with a grunt.

Stella glanced into the suite to check on her frightened little girls, relieved to see Leticia dragging them away from the door.

"Think iceberg!" Brinke shouted, as she grabbed Stella's hand.

A starburst of blue light sailed over Ysabella and fell on Violina like a boulder, spreading across her body. As the glow died, ice remained, trapping Violina, the momentum knocking the frozen witch statue onto her back.

Ysabella struggled to her feet and stumbled toward the other witches. "It's not enough! We three must…!"

A tinkling sound told them Violina had already broken free. She rose like a catapult, her left hand extended and cupped. A violet bubble grew and flew from it, enveloping Ysabella.

Brinke and Stella watched in horror as the energy blister began to close in on the elder witch like shrink-wrap. Ysabella's scream was silent within the vesicle, but her pain and terror were plain for all to see.

The bubble trap crushed in on the old woman at alarming speed.

Brinke knew how this spell worked, knew that Ysabella would soon be a basketball-sized bag of crushed flesh. "Stop it, damn you, Violina!"

"Why, of course!" said Violina. "Just relinquish your magic energy to me, and I'll let her hobble back to bed."

"What is she talking about?" asked Stella.

"There's a spell of transference," Brinke said in a defeated voice. "I used it to revive Ysabella."

"You too, my fledgling friend," Violina said to Stella. "You will repeat her chant and grant me your powers…such as they are."

Stella glanced toward the little girls and saw they were huddled with the terrified Leticia against the bedroom's far wall. "All right."

Violina stopped the bubble's shrinking by turning her cupped hand sideways. "Begin."

Brinke wept as she did. "Crotus Keemay Kah…"

Stella regretfully repeated.

"Sunoo Gemma Kah…"

Stella felt a pull, a draining from her solar plexus, like a powerful vacuum hose was pressed to it. "Sunoo Gemma…"

"'Scuse me." She was shoved to the side.

Dennis stood beside her, his chin and shirtfront drenched in blood from his broken nose. In his right hand was Matlida Saxon's athame, held aloft.

Dennis slung his arm like a baseball pitcher. The athame appeared in Violina's throat. As if by magic.

Stella stared at him in astonishment.

"I took a mail order ninja course when I was Stuart's age," he said, sounding congested.

Violina grabbed the handle of the athame and began reciting an incantation, which came out as mere lip movement. This quickly trailed off as the baneful witch toppled face-forward, plunging the knife point through the back of her own neck as she landed face-first.

The bubble around Ysabella dissolved to a fine mist. She gulped fresh, glorious air. Dennis went to her, offering a helping hand. "I ain't trying to be no nick-of-time cowboy here," he said, "but I owed that bitch."

He took a black bandana from his pocket and wiped his bloody nose and chin. "Besides, you ladies are gonna need all the magic you got for our real problem."

Jill blindsided him, driving him against the wall as she laid a kiss on him that seemed shockingly violent to the onlookers. Their age of celibacy was quickly coming to an end.

Chapter 31

Walk Among Us

Trapped at dead center of the Community Center's gym floor, Reverend McGlazer, the Stuyvesant siblings, Bernard Riesling and Timbo formed a tight circle facing out. Timbo chambered another round in his rifle but held off from shooting, considering the ratio of bullets to assailants.

The pumpkin goblin at the window just above them opened its mouth so wide its unsettlingly human teeth began to space out from one another. It squeezed its eyes shut in a sick farce of human pain—and vomited.

Reflexively, the survivors stepped back from the yellowish splash of pungent water and pulp. Kerwin's grunt reminded them that there were tentacles waiting for them if they fell within reach.

Then came another stream of pumpkin puke. Then another. The goddamned squash monsters were trying to hurl on them for some reason. Timbo raised his rifle, gratified to see the wretched, retching horrors quickly duck out of range.

"Oh, God," Mayor Stuyvesant whispered. "No..." She clutched her brother by the sleeves.

The first puke puddle was...doing something.

The seeds clumped amid the pools went into a hyper-fast growth stage, expanding to small mottled green spheres, then yellow ovoids, quickly darkening to orange as they swelled.

"They barfed up babies or something!" Stuart exclaimed, nearly running backward from the weight-room window.

Pockets set off a choir of frightened whining.

"Oh, man…" DeShaun saw for himself, and instantly regretted, for the kids' sake, the defeated tone in his voice. "I mean…um, this might take some…wait!"

"What!?"

"In your backpack. The…"

"Atomic Corndog!" Stuart interrupted. "Hells, yeah!"

DeShaun knelt and grabbed Pockets by the shoulders. "Listen, buddy. There's a job you gotta do, okay?"

Pockets shook his head vigorously. "No!"

"Everybody's depending on you!"

Pockets started bawling as he nodded his affirmative, regretting that he was rising to the occasion.

* * * *

"What about your friend?" Ophelia asked Pedro, as he pulled up in front of the sheriff's office.

Wrapped in a blanket, Deputy Yoshida lay in a cramped heap in the back of Pedro's Honda, while Ophelia and her mother sat crunched together in the passenger seat.

"Keep it down. It's been a while since he had some decent shut-eye."

Thunder sounded. Pedro glanced back at Yoshida, both relieved and concerned that the crash did not wake him. "Come on, ladies. Let's get you inside."

"Will you stay with us?" Ophelia asked.

Pedro saw the memory image of the girl's father, lying broken and dead in their living room. He realized she probably didn't even know what had happened to him—or wasn't facing it. "I'll catch up with you in a little while," he answered.

Pedro wrestled Yoshida onto his broad shoulders and ran though the rain with Ophelia and her mother to the station-house door, where they were met by Hudson and Deputy Astin, both lugging boxes of ammo. Military-grade guns were strapped across their backs.

"Petey!" Hudson said. "Am I glad to see you. Is Yoshi okay?"

"He's done his fair share for the night."

"All right, then. Get these girls and that sexy sack of Kobe beef back there safe in a cell and come with us."

As Pedro started toward the holding area, Astin stopped him. "Thought you might want to reunite with your old friend."

Pedro had not seen his scarred ten-gauge in a year.

* * * *

"Okay, Pocky." DeShaun death-gripped the weight room's decades-old push broom and set it like a hockey stick. "On three, you open, we're out, you close it. I'm on defense, Stuart bolts next door to get that backpack, we scram straight back. You open and close it fast."

Stuart took up a runner's starting position a few feet back. "If one of 'em gets in…" The other kids raised five-pound plates, dumbbells and short bars. "Right."

"One…"

Pockets clasped the weight-room doorknob in both little hands.

"Two…"

He swallowed such a deep breath it made his eyes open silver-dollar wide.

"Three!"

Pockets screamed like Debbie Rochon as he jerked the door open. DeShaun went first, with Stuart barely out before Pockets slammed the door behind him.

DeShaun ran to the nearest cluster of baby pumpkins and bulldozed them with the broom, sending a half dozen sliding across the floor.

Stuart jumped over one and hit the office door in one motion, calling, "Behind you!" to DeShaun.

"Got it!" said the other boy, as he sideswiped the creature with a golf swing that sent it into the wall—and into pieces.

Stuart was out the office door with the backpack. "Aaaaagh!" he cried, as he fell to his back to avoid the leaping arc of a screeching squash.

DeShaun intercepted it in a perfectly timed smack with the wooden side of the broom head.

Red blood and white seeds splashed across the weight-room door. Hearing Pockets's muffled squeal, the boys hoped he hadn't abandoned his post.

DeShaun helped Stuart up and shoved him toward the door. Pockets was as good as gold, swinging it open as he called, "Hurry up, you guys!"

DeShaun dove in, breaking his fall on Stuart's back.

More panicked cries rose from the children. DeShaun and Stuart turned to see one of the basketball-sized monsters halfway in the door, its vines flogging at little feet. Pockets pushed the door against it but froze when two vines, then a third, wrapped around his leg.

"You know what to do, Pockets!" DeShaun yelled.

Pockets looked at DeShaun and, in that microsecond, went from terrified to determined. He took a step back with his free leg and thrust it into the door with all the power his fifty-pound frame could muster. The would-be invader was reduced to mush.

"Good job!" praised the big boys. "You're a hero!"

Pockets stared at the dead strand around his leg. Stuart yanked it off and tossed it behind him with as much nonchalance as he could muster. "This time, everybody's gonna hafta soldier up."

Chapter 32

Children of the Damned

The vomited seeds grew to normal-sized pumpkins in less than two seconds.

Realizing what was happening, Timbo quickly loaded and raised his rifle—then screamed to wake the dead, as a volleyball-sized assailant leaped ten feet and clamped onto his shin with its jagged baby teeth.

Kerwin yanked the rifle out of his hands and swatted the thing away with the butt.

Before Timbo could thank him, another had jumped onto his back and wrapped a thorny clothesline-vine around his throat.

Mayor Stuyvesant, a soccer forward in college, caught an incoming monster with a powerful punt that sent it into the wall, where it burst apart in a gory explosion.

Bernard swung a pallet board, hoping to catch his attacker with the same athletic timing and finesse as the mayor. He missed.

The thing bit into his forearm and quickly wound its tendrils around his wrist. The engineer stumbled backward, bumping into McGlazer and knocking him into the waiting, writhing tangles of an adult demon.

It hauled him up to the window with dizzying speed. McGlazer braced himself on either side of the window frame with his feet, immediately feeling his thighs and hamstrings tingle from the stress of fighting the pumpkin thing's strength. Soon, his legs would fail, and he would be raggedly ripped in at least two pieces, starting from the groin.

The creature's face appeared in the window—and McGlazer realized, with blooming despair, that he recognized it.

Below, Kerwin crashed to his back—atop a newborn monster—as he caught the next attacker in both hands, just inches from his face. Despite his peril, he felt both disgusted and gratified that he had crushed one of its siblings underneath with his fall.

Thin vines circled his arms, then wound around his throat, generating leverage that brought those awful little square teeth ever closer to his face. Kerwin jutted his false chin up like Stallone, allowing the little monster to bite into it harmlessly. As it applied pressure with its teeth, he did so with his hands. Terrified surprise crossed its face just before Kerwin crushed it into bloody pie filling.

Pain exploded at his ear as a newborn nightmare bit into it—and tore it off.

His sister, the mayor, lined up another big kick right into the thing's mouth, but this more-mature fiend had faster reflexes. It snapped down on her toes with perfect timing, piercing Doris's shoes, bringing instant, exquisite agony.

Kerwin rolled behind her to break her fall, coming within grasping range of one of the adult horrors' flailing tendrils. He wished for a scream to mourn his leg, as the vine squeezed into it like thin twine wrapping sausage.

The fearsome face that McGlazer knew from his tortured inner vision projected centuries-old scorn at him, as its tiniest strands entwined his head and stabbed into his temples. McGlazer shrieked in an agonized falsetto.

"Silence," said the familiar invading voice, that of Conal O'Herlihy.

McGlazer could not quiet his own anguish, yet he heard Conal above it, nonetheless.

"Within you again, I am!" mocked the sinister Celt. "This time, I have no need to share your body, preacher." The steel-cable vines pulled McGlazer nearer the window. "So I will simply shred it to bits."

The weight-room door burst open just ahead of a high-pitched war cry. DeShaun held a lighter to the end of the thick, gray mega-sparkler the boys affectionately referred to as the Atomic Corndog.

With the stamping of little sneakers, a horde of yelling children swarmed through the door, each wielding a bar or dumbbell or plate, cylinders and circles of heavy metal.

"Remember, you guys!" DeShaun said, as the sparkler burst into cascading flashes. "Don't look at it!"

"Now go make the biggest mess ever!" added Stuart.

The army of evil orange gourds dispersed, clearing away from the brightness that blinded them.

Pockets was just strong enough to swing the four-foot curl bar he held, scoring a hit with his first at-bat that shattered his blinded demonic target into many disgusting pieces.

The other children, finding fun where there had just been fear, followed suit, smashing pumpkins with relish and aplomb. Stuart brought up the rear with the push broom. He slid it into the scrambling pumpkin babies, robbing them of leverage to leap away. Their little vine legs intertwined the broom handle as they accumulated against the advancing bristles.

Stuart gained speed as he deftly swept them toward the foot of the stage. Then a mighty final push sent most to abrupt and messy deaths. A few of the goblins escaped, rolling and sliding in all directions.

The children grew bolder, descending on the disoriented demons, stomping and squashing them as they essayed high-pitched war cries.

Conal's giant orange face, bleached white by the mega-sparkler's blaze even at this height, twisted into a furious grimace.

He dropped McGlazer like a bag of trash.

The minister hit the hardwood floor with a sick thud, landing mostly on his hands and knees. The former stung, and the latter radiated more dull pain than McGlazer thought possible. But experience told him he would be all right and ready to rejoin the battle in a few minutes.

Conal lashed his longest tentacles at the kids who were destroying *his* kids.

DeShaun rushed in front of the children protectively, waving the mega-sparkler to ward off Conal's grasping tendrils.

Freshly promoted General Pockets and a pair of his new soldiers skirted around DeShaun to destroy the blinded baby pumpkins.

Stuart yelled like a berserker as he ran to Kerwin's aid, slamming the sharp corner of his push broom onto the vine that constricted his brother's ex-manager's leg. The vine splintered and went limp.

Stuart helped Kerwin to his feet.

* * * *

Once they got Jill and Dennis pealed apart—a group effort—Ysabella marshaled her troops for a brainstorming session. She needed a large space that was sheltered, yet open, with a roof but no walls. There was a circle to be drawn, using salt and chalk, and it had to be safe from the supernatural torrent Violina had raised.

Dennis broke the news about Maisie. For a moment, it seemed that Ysabella's rejuvenation was nearly reversed. Brinke had to help her to the bed, where they sat together. Ysabella gripped Stella's wrist and closed her eyes to dam tears. "Poor, poor wonderful Maisie."

They were soon joined by Brinke, who laid her long arms across their shoulders. "She'll come to us in time."

The three of them sat and wept together for little more than a minute, which was more than they could spare.

Ysabella had a job for Dennis and Bernard. "You know where Violina cast her sigil?"

"Yeah," Dennis said grimly. "Right around Bennington's stone."

"I need you to go there and erase it."

"We're on it."

Turning to Stella, Ysabella took her hand and held it like a sister. "I want Candace to go with us, but there is some danger."

It had been little more than a whisper, yet Candace heard. She went quickly to them, eyes imploring. "Yes. I have to go, Mom. The town needs me."

Stella swelled with admiration for the little girl and realized how valuable her courage and strength would be. "You will stay right by my side every instant!"

Finally, Ysabella turned to Leticia and Elaine, who would remain there with Emera and Wanda. She gave them very specific instructions.

Emera was set to protest vociferously, until Candace told her that Bravo would stay with her.

Then the witches piled into Stella's car to head to the Grand Illusion Cinemas.

* * * *

Settlement era

The house where the nice big man and strong lady let Everett rest had been warm and comfortable. Better than any of the little shacks where his parents made him live. Better even, than his very own bedroom in the big house, from when he was a little boy, before the priests.

The scarecrow clothes made for a great costume, but they were itchy and dirty and not very warm. Everett knew someone in the odd little town had to have something better. Now that they were all out admiring the wonderful decoration he'd made, he could go into their houses and get warm and find stuff to eat.

Peering in the window of Marion Stansler's house, Everett saw a nice fire burning in the fireplace.

Corn was growing in the field behind the house. Everett went to gather a few ears. When he came back, he found something very nice, hanging on a nail on the back of the warm little house.

It was so shiny at the top. It was like a bird with a long beak that pointed back to the town, where all the people were surely marveling over the man-in-half display he had made.

The handled scythe, many times larger than the hand sickle he used when he first got to this funny little place, called to mind another of his favorite Halloween figures—the Grim Reaper.

Everett laughed, and even checked above his head to see if a light bulb had appeared there, like in cartoons, because he had had a good idea.

He went in the horsey barn, where people always kept nice blankets for their animals for the cold days that came not long after Halloween. Sure enough, there was a nice big brown one lying across the gate that kept the horse inside. The horse on the other side of it scooted and scooted until it was against the wall, far away from Everett, but that was okay. He would bring it an apple later, or some fingers, and see if it would be his friend.

Everett found some rope, too, and used it to tie the blanket around his waist and his neck to make a hood. Then he picked up the scythe and studied his moon-cast shadow. It was just like the Reaper!

Wait. He needed more. No one had face paint or decent plastic masks around here, but that was okay. Everett was a big boy. It was time to move on from kid costumes.

Everett thought of the witch and the motorcycle people from the last Halloween, and how he made masks out of their faces, but the best part was the skull part, under the skin.

Everett had a skull too. But his face was in the way.

Everett went inside Marion Stansler's house with his ears of corn and his new costume. There, he found a really nice knife to help him with both.

Chapter 33

You Always Stand In My Way

Adonijah Cooke stood facing Conal, now behind the skinned-maple bars of the town jail, as though his candlelit glower could bypass Judgment and send the Irishman plummeting into hell.

"Adoni, why don't you leave this to me?" Bennington stepped between Cooke and the cell, placing loving hands on his friend's shoulders. "Go and mourn your boy. When you're ready to bury him, I'll pay for the box."

"This scoundrel would just as soon have seen you hang, Bennington," said the grieving father.

"Yes. We cannot let ourselves descend to such a state."

Adonijah finally turned and shuffled out, followed by his devastated sons.

"It wasn't me who…killed Jonas, Bennington," hissed O'Herlihy. "Your old house whore lied."

"Guilty of this murder or not, your sins have found you out, Conal."

Bennington checked that the door of the jailhouse was closed tight, then slid the flimsy chair, last occupied by Jonas, against it. "Just count yourself lucky you're locked in here now."

"You know the killer?"

"I only know there are worse men than even you loose in the world, Conal."

Conal opened his mouth to boast of just how much worse he could—and would—get, but stopped himself.

* * * *

Two full cups of his own corn whiskey had become a nightly habit for Schroeder, the only thing to silence his increasingly troubled mind as the settlement's turmoil filled his thoughts.

For the last week, he had been preparing a special batch, though he was certain he could never gain the courage to distribute it.

Even so, when he heard the knock, he sat up so fast his addled mind swam.

"Good heavens!" said his wife, Olga. "Between you and the door, I might have died of fright."

"Hush, Olga!" Schroeder tossed off the quilts and reached for his rifle.

"You hush yourself. It's only your…'customers.'"

It was unlikely to be anything so mundane.

The floor's cold planks against Schroeder's bare feet made him curse, fully waking him from the nightmare image of Hezekiah Hardison—first hanging in his field like a crucified corn god, and then lying pale and bloated as he and Conal rolled his corpse in the oilcloth.

He skimmed a mental list of all possible visitors, the first space on this list occupied by a black question mark for the unknown killer-on-the-loose.

The knock had come from Gregor Tiernan at the door, with Theodore Blaisdell mounted on a restless mare behind him. "We need you, Friedrich. Conal needs you!"

"Conal? What has…?"

"Bennington and his fellows have moved to blame Conal for murder," said Gregor.

"Jonas Cooke!" shouted Theodore. "Cloven in twain!"

"He's in the jail now, Conal is," Gregor explained. "We're gathering in the secret hall."

"We go now!" Theodore yelled.

Schroeder turned and peered into the darkness of his house to buy a moment of thought. "Move on to the next man, and I'll be on your trail," he said. "I'll bring something useful."

* * * *

Schroeder's mother had been born with a caul, a sign of clairvoyance.

She had never spoken of it, until the day Friedrich told her he was leaving for the new world. Then she wept with despair, telling him Sensenmann would follow him there.

Schroeder's horse was small and old. With the dark seeming to slowly enclose him like a crushing chrysalis, Schroeder was tempted to push the nag to hurry, fearing that moving too slowly would make him a tempting target to whom or whatever (Sensenmann) was doing all the killing.

He had been dismissive of his mother's reaction, right up until this very moment when dissension was coming to a head, the leaves were dropping like frogs upon Egypt in the book of Exodus and a very real Angel of Death was creeping among them.

The night ahead bore a weight of fatefulness that made him regret leaving Holland, of ever even meeting with the ambitious Anglos who had mapped this leaf-covered corner of hell.

Yet turning back to his settlement home was no more an option than turning back to Europe.

Olga would be up worrying very late this night, and a good many after.

* * * *

Modern day

With Dennis and Bernard drawing the few pumpkin demons that hadn't made their way to the Community Center, the witches' drive to the theater was uneventful.

"I'd hoped for something open all around," Ysabella said, "but we'll make this work."

The Grand Illusion Cinemas was Ember Hollow's most recognizable landmark other than Saint Saturn Unitarian and had been its most popular social spot—before Dennis almost died falling from the top of the marquee.

Supported by a pair of thick cement columns, it projected out over the ticket-queue area and main structure about fourteen feet. Except for the glass-face front and doors, it was all clear, open space.

A crashing sound and a nerve-splintering shriek, only a couple of streets over, startled the newly-extended coven. At least one of the pumpkin monsters was close.

"Let's get to work." The women went about drawing a circle with chalk, spreading salt evenly outside the perimeter. Stella listened to the invocations the witches spoke and repeated them. Candace joined in as well, falling easily into the role of white witch as if she had done it all her life. The look she gave Stella, the search for guidance, told the adoptive mother it was her commitment giving Candace courage and confidence.

Chapter 34

Back to the Cemetery

"This thing could use a cowcatcher right now," noted Bernard, as Dennis veered the hearse toward a tractor-sized orange ogre that was advancing toward them on a dozen thin multi-jointed legs.

"Like that truck in *Jeepers Creepers*?"

The hearse bashed into the crawler doing forty, hurling it thirty feet into a sidewalk planter, where it broke apart on the red-brick corners.

"Careful." Bernard lowered the forearm he had reflexively raised when Dennis accelerated toward the miscreation. "*Jeepers Creepers*. Is that the one with the pervy gargoyle?"

"Yep." Dennis stopped at the intersection.

"You and I could slap one on this baby in a single afternoon," Bernard noted.

Dennis raised an eyebrow and nodded. "Might look pretty badass."

The hearse shook with the boom of something landing hard on its roof.

"Aaah, cripes!" exclaimed Bernard.

A firehose-thick scorpion's leg bashed the windshield, cracking a spiderweb network of white lines right in Dennis's line of sight.

"Dammit!" Dennis swerved. "Get off my car, you big tick!"

"Watch out!" Bernard's side of the windshield was mostly clear. He was able to see the light pole coming at them with terrifying velocity.

Dennis braked, hoping to throw the thing into the pole. But it stayed in place, bashing at every window with its claws.

"How are you gonna...?" Bernard didn't finish his question. Dennis ducked to see under the breakage and gunned it. Seeing that he was torpedoing toward the church drive's iron fence like a bullet, Bernard raised both forearms this time.

The hearse crashed into the black gates with a roar to match the hitchhiking demon's. Dennis, having wrecked a few times before, knew to lean right so his head wouldn't hit the wheel.

There was a split second of relative silence. Then Bernard screeched like a monkey.

Dennis popped up, "What!?"

Bernard took a deep breath of relief. "When your head hit my lap, I thought it was…no longer attached."

Their horrific hijacker recovered as well and shrieked its rage.

The rear window cascaded inward. Then Bernard's.

Now it was Bernard's turn to crowd into Dennis's side. The windshield caved in as a single piece, covering the pair like a blanket.

A shout, in a familiar voice, said, "Get down as much as you can!"

Dennis pushed Bernard's head down and lay over him.

Staccato gunfire punched the air, plunking pumpkin flesh. The stalks withdrew, then the hearse rose six inches as the abomination leaped off with an enraged roar.

"Come on!" Dennis dragged Bernard toward him as he opened his door.

* * * *

"Good boy!" Elaine told Bravo.

The dog had posted himself at the door as always, his tail held high. It was clear that the thunder frightened him, but duty called. His pleasant-smelling charges came first.

Per Ysabella's instructions, the little girls were given lots of paper and colored markers from Brinke's bag—a step up from crayons for the smaller girl. "Girls, can you draw me a picture of a storm, like this one over the sky of our town?" Leticia asked.

The little ones quickly set to work, losing their fear of the storm as they drew. As Emera raised a red pen, Elaine stopped her. "Hey, I have an idea! Let's make the lightning green, like pretty trees!"

"Okay!"

* * * *

As the latest and loudest burst of thunder boomed, Elaine turned to Leticia. “I’m sorry I was ever angry with you about leaving. You certainly can’t be blamed.”

Leticia smiled at her friend. “Don’t think I’m gonna give up on trying to get you to come too.”

“Wook!” Wanda raised her and Emera’s latest drawing, completed in minutes. It depicted the Green Man on Emera’s bracelet, smiling placidly as he blocked red lightning with one hand and projected green lightning with the other.

The mothers stared at each in astonishment. “That’s...brilliant.”

* * * *

Conal, the pumpkin demon, forced his giant face into the window frame and opened his jagged-toothed maw with a cry of rage. He blasted another stream of pumpkin-seeded placenta onto the gymnasium floor, dispensing hundreds of his horrific offspring.

Much of the mess landed on McGlazer’s back, shocking him out of his pain trance. The spores spread instantly and wound their tiny twine vines around his face and neck before they were even out of their shells, drawing lines of blood and trails of pain.

McGlazer dug his fingernails into his own flesh to gain purchase under the wire razors, breaking them apart at the expense of deep gashes in his fingers.

“How much longer on the corndog!?” Stuart shouted.

“Half!”

Three full-grown pumpkins reappeared at the high windows and reached in again. Their vines, having grown longer from the mystical rainwater, brushed against the embattled Community Center occupants now.

Soon their prey would be within easy reach to strangle and drag across the broken glass of the window frames, to consume or simply dismember as they saw fit.

The rain suddenly ceased.

Chapter 35

Hellstreet

With its mother dead, the red-lit storm quieted quickly under the influence of Ysabella and her apprentices.

The bright red flashes softened to a rather mute pink, the thunderclaps to subdued grumbles.

But the oddball cadence of vine-tacles and tree-limb spider legs making their way over and through Main Street's structures only grew louder.

The witches, old and young, kept their eyes closed as they spun leftward and repeated Ysabella's passionate words, having fallen in sync with her long before a reasonable learning curve.

The witch queen stopped mid-spin, unaffected by the law of momentum. Without opening their eyes, Brinke, Stella and Candace followed suit a split second later, all facing toward the Community Center.

The first leering, fiendish face, peering down from the roof of the now-closed sporting-goods shop, put a serious dent in their collective resolve and courage. Stella felt Candace grip her hand harder.

When it roared down at them, yellowy saliva spraying from its unnatural maw, a withering wave coursed through the coven. Ysabella's power and determination quickly brought everyone back.

She began to turn again, in the opposite direction. "Spirits! Bring down the rain!" they all intoned. "Reverse the tide of infection! Halt the impetus of evil!"

The sky began to rumble again, sounding less like invasion, more like cleansing.

The horror on the roof leaped to the ground and charged, only to be bounced back violently by the invisible wall of the magic circle.

Gaelic flowed seamlessly into Greek, then Chinese, then Arabic, the feminine chorus a perfect harmony of goddess-mother intention, with no hesitation or lag time from one woman to the next, child or crone.

A half dozen more orange goblins appeared, all eager to test the circle, all quick to learn their lesson.

Clouds that had just separated and dispersed now rejoined. Flashing within was a vital bright green.

Now smaller pumpkins, soulless children of the original horde, began to appear and crawl toward the circle, threatening, but for the moment harmless.

"Strike down the pestilence!" said Ysabella/Candace/Stella/Brinke.

The first strike turned the autumn night to a brief green day.

The living pumpkins skittered back, but quickly regrouped, congregating and mingling in a way that suggested a hive-mind.

* * * *

The pumpkin things swarming around the witches' circle numbered well into the dozens. Ranging in size from normal to the diameter of a delivery truck, the Halloween hellions crawled between and over one another to get to the border. But they could not cross.

They voiced their frustration with crusty croaks that scratched at the witches' ears like broken glass.

Candace understood why Ysabella had suggested it be her hand that Candace held as they performed the ritual. Her mom, Stella, was as brave they came, but as a novice witch, she was probably trembling hard enough to shake teeth loose by now.

Ysabella's hand was soft, strong, loving, determined and unwavering. The predatory shrieking and scrabbling taking place just a few yards away was impossible to ignore. But thanks to the crone, it was manageable for Candace.

Ysabella thrust her hands out in a command to stop.

The brisk, chaotic winds that blew from the south as part of Violina's maelstrom went dead still, like a wall of thickened air.

In this quiet, the song of the witches was distinct, its harmony both soothing and enervating.

Distracted by this sudden shift, the demonic pumpkins went still.

Ysabella began a new chant. As before, all the enchantresses joined without hesitation.

By the third repetition, a new wind, steady and smooth, began to blow from the north. It smelled like a clean mountain stream.

The monsters raised a collective roar of rage, jostling one another as they surged against the invisible barrier of the circle.

Behind the witches, the theater's entry doors exploded. Vein-severing shards rocketed at the witches. The spell had not accounted for the intrusion of such a mundane material.

Candace felt the glass missiles punch into her back and legs like a coordinated hornet attack.

Flying fragments cut across the chalk and salt, opening the circle. Demonic, demented faces bobbed from the shattered doors.

Stella eyed the crone with defeated horror. "They came through the th—"

"Do not stop the chant!" Ysabella called, to Stella and everyone, as she turned her diminutive body to face the cinema entrance. She directed her hands at the demons and issued an incantation that blew the monster mob back into the building.

It took a second before the women fell back into their rhythm. With the circle broken, they spoke now with less assurance. Brinke gasped at seeing one of the things doing its best to wipe away a section of the salt and chalk to create a weakness.

"Broma Hasha!" she exclaimed. The invading tentacle burst into sparks like a fuse that traveled back toward the pumpkin demon. Squalling, it dashed its tendril on the ground, trying to extinguish it before it traveled to the thing's misshapen body.

It was unsuccessful. The thing became essentially an enormous smoke bomb, fizzing away to nothingness the same way Everett Geelens had when Matilda Saxon's powdery mix met his skin. Lacking the time to designate a destination for the unwilling time traveler, Brinke could only hope it emerged into the ocean or desert, somewhere it could not hurt anyone.

It was not the best spell for the job. She had panicked. The execution was taxing for someone who had just given up twenty years of her life less than an hour earlier. Brinke dropped painfully to her knees, her head spinning.

Yet she did not stop chanting.

From the right of the circle, one of the monsters ejected a stream of seeds and hate. It passed over the circle but immediately steamed away to nothingness.

Ysabella leaned down to Candace. "Imagine the strongest, most powerful and loudest lightning you can!" she commanded. "Not red but green."

Ysabella patted the girl on the head and returned to the chant.

Candace whispered, pointing at the nearest of the demons. "That one!"

The fierce green streak fell with a deafening crack, blasting the creature to bloody pieces.

The other monsters recoiled from the ruins of their comrade.

Candace pointed at one that was opening its mouth to try to vomit over the circle.

It was disintegrated in an instant.

The other witches placed hands on Candace to transfer courage and power.

Lightning bolts fell like the rain itself, vaporizing the assailants every split second, then several at a time.

They scuttled away like frightened crabs but could not avoid the focused imagination of the little girls and their adult batteries.

* * * *

Settlement era

Gregor and Theodore quietly maneuvered their horses in the forest far from the main street, careful not to alert the already-addled townies.

Conal had gone over the procedures for this eventuality carefully and frequently, hammering home every detail for his loyal followers. The plan was to ride around the back of the hill at the end of town and come up behind Conal's house for secrecy. They would use the secret entrance into Conal's underground chamber, make preparations, then begin the tactical assault that would place the town under their control, killing Bennington and his loyalists along the way.

They had not expected to have to break their leader out of jail, but the Celt had them well prepared. It was only a minor contingency.

The three candles that were their signal burned low up on the hill, discernible only to anyone searching for their glow. Seeing it, Gregor and Theodore exchanged a nod of determination.

Theodore, riding in front, had just turned to face forward when his horse stopped dead in its tracks so abruptly, Gregor's steed ran into it.

"Ho!" Theodore whispered harshly, whipping the beast across the neck with the reins. "Move along, girl."

Gregor's horse tensed as well, backing up until its hindquarters met a hickory.

"What's the matter with these godforsaken—"

Theodore's complaint was severed by the crashing patter of footfalls—someone coming toward them, fast.

Theodore reached for the weapon on his saddle. His horse threw him, before he could grab it, and bolted away at full gallop, leaving the dazed rider on his back.

Gregor's horse was clearly of the same mind. Gregor hopped off and threw its tether around a sapling, then went to help Theodore.

"I heard someone," whispered Theodore.

"Some…one?"

"One pair of feet only."

Then it emerged into the moonlight, its black robes flowing, its sickle arcing back and forth, its gleaming white-and-scarlet face reflecting moonlight at the men like some cursed mirror.

The Death Angel.

"God!" Gregor tried to help his friend to his feet, right up until the instant the long blade sunk into his torso.

As he fell to his knees, the Reaper wrenched the blade free, shouting "Tricks and treats!"

Blood pumped onto Theodore's face, into his eyes. It was like a splash of cold water, shocking him awake.

Everett arced the harvesting blade into Gregor's side.

Theodore sat up, ignoring the pain of his fall, and ran toward the low signal light, as he heard the meaty *thunk* of the third and final cut for Gregor—the one that removed his head.

Chapter 36

Dream Forever

As he stopped his horse alongside the two dozen or so others already tied to the trees behind Conal's home, Friedrich Schroeder briefly considered turning around and going home. That was before he saw Beaufort Grandy step out from behind his horse. "Have you checked your horse's shoes, Friedrich?" he asked.

"Yes," Schroeder lied, as he eased off his horse and patted it.

"Come tomorrow," the blacksmith said, "you'll likely have a good spare mount or two."

Schroeder grimaced at the remark's implication—that men would die tonight and leave behind spoils.

"Shall I check your weapon?" asked the blacksmith.

"I haven't loaded it yet."

"We're to be loaded and ready every minute," Grandy rebuked. "Conal made it plain."

"Yes, I…it's been such a hectic night. I was lazy."

"Let's have it, then." Grandy held out his hand. "I'll make it ready."

Schroeder went to his saddle, as if he expected to find his matchlock pistol tucked into it. "God help me. I've forgotten it."

"Good God." Grandy was disappointed but did not seem suspicious. He pointed at the wagon hitched to Schroeder's horse. "Well, what did you remember?"

"It's…wine. For preparation and celebration."

"You think we'll go on the attack with a headful of fire?" Now Grandy seemed suspicious.

"No, but…I'll just need a small measure first." He held out his hands, making them shake. "To steady my nerves. Thought others might need the same."

Grandy cocked his head to regard Schroeder, appearing ruthlessly judgmental. "Let's tote it in then."

* * * *

Kemlin Farrady immediately came to meet Schroeder and Grandy as they carried in the crates of booze. "What useless clutter do you bring us, Friedrich?"

Farrady whipped away the cloth covering and glowered at the clinking jars. "We have serious business tonight, men. Take your swill out of here."

Schroeder was searching for excuses to stall when the sounds of breakneck galloping sifted through the door. The men hurried outside to see Theodore arrive, his horse's hooves tearing up the ground to stop.

"You'll rouse the town, you fool!" Farrady hissed.

"The Angel of Death!" exclaimed Theodore, as he dismounted. "It's come!"

Theodore dashed inside without tying his horse, leaving Farrady to do it.

"Get inside here and shut that door!" Theodore demanded. "Damn the horses!"

"You've taken leave of your senses, sir."

"No! It took Gregor!" Theodore broke into a coughing fit, bending to put his hands on his knees. His gaze fell upon the liquor. "Give me that!"

"No! Not yet…" said Schroeder. "We have to…"

"What?" asked Farrady.

"If you had seen it, Friedrich. Its face…" said Theodore, worry lines filling with shadow.

"You've already drunk tonight, haven't you?"

"I've never had a drop!" Theodore lunged past them to close the door.

"Stop this now, damn you!" Farrady tried to restrain him, but his fear-born strength was too much.

"It's coming!"

Farrady ordered two of his men to go to the edge of the woods on horseback and have a look.

"No!" Theodore grabbed one of the men and tried to wrestle him to the ground. "You will die!"

Farrady turned Theodore around and slugged him hard, sending the younger man to his back on the stone floor. He took a matchlock from one of the men and pointed it at Theodore, inches from his face. "I'll go myself. Keep this coward from moving."

"Don't go, Kemlin! Shut that door, and let's all stay here till dawn."

"You've joined with Bennington, haven't you, son?"

"I don't care about that any longer! I am not ready to die!"

Farrady arced the butt of the rifle into Theodore's forehead, knocking him unconscious. "It'll be sheer luck if you don't, idiot."

* * * *

"We can't go!" Theodore repeated, hurrying to close the underground chamber's door as a new arrival entered. "We'll die!"

"If you won't be silent, I'll throttle you myself, Theodore!" threatened Farrady.

"It's waiting out there to claim us all!" Theodore said.

"For God's sake. Give him some of your accursed wine, Friedrich," Farrady ordered.

Schroder stood frozen. His grandmother's prophecy was coming true.

"Friedrich!"

"Wha…? It's…not time yet."

"You are both trying my patience. If you don't give him the drink and calm him down, our plan will be compromised. And Conal himself will hold you accountable."

Even in the candlelight, Friedrich could see suspicion forming on the faces of the men. He found a loose, fist-sized stone on the floor, picked it up and bashed the whimpering Theodore over the head with it, sending him to his knees, then to his face.

"Heaven above!" stage-whispered Farrady. "Have you killed him?"

A trio of the crew knelt to check on Theodore.

Farrady pointed at Schroeder. "You are as mad as he!"

"I…won't waste my hard labor on a madman" was Friedrich's excuse.

"We need every man, you miscreant," Farrady chided. "Are you trying to sabotage us?"

"No!" Friedrich said. "It's just…my nerves…"

"Why should we chance it?" asked someone behind Friedrich as he grabbed the Dutchman's shoulder.

A knock came, neither in their secret, coded rhythm nor at a discreet volume.

Farrady stared at the door as he reached for his rifle. He motioned for the nearest man to open the door.

Remembering when he had found Hezekiah Hardison hanging in the stead of his crow-repelling effigy, Friedrich wanted to back away, to get behind every man he could. In that instant, he became convinced that Theodore had indeed seen the very personage of Death.

Someone swung the door open and lunged backward. Farrady tensed as stiff as his weapon.

There was only darkness—and the sound of disturbed horses.

"Go and look," ordered Farrady.

The opener regarded Farrady as if he was insane.

"I'll be with you," Farrady promised. "Just behind."

The man drew a deep breath, his countenance still doubtful, as he took up his own rifle. The other men began to follow suit. Friedrich took the opportunity to distance himself from the entrance.

With Farrady pointing his rifle over the opener's right shoulder and holding the candle lamp high, the duo crept out into the silent darkness.

Three yards out, a flash, a boom and a truncated cry loosened the bladders and bowels of the heartiest settlers present.

Farrady's groping hands and tan shirt were the first things to break through the dark, as his body ran back through the door and fell forward, squirting blood from his neck stump onto the stone floor and the nearest feet.

The clamor of panic had barely begun before a loose pattern of bangs and powder flashes filled the room; guns discharged pointlessly. Amid the yelling and stumbling, someone thought to close the door.

"Shoulders to!" cried the man, and four complied, smashing into one another and the door to keep it from being opened by whatever it was that…

Death.

It was the Angel of Death.

"God's punishment!" called Schroeder. "For our chicanery!"

If anyone heard and believed, they did not resign themselves to their fate. Survival was the one and only consideration.

"Wait!" shouted Benjamin Gaffney. "There's a knock!"

Dead silence fell like fast fog. Then, barely muffled by the all-too-flimsy door: "Triiiiiick or treeeeat, you funny men!"

The voice was at once that of a child and a demon.

"Don't let it in!" cried Gaffney, just before the point of a two-foot scythe blade stabbed through the wood—and into his forehead.

The other men at the door swarmed backward, crushing each other and Schroeder into the rear wall.

"Trick it is!" Everett Geelens/the Grim Reaper excitedly announced through the bloody hole he had made. He yanked the scythe out fast and hard, smashing Gaffney's head against the door hard enough to crack the wood.

A pale fist crashed through the weakened spot. The hand opened to give a "howdy" wave, then withdrew.

An eternal instant later, a face was framed in the splintered hole, and they all knew Theodore was right.

A blood-slick skull, to which bits of leaves, dirt and flesh stuck, grinned at them, hanging gristle dancing in the candlelight.

Its maddened eyes provided no suggestion of life. "Heeeere's Evvie!"

The hole went black. A residual negative image of a skull remained, stamped on every mind's eye.

"Out of my way!" Schroeder knew what he had to do. He wrestled past the men to get to the crate of liquor he'd left terrifyingly close to the failing door, sparing an instant to reflect on the irony that in his original plan, Schroeder was to be the only one not to imbibe the poisoned spirits.

The others stood silent as he uncorked a jug and drank mightily from it.

Schroeder gave them no thought, hoping against hope that it would be only oblivion, and not yet another unearthly angel, that met him in the coming minutes.

Chapter 37

Under Saturn's Shadow
Modern day

"They're clear!" Pedro called, holding a spotlight toward the wreckage of the hearse and gate.

"Hit it with the gas," Hudson told Deputy Astin.

With a thunk and a whoosh, a gas grenade flew from Astin's M4A1 into the growling jack-o'-lantern terror's mouth and ignited with a flash.

The monster issued a cry of pain as it leaped eight feet in the air and came down on its back, scuttling and slashing helplessly at the air with its bizarre appendages. Light and smoke emerged from its mouth, making for the most horrific jack-o'-lantern ever.

"Good job." Hudson brought his Famas bullpup to his shoulder and let loose a strafing line of rounds, tearing open the damned thing. "Go, Pete."

Pedro got a few feet closer and took a knee, raising his sawed-off shotgun. "Stay down, Denny!"

He opened up with three shots, blasting off a leg and two massive chunks of bloody orange flesh.

The remaining legs extended, twitched and then folded in on the ruins of its bulbous body.

Pedro smiled as he wiped rain from his eyes. "K.O.!"

* * * *

Pedro jogged to them, followed by Hudson. “You dudes okay?”

“We are, but…” he gestured toward his ruined hearse.

“Maybe we can buff all that out when we do the cowcatcher,” Bernard told Dennis.

“You guys should get over to the Community Center,” Dennis told Hudson. “That’s where most of these things are going.”

“Way ahead. What about you?”

“I gotta clean off some graffiti,” Dennis said. “Trust me. It’s high priority.”

“As you say.” Hudson tossed his .44 to Dennis and unslung his night-vision-equipped hunting rifle for Bernard.

* * * *

“I see ’em!” Hudson, leaning out the window, handed his bullpup to the driving deputy. “Hand me the scope.”

On the opposite side, leaning out from the rear, Pedro squinted into the wind and rain, scanning for would-be ambushers.

Hudson raised the rifle and scanned for the most feasible target. “Looks like they’ve all mostly converged on the Community Center like Dennis said.”

He fired, then turned to smile at Pedro. “Got one!”

“Lemme have a turn.”

“It’s not a game, Petey.” Hudson re-chambered. “Get one of those grenade launchers ready.”

Pedro ducked into the vehicle and found the fitted M4A1 among the weapons aligned on the seat.

As he rose, Hudson leaned in. “Gun it, Astin. Those things are about to get into the building, if they haven’t already.”

As Deputy Astin accelerated, Hudson yelled at Pedro. “Start shooting as soon as you see the whites of their eyes.”

* * * *

As they crested the hill and came to Bennington’s towering obelisk tombstone, Bernard stopped in the driving rain to lean on his knees and catch his breath. “Damn you…Barcroft boys,” huffed Bernard. “You’re determined to kill me on this very hill.”

Dennis took a bandana from his back pocket and trekked to the obtrusive grave marker. He ripped away the plastic sheet Violina had made him place over the summoning sigil and scrubbed the blood mark until it was a brownish blur.

By then, Bernard had caught his breath and gone to work kick-cleaning the circle Violina had cast, reducing it also to a meaningless mess.

He and Dennis exchanged a triumphant smile, as the storm began to quickly subside.

"We get a medal or something now, I guess," said the rocker.

"A paid tropical vacation would be better," said Bernard. "But finishing October without any more Sam Raimi–type shenanigans will suffice."

Dennis took a bag of candy corn from his jacket pocket, ripped it open, tossed a few pieces at the base of Wilcott Bennington's grave and sat on the wet stone base, holding the bag out to Bernard.

"Hey, is that harvest mix?" asked the engineer/chemist/warrior.

* * * *

McGlazer's grimace of pain vanished when he saw the new storm pattern setting in and the blast of green lightning staking its claim on the sky and against the hate-fueled pumpkin mutants.

This wasn't a warning. It was an announcement.

The horrid, human-esque faces of O'Herlihy's displaced followers withdrew.

It was hardly a relief; the smaller squashes remained inside the Center, undeterred from their slaughterous directive.

McGlazer barely had the strength to raise an arm against the toothy terror that rocketed toward him. The next one would find his throat or heart, or whatever it wished.

He looked toward Timbo, hoping for the tried-and-true, last-second salvation of hot lead.

The rifleman was swinging the empty weapon like a cricket bat, mostly hitting nothing.

Kerwin swung his board at the crawling creepers as Stuart raised and dropped the ten-pound dumbell repeatedly onto each foe that got close enough.

DeShaun bashed the rushing pumpkin spawn with his push broom. But each thrust was less effective as the strange creatures grew more savvy and savage. They were quickly learning to dodge to the side and around the oncoming bristled bludgeon.

DeShaun dropped the broom to duck as two of the little bastards sailed toward his face. Pockets and his young troops rushed to protect him, blitzing the sentient spheres. Their blows missed, landing sharply on the hard wood floor, leaving their young bodies exposed to snarling, flying counterattacks.

The children screamed in pain and terror, breaking ranks.

McGlazer wished for the nostalgic hopefulness of two minutes earlier, when they had only the overlarge adult creatures and their just-too-short tentacles to contend with.

Chapter 38

Trapped Like Rats

Settlement era

"You all saw it," whispered John-David Pewter, his face nearly as white as the skull of the demon that lurked outside. "That was the Lord's angel."

"We were wrong…" said Nicholas Weber. "We were led astray by Conal. And now the Lord has judged us."

Farrady stared at the hole in the door, shaking his head. "But…how? We worship the one true God. Bennington would have us devote ourselves to whatever god we wish. Like heathens."

"Do you really think a man can know the truth of God in a single lifetime?" asked Schroeder. "We are mere children."

He drank deeply from the jug of his poisoned liquor. "In this moment, I pray only for oblivion." He lifted a fresh jug and tossed it to Pewter. "You're welcome to join me."

"You…sought to poison us tonight?" asked Farrady.

Schroeder issued a bitter laugh. "Call it a mercy." He took another deep swallow, finishing with the jar, then set it aside and lay down like he was taking a brief doze. "There's enough for all of you." He interlaced his fingers and straightened his neck. "Or you have only to step outside, if you prefer."

Farrady beheld the matchlock in his hands as if it was a mere toy. "God's will is not to be hindered by powder and ball shot, I suppose."

Weber had stared at the jug since catching it. Now he uncorked it, drank deeply, took a breath and drank again. "I renounce my own soul." He handed the jug to his nearest comrade and knelt, staring at the useless barrier of the door almost placidly. "Thy will be done."

Farrady leaned over to check on Schroeder and found that he was not breathing. "I say we fight the demon."

"Fight the Reaper?" someone responded. "May as well fight God Himself." The man went to the crate and took up the jug of tainted whiskey. "He's given us a choice in Schroeder's elixir. Quiet, eternal sleep..." He motioned to the door. "Or the cold edge of the scythe."

He uncorked and drank, swallowing mightily, then handed the jug to Farrady. "It was a brave thing we all tried, coming here to this land, the Stronghold of Death Itself."

The man lay down beside Schroeder, patting the dead man's arm with gratitude, then closed his eyes and breathed his last.

* * * *

Modern day

As he ran at a cluster of cowering killer-pumpkin toddlers, DeShaun's mega-sparkler abruptly died.

The timing was perfect, as it turned out. The blinded baby demons ran almost comically into the walls and bleachers and under the gleefully stomping feet of yelling children.

Kerwin Stuyvesant, releasing pent-up frustration from two years of painful silence, might have scored the greatest number of squash-squashings, relentlessly going from one to another as if playing a life-or-death game of whack-a-mole.

McGlazer, his hands and legs still stinging, could only act as a spotter for the mayor. He knew every corner and cranny of the center as well as the back of his throbbing hand. He could reasonably predict what hiding places the blinded pumpkins might luck into.

The mayor made good use of her soccer-trained muscle memory, landing a good many full field-goal kicks.

When McGlazer heard the *foosh* of a propelled grenade and the flat rhythm of Hudson's bullpup, he had to smile, despite his pain. The cavalry had arrived.

A green flash and a louder boom offered even greater reassurance. Devil's Night had just become Witches' Night.

* * * *

Deputy Astin careened into the Community Center's parking lot, calling, "Hang on, boys!" sounding for all the world like Bo and/or Luke Duke.

Pedro already had a shot lined up with the grenade launcher on one of the horticultural horrors crawling at the edge of the roof. Though it was a gas grenade, the impact knocked the thing loose. It landed deftly on its four legs, but one of these splintered on impact.

Screeching, the thing began a lopsided charge at the cruiser. Hudson sprayed it with the bullpup, just as Deputy Astin drove up onto the fringe-tree island.

Three more slayer-squash crawled toward them, zigzagging deftly to avoid the bullets.

The nearest made a ridiculous leap, covering forty feet. Pedro tried to intercept it with a grenade, but the shell flew off harmlessly toward the ball fields.

The monster landed on the roof of the vehicle, its mouth open, ready to clamp onto Pedro's head.

He held it off with every ounce of his significant strength, pushing against the edges of its mouth.

Hudson knew he couldn't shoot. He and Deputy Astin leaped up onto the vehicle and started battering the thing with their weapons. Deputy Astin was smacked away, absorbing the full impact of the beast's tree-trunk leg and sent sailing into the parking lot, where he slid several feet—before an elephantine foot at the end of a foot-thick vine leg descended, crushing the deputy's torso.

It was Conal.

The devil rushed toward the struggle between Hudson and his follower, catching Hudson completely off guard. The Conal demon snatched Hudson and hoisted him high, relishing his helpless state as the bullpup clattered to the pavement.

A sound grew, a purposeful chanting, a multitude of female voices coming toward them from Main Street. The chant was accompanied by green lightning bolts, landing in near-straight lines upon Conal's monstrous troops, blasting them to smoking bits.

Conal turned his hideous visage to see them, slowly lowering Hudson to within…

Pepper-spray range. "Hey!"

Conal turned and caught a decent stream in at least one eye. Roaring with fury, Conal flung Hudson toward the Community Center to smash him to pieces against the wall.

The high branches of the fringe tree stopped him, slowing his momentum before bouncing him back to the pavement.

The witches came around the corner of Ecard Street, all holding hands and chanting together.

Chapter 39

I Do Not Fit

Settlement era

Everett did not mind the pain so much, since it was for such a good cause. Besides, he still had his face, folded up neatly in his pocket. He could put it back on later, after Halloween.

Right now, there was a whole roomful of silly men having the stupidest Halloween party he had ever seen. No masks, no music, no scary decorations, just the same ol' boring pilgrim costumes everybody around here wore. Pilgrims meant Thanksgiving, and it wasn't Thanksgiving. It was Halloween, gosh dang it!

Everett knew there would be resistance. That's just how grown-ups were about Halloween. But then, when he got them ready, they sat still and made for good decorations, with their blood and guts and stuff like that showing. Well, they were also dead, but that was just part of the fun.

Everett wanted to pet every one of the horses, but they all whinnied and got spooked and kicked and tried to run away, so he left them alone. It was kind of like his sister's dog, Bravo. They just didn't like him.

Oh, well. He didn't need to be liked. He needed to have Halloween, and for everyone else in the world to have it too.

Everett could barely contain his excitement as he counted to thirty-one, long enough to build suspense, he figured, then charged the little wooden door and burst in, scythe held high like a real reaper!

"Boo!" he shouted, then "Happy Halloweeeeen!" and he swung his scythe in an arc wide enough to cut off five heads—maybe six!

But all the pilgrim guys had fallen asleep. No wonder, with this boring party. Everett knelt down and inspected the men. They weren't breathing, let alone snoring, and they did not respond when he shook them or poked them with the scythe.

Everett was sad. He sniffed one of the jugs of punch or whatever, and it didn't smell very fruity, just pungent and yucky.

With a sigh, Everett stood up and removed his hood. He was tired of this smelly town and its lack of Halloween. Plus, his face hurt now, and for nothing.

Everett wandered outside and waved goodbye to all the spooked horses. At least they were having fun.

He decided to walk and walk until he found a real place where people wore costumes and sang "This is Halloween" and put cardboard skeletons on their windows. Maybe he could even find Candace.

Everett stuck his face back on to the front of his skull and walked toward the moon.

* * * *

Bennington kept a respectful distance, as Jonah Cooke released Conal from the dirt cell.

"Chloris admitted it was likely someone else who killed my boy." Cooke stepped away from the door and stared at Conal.

"You'll kill me, won't you?" Conal asked. "Say I tried to escape."

"No, Conal." Bennington came closer. "There are other bodies. You could not have killed them all."

"You're not…not strong enough to…do what was done to my son," Cooke said.

Conal stood but remained in the cell, still wary. "Who then?"

"I know who," Bennington admitted. "God forgive me, I… helped him heal."

"It would be best if you would consider going out on your own, though," said Cooke. "Or with your followers."

"Have you any idea where they might have all gone?" Bennington asked him pointedly.

Conal shook his head and exited the cell, certain, after all this time, that they had all abandoned him. Perhaps they had even been planning a separate colony of their own, without his knowledge. He did not know whether to feel relieved or dejected.

Cooke took him by the arm. "Move against Bennington or this town," he intoned, "and I'll kill you. You can be certain."

Conal left, fearing that, until he was well away from the jail, Cooke would shoot him in the back—for that is exactly what he, Conal, would have done in his shoes.

He made his way up the hill and found the horses tied among the trees near his house. His friends were here, after all, for whatever reason, and had been for a good while.

So why hadn't they tried to free him?

He found the answer in the secret rooms under his house and recalled the message of the mushroom. This was not his time.

Buoyed by the knowledge that he would soon be resting longer than he ever had, Conal labored well past dawn, dragging the corpses of his soldiers to the stone coffins they had prepared, filling then with mushrooms and pumpkin seeds that offered the promise of resurrection in an age to come.

Then he drank Schroeder's poisoned wine and lay down with a sad smile, anticipating his chance to live again.

Later that day, Bennington, Cooke and a wary posse of recruits would find the strange mass grave. Respect the dead, they decided, and leave well enough alone. The subterranean chambers were sealed off, the stairway and doorway covered over, until the year 1923, while the empty house was expanded into a gathering hall for the town and a sanctuary for those seeking spiritual solace—the town's church, open to all.

The rest of the town concluded that Conal must have fled with his followers. No one missed them, and indeed an annual celebration of his defeat and exile began to take place. In time, this would evolve into the annual Pumpkin Parade.

* * * *

Modern day

The Conal demon, its awful face twisted into a pained orange grimace from Hudson's pepper spray, spun around twice, like a broken wind-up spider. But Ysabella's cleansing rainstorm favored him in clearing his eyes of the irritant more quickly than common water.

Pedro pushed and pushed, but his massive arms only gave way more and more as the giant mouth of the pumpkin inched ever nearer to snapping shut on him.

"Petey!" called Jill.

Brinke broke the chant. "Don't use the lightning!" she said. As she ran toward the parking lot, Jill lamented that the witch's statuesque grace and athleticism were a few degrees diminished now.

The other women closed their line as they continued walking, trying not to show alarm at the size and maddened motions of Conal O'Herlihy, the Anti-Great Pumpkin.

"Numa Heeyosh Numa!" Brinke called breathlessly, as she came to a halt some six feet from the vehicle and the Pedro-pumpkin struggle, emitting a stream of pink light from her fingertips.

Pedro's assailant growled with confidence, barely affected by the repulsion spell.

Jill began the beat of the march again.

Brinke took a deep breath and stood tall. "Numa Heeyosh Numaaaaaaa!" she repeated, bringing the back of her hands together, and then violently separating them, as if…

…Ripping the pumpkin in half.

Pedro fell forward as resistance against his exertion suddenly stopped. For the second time of the night, brains, seeds and stringy pie filling splashed down on him like pig blood from the gymnasium rafters onto poor Carrie White, off in some subtler universe.

"Yuck!" he squeaked, shaking his hair and holding his arms out to catch the cleansing rain shower full on.

Conal rose on his spidery legs, larger than ever now—and fully recovered.

He skittered toward the cruiser and easily raised it over his head with his two forward legs.

Ysabella stopped. "Sisters! Now!"

Jill dropped her ersatz drum and helped the weakened Brinke back to the street to rejoin the formation.

Conal hurled the car. Brinke raised one hand as she called, "Faitu yor'na!"

The car fell straight down in front of the witches, less than a foot away.

With a croaking cry, Conal willed giant crab claws to grow from his forelimbs. He snapped them in a threatening display, then gripped the fringe tree planted in the median and hoisted it like a mere weed. Mud rained down on Hudson from the disconnected root system, yet the chief deputy lay dismayingly still.

Conal scrabbled forward with the tree aloft, snarling at the coven.

The witches took steps back, until Ysabella stopped them. "Do not retreat!" she called. "Stand strong!"

Ysabella swung her arms around in wide arcs and held out her fingers, as if to catch the wooden missile in her hands. She shouted, "Bhurashtu!" in a voice starting to show signs of wear.

The women gasped but did not fall back. The tree stopped to hang in midair just inches from Ysabella.

Conal clambered toward them, his pincers still growing out from his forelimbs, inches to the microsecond.

"Faitu nooma!" The tree rocketed a hundred feet up. "Brinke! The shiel—"

Brinke was already in motion, dashing to the crone's side with hands clasped and wedged toward Conal. "Tru-ah Ka-nah!"

Hitting Brinke's invisible wall, Conal slowed but did not stop. His massive pincers darted toward the witches, testing Brinke's strength.

Ysabella dropped to one knee and brought her hands down with a snarl of her own.

The fringe tree crashed atop Conal, smashing him down to half his height.

He screeched like the damned—and pushed himself up, raising the tree.

"No, Conal." Ysabella barely murmured the sentence.

Like automatons programmed in perfect sync, the sorceresses pointed at the monstrosity, shouting no particular words.

Lightning as bright and green as a sun-soaked grass field arced onto and into Conal from all directions. For the second time in less than a millennium, Conal had time to realize that his lust for power would go unfulfilled.

The sustained strikes pierced and pounded Conal O'Herlihy into a million sparking, flaming flying pieces that scattered for hundreds of yards.

Weeping, Stella lifted Candace into her arms, as if trying to regress her to girlhood from the hyper-speed maturation she had been forced to do.

Pedro covered his head as he ran to check on Hudson. He smacked the heavy clods of mud off his friend and turned him over. "Dude, you better n—"

"Don't!" Hudson's eyes popped open in terror as he grabbed Pedro's jacket. "Don't mouth-to-mouth me!"

* * * *

DeShaun and Stuart hit the Community Center doors together, knocking them open with a steely echo.

"Dad!" DeShaun cried, seeing his father on the ground and Pedro kneeling to hold him.

"He's okay, dude!" Pedro said.

"Candace!?" Stuart strained to see into the center of the witches' circle—and there, in Stella's arms, was the girl with the familiar streak of white hair; it was flowing amid the wet and messy chestnut locks of his best and only girl.

Still loosely under the command of Pockets, DeShaun and Stuart's army of pint-sized pumpkin smashers continued to patrol the corners for any ghoulish gourds that had escaped their wrath. For a wild, sugar-fueled mob, the children had been surprisingly thorough.

Unlike the previous year's mushroom zombies, though, the killer squash did not smoke and melt away to black goo but remained as a litter of broken shell, scattered seed and, more disturbingly, teeth, eyes and brain matter.

The triumphant children essayed prolonged disgusted expressions of "eeeww" and the like, but they also seemed eager to play in the bloody mess like it was a fresh mudhole, daring glances at the grown-ups to see if they were going to be shushed or made to sit.

"It's Halloween. Let them have their gross fun," was the collective opinion.

McGlazer finally felt like he could see the light at the end of his pain tunnel.

He'd be in bed for a few weeks, maybe even need his cane again for a while. He would probably come to curse cold days. But he'd live.

Kerwin came to sit beside him, just being someone's old friend for the first time in years. Maybe for the first time in his entire life.

McGlazer patted Kerwin on the shoulder and raised his weary head to smile—his blood freezing at the sight of a shadow writhing behind the sound system's massive amplifier.

"Get back!" he cried, yanking Kerwin away. The speaker fell face forward with an echoing thud, as the last remaining pumpkin demon, a beachball-sized specimen with gleaming yellow eyes, crawled out into the open, and hiss-screeched at the two men.

In the dark, something about its shape seemed, even for a demon squash, wrong…

Pockets's soldiers stomped toward it with shrill battle calls, raising their fitness-themed weapons.

The thing didn't run from them, though, but toward the double doors. Just before a barrage of small weight plates could smash onto it, the thing leaped into the air and spread two gigantic leaves from its back.

Pushing off with its tendrils, it began flapping these bizarre wings furiously. All watched in horror as it gained height with unnatural speed.

"Stop that goddamn thing!" McGlazer heard himself say, as all his pains flared worse than ever from pure, sudden, hopeless stress.

The pumpkin-bat, seeing the witches below, veered east to avoid lightning spells.

Chapter 40

Where the Sky Ends

Dennis and Bernard, having made their way down the cemetery hill, stopped for a moment to examine the wreckage of the hearse and the gate.

"Metal as hell," said Dennis.

But Bernard was frowning toward the sky. "What the…?"

Dennis followed his gaze to the odd black spot that crossed through and around patches of fog and smoke. "Moving fast, whatev—"

A jagged green bolt missed the thing by a few yards. Voices from Main Street were faint, but the context was clear. The witches were trying to bring it down.

"The rifle, bro!"

"Huh?" Bernard just held it out and stared at it.

Dennis pushed it up to his shoulder. "Shoot it down, man!"

Bernard peered through the scope—into utter blackness.

"Judas Effing Priest…" Dennis clicked a button on its side, and a green-black sky came into Bernard's view, framing the flying object.

"Holy rock and rolly!" exclaimed Bernard. "It's a—"

"Just shoot it before it gets out of range, dude!"

Bernard tracked it for a second or so, then pulled the trigger. Dennis winced at seeing the rifle barrel jump.

"It's too small!"

"The wings are bigger," Dennis said. "Just time their rise and fall."

As Bernard followed the thing, it grew smaller and fainter behind the fog.

Dennis wanted to take the rifle away, yet knew he would never line up the shot in time.

Bernard fired, re-chambered and fired again, almost immediately.

Dennis felt a rush of relief—the tiny black shape abruptly began to fall.

Even at this distance, the satisfying sound of its thunk onto some hard roof reached their relieved ears.

"My hero!" Dennis hugged Bernard so hard it drew a squeak from the chemist.

* * * *

McGlazer lay in his hospital bed, floating on the cloud of painkillers in his system, but wide awake.

The television news was locked on the incoming reports from Ember Hollow, how the world was being forced to reconsider all notions of the supernatural, all because of three strange autumns in one sprawling farm town.

His name rose occasionally, in tones of admiration. But he wasn't interested.

He switched it off and thought of all the strangeness of Ember Hollow and his life, gratified in a way that he had been a part of it, hoping with every fiber that he never would be again. He saw the Gideon Bible lying on the nightstand next to his bed and picked it up. Too zonked to try to read, he just held it and considered the tactile sensation of its weight, its smooth leather binding, its delicate pages.

A light knock, the nurse's kind face. "Want some visitors, Reverend?"

McGlazer smiled.

He put the bible back on the nightstand as Stella entered, appearing as exhausted as he felt. "Can't believe I get to be first." She eased the door shut. "So many people are here to see you."

"What about the family?"

"Candace is helping the witches with a cure ritual for Yoshida. Emera is with Wanda, sound asleep."

"And Bernard?"

"He said…you might have something to tell me?"

McGlazer sat forward and immediately fell back. "Ouch."

Stella held his hand. "You can say it perfectly fine lying flat on your back, Abe."

"So I can." He shot a glance at the bible. "I want you to take over the church."

"As...minister?"

"If you want the job. You would be great."

"What about you?"

"Mostly a mystery to be solved later, I think," he told her. "Maybe I'll be your assistant for a while, scheduling appointments and making coffee."

She smiled, but her expression was a little bit sad.

"Maybe I can convince one of our fellow survivors to partner with me on a café and bookstore, or some such quaint idea."

Stella pulled up a chair and leaned close. "I get the idea you were thinking about this before tonight."

"This town needs Saint Saturn's, and Saint Saturn's needs you."

She waited, knowing he would elaborate in his own time.

"I'm not...thinking about God right now. I realize that lack of faith doesn't mean lack of character. I'm going to...keep searching—not necessarily for 'God.' Just for whatever might be behind the curtain." He raised his gaze toward the ceiling. "If anything."

The hospital's lobby areas had quickly become crowded, as members of the press and the civil services learned of the latest chapter in the ongoing Ember Hollow horror show.

DeShaun and Stuart stayed in Hudson's room and watched some of the news coverage with the volume low. When he'd been admitted, Hudson had insisted he didn't need treatment; he wasn't that banged up. Staff firmly placed him in a wheelchair and made him take a handful of acetaminophen. "You are suffering from exhaustion," said the doctor. "You're not going anywhere but one of our beds. No visitors for ten to twelve hours."

Epilogue

Pedro hadn't really known Maisie well enough to reasonably predict if they could form a lasting couple. If so, it would be the first in Pedro's troubled life.

Certainly, he did not get to know her well enough to weep with such violence, to mourn her like a lifelong lover.

He wiped his tears with the Sex Pistols T-shirt she had somehow cleansed of bloodstains. He had washed it in a way that was ceremonial, in the sink of Hudson's bathroom, with a white candle burning, hung it to dry and folded it as close to the way she had that he could remember.

He scooped out a small rectangle in the fresh reddish mound over her grave and placed the shirt there, then covered it over. "Hey, I'll keep an eye out for it—and you—in the…whatever"—Pedro scanned the grave-dotted hills that surrounded Saint Saturn Unitarian Church, soon to be Saint Saturn Interdenominational Temple—"next place."

He stood and stared at the mound, narrowing his eyes as though he could see the petite smiling beauty's light beaming through the earth. Perhaps some part of him could. "I guess you ain't got no choice but to have that picnic with me now, huh?"

He found himself strangely wishing for her delicate hand to burst through the earth and clutch his leg. "Jeez, what's wrong with me?" he chuckled.

Nothing changed.

"Whatever it is, I get the feeling you'd be okay with it."

Pedro kept himself from crying and walked back down to the street, where Dennis and Jill waited, both weeping on his behalf.

ACKNOWLEDGMENTS

Michael and Maureen Crosby are inspiring to me for reasons no one, not even I, can fully understand. I can't help but believe they've accrued fantastic karma.

Too many of the people who have, in their own way, inspired or encouraged me are no longer with us.

Joel Mullinax, my first school chum ever, fell to his own demons, leaving me with memories of his fierce sense of loyalty and acceptance.

Johnny Huskey, a superior martial artist and human being, was also a talented imaginer, something he kept mostly a secret. I was among the lucky few who were privy to that side of him.

Finally, my father Lewis W. Green, was a brilliant writer and journalist. In ways plain and strange, he was as fine a teacher as any student could want.

Don't miss all the fun of the Haunted Hollow Chronicles!

In case you missed the beginning, keep reading to enjoy an excerpt from Book One, *Red Harvest.*

All the Haunted Hollow Chronicles novels are available from Lyrical Press, an imprint of Kensington Publishing Corp.

www.kensingtonbooks.com.

Chapter 1

Ember Hollow, North Carolina
October 29

"Helen, a few weeks ago, the empty field you see behind me was home to roughly twenty-five thousand Autumn's Pride pumpkins," pronounced local reporter Kit Calloway. "They're all gone now, on their way to markets and homes around the country. But a good many are staying right here in Ember Hollow, where they will be carved and decorated for the town's annual Pumpkin Parade on Halloween night."

Viewers were treated to stock footage of parades past, with costumed bystanders hooting and clapping while spooky floats crawled by with more elaborately costumed performers aboard.

"For, you see, come Halloween, Ember Hollow becomes *Haunted* Hollow, Halloween Capital of the World." The handsome reporter gave a charming raise of his eyebrow. "And this year promises a little something extra, as the town's very own homegrown rock band The Chalk Outlines takes the stage above The Grand Illusion cinemas to play a full set. Now the band has taken the local club scene by storm, but this year, with their performance at the theater, they hope to garner the attention of a special guest."

"Kerwin Stuyvesant—Talent Manager" read the screen caption under a man in his fifties who wore a bright green suit and funny-looking little hexagonal spectacles. He smiled into the camera with huge teeth that made the tiny glasses seem like toys. "The kids have been rehearsing and hitting the gigs hard, and if I didn't believe they had what it takes to make it to the top, I wouldn't have signed on to manage 'em!"

A quick snip of the trio of Halloween-themed punk rockers, awash in strobe-lit fog at some dive club, flashed on the screen before a cut back to Calloway, who concluded the report with a graceful nod. "Helen, as always, I'll be right here in Ember Hollow covering the parade and enjoying the company of these great citizens! Back to you!"

* * * *

Thirteen-year-old Stuart Barcroft woke to the sound of his mother's low humming as she breezed past his door to the room of his older brother, Dennis. He hopped from his bed and hurried into his clothes, eavesdropping on the conversation between mother and brother.

Ma—Elaine Barcroft to you and me—exclaimed, "Oh my word, Dennis! Is that going to wash out of my sheets?"

And he knew Dennis had blood on him again.

As Stuart headed toward Dennis's room, he saw a sheet of sunlight spill onto the hallway floor from the doorway—Ma opening the curtains on his poor brother.

"That makeup is a mess," she huffed, but was not really that sore about it.

At the doorway, Stuart looked his big brother over to make sure he was okay. Dennis, taking a long drink of water from the glass he kept at his bedside, was still in performance attire. His hair, already way too long on top, was disheveled and sticky. Surely exhausted, he hadn't changed out of his stage attire of torn black denim pants and a hospital scrub top spritzed with the offending stage blood, over a black long-sleeve T-shirt with bones printed on the arms.

"Oh yeah, Ma. I checked the package. Washes right out." Despite his exhaustion, he was as patient and respectful with his mother as always.

Spotting Stuart, Dennis raised the glass. "Hey, dude."

"Why didn't you clean it off?" groused their mother. "And you're still dressed!"

When Dennis had moved back in (at the ripe old age of twenty-six) it was into a room his mother had kept essentially as he had left it when he moved out at eighteen. The walls remained plastered with punk posters: Misfits, Black Flag, The Addicts, Sex Pistols, Order of the Fly, Nekromantix, and, of course, Elvis.

"Our gig went over," Dennis explained in a scratchy voice. "Had three encores."

"You're sure that's all?" probed Ma.

"*Ma!*" Stuart called. When she spun with a quick squeal, Dennis and Stuart broke out laughing. Stuart was just trying to get her off Dennis's case. Giving her a start was a bonus.

Ma was a good sport about it. "Just how many scares can I expect this Halloween?"

Dennis gave her a tight hug and a kiss on top of her head. "All of 'em."

Ma took his wrist and pushed up the long sleeves of his black undershirt. "Let me see something."

She turned over his heavily tattooed arm and examined his inner elbow. Dennis pulled away. "What the hell?"

"I hear so many things about punk music people," she said in a grim tone. "Promise me you're not using any hard drugs?"

"*Ma!*" Dennis and Stuart rebuked in harmony.

Ma clapped once, holding her hands together as she gave a satisfied chuckle. "Guess your ol' Ma can still pull off a Halloween prank herself every now and again, huh?"

Dennis walked to his dresser, picked up a crumpled orange flyer, and handed it to Stuart. "I'm a drunk. Not a junkie. There's a diff."

"Don't *say* that!" she rebuked. "You're not either one! Not anymore."

Stuart read the flyer and grinned.

Ma sniffed at Dennis's water glass.

THE CHALK OUTLINES! ON STAGE TONIGHT! read the flyer. It was a rough, old-school mimeograph job, featuring a grainy photo of Dennis with his bandmates, a muscular Hispanic and a petite sneering alt chick, all of them dressed in campy Halloween-inspired rockabilly gear.

"Once a drunk, always a drunk, Ma. That's the deal." Even this sounded cool coming from Dennis.

She patted his back. "You're doing so well, Dennis. I'm proud of you."

Stuart offered an agreeing smile, not sure if he should say anything.

"Now *hurry*!" Ma squealed. "You shouldn't keep Reverend McGlazer waiting."

She kissed him and turned to leave. "Oh! Can you drop Stuart at school? You want to hear how Dennis's jig went, don't you, Stuart?"

Stuart and Dennis snickered at her word choice. "Sure, Ma. No prob."

* * * *

Beaming, Stuart raised the luchador mask off his face and amped up the volume. His favorite part of autumn mornings was this: riding in his brother's tricked-out hearse as leaves blew across the tree-lined streets and swirled in mini twisters, chasing each other under an umber haze.

The trees, fences, and mailboxes along the street all wore such elaborate Halloween decorations, it was like a high-stakes contest. Nylon witches and ghosts floated in the trees, wooden black cat cutouts stood in the flowerbeds, wittily inscribed Styrofoam tombstones jutted from front-yard displays.

Dennis's 1970 Cadillac hearse was a mobile advertisement for his band, with flames painted on the hood, cartoonish chalk outlines of a voluptuous woman's corpse stickered on the doors, and a V8 472 cc engine that could roar like an enraged lion. Stuart loved to ride in it, especially to school.

The familiar punkabilly music emanating from the speakers had Stuart bobbing his head, tapping his fingers on his thigh.

Dennis looked at him, pleased. "You really dig that track, huh?"

"I think it's your best ever."

"Let's hope the record company suit agrees."

"She *will,* dude!" Stuart insisted. "I'd bet on it!"

The chorus began, and Stuart sang along with appropriate facial contortions.

"I better watch you, man," Dennis said. "You'll end up replacing me."

"Yeah, right," Stuart said and scoffed with a sideways glance at his brother. "Maybe I can be in the band one day though. Keyboards or something."

"No way, daddy-o." Dennis shook his head, as he always did when Stuart raised the topic. "College. Then some more college! After that, college. You'll be going to college—beyond the grave!" Dennis goosed his brother, right in that spot under his ribs that made him giggle like a baby. But for Stuart, the appeal of one day being like his brother was near irresistible. "We'll see."

"For real, Stuart. Mom's had plenty of guff outta me. She doesn't need it from her widdle baby bubby."

"Shut up. You're doing okay. Pretty good, actually."

"Maybe." Dennis took his eyes from the road to give Stuart an earnest, penetrating gaze. "But you're gonna do better."

A dozen yards ahead, burly Mister Dukes cast a scowl at them, which seemed reasonable given that he was in the midst of unwinding moist toilet paper from his mailbox. His morning's labor was only beginning; more of the soggy bands lay draped across his shrubs.

Dennis slowed the hearse and rolled down the window. "Morning, Mister Dukes. Ya got hit?"

"Yeah, yeah, yeah." Dukes waved to Stuart as he wadded the tissue into a handful. "Hey, it wasn't you, was it, boys? Be honest."

"Come on, Mr. Dukes." Dennis stayed cool, as always.

"Aaah I'm sorry. It's just … that weird music, and whatnot." Dukes squinted like the concept was a literal indecipherable blur to him. "What d'ya call it? Junkabilly?"

Before Stuart could stop himself, he explained, "It's called horror punk!"

Dennis nudged him. "Easy."

"No offense, boys." Dukes frowned at all the unpapered yards surrounding his. "Guess I'm just too old for all this Halloween crap."

"Never too old for Halloween, Mr. Dukes!" Dennis called, waving. "Hope you make it to the Pumpkin Parade!"

"Maybe." Dukes waved, mumbling something they couldn't hear.

As they pulled away, Dennis gave Stuart a reproachful glare. "Gotta build good rapport with the public, Stuart."

"He doesn't respect our music!"

"Nobody does. That's why it's called punk, genius."

Stuart had this thought and the music to fill his mind for the rest of the ride to Ember Hollow Junior High. If they had stayed at Mr. Dukes's place longer, they would have seen him open his mailbox and find a single piece of orange-and-black-wrapped candy.

About the Author

Photo by Scott Treadway

Patrick C. Greene is a lifelong horror fan who lives in the mountains of western North Carolina. He launched his Ember Hollow series with *Red Harvest* and *Grim Harvest*. He is also the author of the novels *Progeny* and *The Crimson Calling*, as well as numerous short stories featured in collections and anthologies.

Visit him at www.fearwriter.wordpress.com.

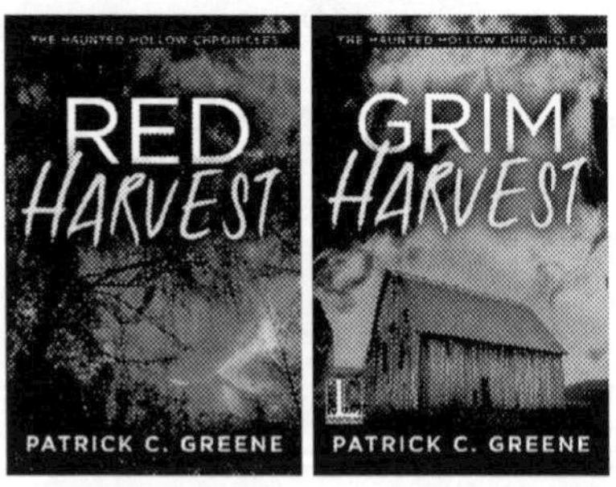

Printed in the United States
by Baker & Taylor Publisher Services